# Treasures of Time

PENELOPE LIVELY

PENGUIN BOOKS

PENGUIN BOOKS

Published by the Penguin Group
Penguin Books Ltd, 80 Strand, London WC2R ORL, England
Penguin Group (USA), Inc., 375 Hudson Street, New York, New York 10014, USA
Penguin Group (Canada), 90 Eglinton Avenue East, Suite 700, Toronto, Ontario, Canada M4P 2Y3
(a division of Pearson Penguin Canada Inc.)
Penguin Ireland, 25 St Stephen's Green, Dublin 2, Ireland (a division of Penguin Books Ltd)
Penguin Group (Australia), 250 Camberwell Road, Camberwell, Victoria 3124, Australia
(a division of Pearson Australia Group Pty Ltd)
Penguin Books India Pvt Ltd, 11 Community Centre, Panchsheel Park,
New Delhi – 110 017, India
Penguin Group (NZ), 67 Apollo Drive, Rosedale, North Shore 0632, New Zealand
(a division of Pearson New Zealand Ltd)
Penguin Books (South Africa) (Pty) Ltd, 24 Sturdee Avenue, Rosebank, Johannesburg 2196,
South Africa

Penguin Books Ltd, Registered Offices: 80 Strand, London WC2R ORL, England

www.penguin.com

First published by William Heinemann Ltd 1979
Published in Penguin Books 1986
Reissued with a new introduction in Penguin Books 2010
1

Copyright © Penelope Lively, 1979
Introduction copyright © Selina Hastings, 2010

The moral right of the author and of the introducer has been asserted

Set in 11/13 pt Dante MT
Typeset by Ellipsis Books Limited, Glasgow
Printed in Great Britain by Clays Ltd, St Ives plc

A CIP catalogue record for this book is available from the British Library

ISBN: 978-0-141-04485-9

www.greenpenguin.co.uk

To Gina and Murray

# Introduction

*Treasures of Time*, first published in 1979, is a novel of serial excavation. With characteristic subtlety and wit, Penelope Lively explores intricate themes of appearance and reality, of the power of memory and of the warping and shaping that occurs with the passing years. In all her fiction Lively shows herself intuitively alert to the influence of the past on the present: in *The Road to Lichfield*, for instance, in *Next to Nature, Art*, in *Moon Tiger* (winner of the 1987 Booker Prize), she pursues the idea of the invisible influence of previous eras, both chronological and environmental, on human experience.

*Treasures of Time* deals both figuratively and literally with disinterment. The point of departure for the plot is the arrival at a country house in Wiltshire of a television team to film a programme on the distinguished archaeologist Hugh Paxton, who died some years ago. Paxton's most famous dig, the one that made his name, was on a local site, where he uncovered a fabulously rich hoard of prehistoric treasure. Now the whole subject is to be unearthed again, this time for BBC television, and the surviving participants interviewed about their recollections. But inevitably the past has been reinvented, and in this delectable comedy of manners Lively adroitly uncovers stratum after stratum of delusion and self-deceit. As well as other participants, three members of Paxton's family were present at the dig: his wife, his sister-in-law, and his daughter, then only a child; and with all of them the official version is interestingly at odds with what actually happened.

Hugh Paxton's widow, Laura, is the most excited about the programme, thrilled by the prospect of taking the starring role. Chic, snobbish and self-absorbed, Laura's life these days lacks excitement: money is in short supply and she has been obliged to share the house, Danehurst, with her sister, Nellie. Now an invalid confined to a wheelchair, Nellie as a young woman had worked closely with Hugh on his excavations, her admiration for him, painful and unspoken, extending far beyond the purely professional. Most reluctantly involved in the present enterprise is Laura's prickly daughter, Kate, down from London for the weekend with Tom, her boyfriend. Kate is decidedly wary of the prospect of a camera-crew zooming in on her family history, with all its subterranean cruelties and betrayals. And yet both she and Tom are themselves professionally involved in investigating the past, Tom writing a thesis on the eighteenth-century antiquarian William Stukeley, and Kate with a career organizing exhibitions of ancient implements in county museums. (For Tom, now, memories of Kate 'would be for ever associated with ploughshares and sickles . . . the sight of a threshing machine or butter churn would, for the rest of his life, bring an expectant lift of the heart'.)

Despite Kate's anxiety, however, when the young man from the BBC arrives he appears to be not threatening at all. Tony Greenway, if slightly colourless, is agreeable and intelligent, skilfully combining professional expertise with a nice line in courteous deference. The latter is particularly appreciated by Laura, who loses no time in showing off about her husband's reputation, keen to impress on Tony the frightfully important part she herself had played and the utterly fascinating life the two of them had led. But as Tony listens and probes, looks at photographs and walks up over the downs to examine the site, more, much more, begins to emerge: uncomfortable memories are revived, awkward situations revisited, and subtly, obliquely, a story begins to take shape of far greater interest and complexity than that originally designed to be shown on television.

Penelope Lively is an outstandingly accomplished novelist, and one of her greatest skills is a deftness of touch. She can introduce a matter of vital importance with a brushstroke so light the reader is barely aware of it: somebody pauses a second too long before answering, perhaps, or the eye is drawn to an apparently minor detail; and yet in that moment everything changes, and almost subliminally we know something significant has been revealed. Thus we absorb the fact that Laura's marriage was far from the flawless union that she promotes, and that there is a crucial but unspoken part in it played by her dowdy sister. Flighty Laura, uninterested in archaeology, had been amused by Nellie's willingness to assist Hugh on his digs, and rarely thinks back to her own first meeting with her future husband; but Nellie remembers it clearly, remembers her ravishing younger sister 'looking, I thought, a bit bored because Hugh and I were talking shop . . . And in the middle of saying something I saw his eyes on her, and how they were, and all of a sudden the day wasn't so nice after all'. Similarly, it is these tiny shards of the past working up through layers of buried memory that gradually reveal how Kate, difficult, defensive Kate, has been irretrievably damaged by what happened between her parents during her childhood.

Each of the main characters is brought into focus in turn, and here again it is due to the extreme sophistication of Lively's art that we learn within a few words all we need to know about them; her possession of her characters is so complete that she can give them to us in little more than a gesture or a glance or a telling pattern of speech.

It is the newcomer, Kate's boyfriend, through whose eyes much of the story is seen. Tom is a good-natured, scholarly young man, not particularly ambitious, and he loves Kate and pities her, too, for her angry self-destructiveness. On his first visit to Danehurst to meet her mother it quickly becomes apparent who is responsible for much of the damage. Laura has developed to a very high level the art of the crushing put-down, employed with lethal effect on her daughter, and indeed on almost anyone, however harmless, who comes within range. 'Are you going to take me for a walk this afternoon,' Tom cheerfully asks Kate, soon after arriving at the house. '"Oh dear," said Laura, "are you that kind of person?"'

Laura is a gloriously comic creation with her selfishness and snobbery and her insufferable insistence on impressing everyone with her own superiority. And yet, although we laugh at Laura, we are also made aware of the sadness of her situation, of her gradual realization that she had failed her husband, of the unpalatable fact that he had married the wrong sister. It is this combining of comedy with a profound compassion for her characters that is one of the hallmarks of Penelope Lively's fiction. She is witty and ironic, but her wit and irony are anchored in a very real sympathy for the human condition. And yet, while sympathetic she is not soft: her characters are never lightly let off, and she is uncompromising over the realities of their lives. In the love affair between Kate and Tom, she conveys its strength and sincerity, while not flinching from indicating the inevitability of its failure.

Like the archaeologist at the centre of her story, Lively is acutely aware of the immanence of the long-buried past. Again and again the eye is drawn to an ancient landscape that is yet an intrinsic part of the modern age. The family house, for instance, is on the Wiltshire downs, close to Avebury and Stonehenge, but it is also surrounded by a network of motorways and industrial estates. Heading back to London after their weekend at Danehurst, Kate and Tom 'drove into the rushing Wiltshire darkness, where the shafts of light from juggernaut container lorries blazed down the Old Bath road (from which Charles II made a detour once, to visit Avebury and Silbury Hill in company with John Aubrey) . . .'. And there is an exquisitely judged episode in which the two young people drive up the motorway with a load of ancient artefacts (Roman coins, a Viking shield) for exhibition at an aggressively modern comprehensive in Birmingham.

Penelope Lively manipulates the passage of time as brilliantly as she manipulates the complexities of her fictional characters. Technically she is flawless: her vocabulary and punctuation are precise, with never an extraneous syllable, and she has a highly developed visual sense and perfect pitch for dialogue. Yet ultimately the quality that defines Lively as such a superb novelist is that rare combination of the artist's necessary detachment with an enormous zest and enjoyment, a powerful personal involvement in the world around her. *Treasures of Time*, moving and very funny, is a testament to all this.

Selina Hastings

# Chapter One

The alarm went. He resisted it, burrowing against Kate's warm back. He felt her reach out, bang the clock, lie in disquieting wakefulness. She said, 'Tom?' He burrowed again.

She sat up, the sheet slipping from her bare breasts. 'Do wake up. Listen, I've been thinking. I shall have to take you to see my mother.'

'Mmn?'

'You'll have to meet my mother.'

'Ah. It's come to that, has it?'

'She keeps asking about you. I can't put it off any longer.'

'Well, fine, then. When do we go? Who wants to put it off, anyway?'

'Me, I suppose.' She had got out of bed now, and stood at the dressing-table brushing her hair. He watched her bottom, lovingly. Dear Kate. Splendid Kate. Her hair stood up in a dark wiry frizz all round her head; at her waist opposing pink curves nicely echoed the shape of white knobs on the dressing-table; below, her bottom rose and fell in time with the hair-brushing. He said, 'What?'

'Do wake up properly, Tom, it's gone eight. I said we'd better go this weekend.'

'Fine.' He yawned, clasped his hands behind his head. 'Great. I like Wiltshire. Cradle of British archaeology. Stonehenge. Avebury. Stukeley's stamping ground – right up my street. Immemorial landscapes. And I'd like to know more about your father, anyway. I suppose the house is stuffed with axe-heads and bits of broken pot. Is it very grand?'

'No, it's not, in fact it's a bit seedy.' She was flinging clothes out of drawers now, quarrying pants and tights and jerseys in a frenzy of irritation.

'Are you staying there all morning or are you going to the library?'

'I love you when you're cross,' he said. 'You go red all up your neck, did you know that? I love you anyway, and I daresay I'll go to the library. Tell me, does your mother know about my humble origins?'

'She knows we're getting married, that's all that's relevant.'

'Ah. What a stern girl you are. Straight to the point and no nonsense. Most people's mums would want things filled in a bit, that's all. She'd be entitled.'

'She isn't like most people's mums. You'll see. D'you want tea or coffee?'

He said, 'She scares you stiff or something, doesn't she? She's the one thing that really steams you up. I want to meet her. Coffee, and three slices of toast please – in bed?'

'*No*,' she said. 'Up, or not at all. And I'm going in fifteen minutes precisely. Some of us have a living to earn.'

His hands, every day, were grimy from books and manuscripts. Seventeenth century grime, some of it, he supposed. He sat in the British Museum Reading Room, picking slivers of dirt from under a fingernail, stared at Stukeley's neat, distinctive handwriting, and read that on an April day in 1719 he visited an 'antient' site where 'as we sat surveying the corn growing upon the spot I did see the perfect vestigia of a temple, as easily discernible upon the corn as upon paper.' Crop marks, clever old Stukeley. And later he had 'met with some excellent Ale.' Ah. It's knowing that kind of thing that makes this kind of thing seem slightly less of a fantasy than it does a lot of the time.

William Stukeley and his contemporaries: a study of seventeenth and early eighteenth century antiquarianism. Tom Rider, M.A., D.Phil. T. P. Rider, M.A., D.Phil. Thomas P. Rider, M.A., D.Phil.

Or not, as the case may be. The little crescents of dirt lay on the manuscripts. And they call this a white-collar job. Stukeley, of course, got his hands dirty – digging, surveying – and his feet, too, plodding around in the muck.

There was a portrait of Stukeley that cropped up in reproduction in innumerable works: a fattish, jowly face, pointed nose, dark, sharp eyes, grey wig, flowing white cravat, jacket of dark, shiny material. From time to time Tom had scoured this for some kind of insight into this person who must occupy three years of his, Tom's life. Three rather crucial years, at that. Occasionally the processes of historical research amazed him: we think we know about the past, learned blokes stake their professional reputations on this or that interpretation of the way things have been at this point or that. Here am I, about to contribute some seventy thousand words which will analyse and pronounce upon the way in which antiquarian studies declined from the intellectual vigour of the seventeenth century into the romantic inaccuracies of the early eighteenth, with special reference to the career of William Stukeley. I know a great deal about Stukeley; I probably know more about Stukeley than anybody else in the world; I know where he was on April 4th 1719 and I know who his friends were and in what language he addressed them and I know the broad course of his life from the day he was born till the day he died. The real Stukeley, of course, is effectively concealed by two hundred and fifty years of gathering confusion and conflicting interpretations of how the world may have appeared to other people. The real breathing feeling cock-and-balls prick-me-and-I-bleed Stukeley is just about as inaccessible as Neanderthal man.

'Sometimes,' he said to Kate, 'sometimes I think of going into industry. A rather dubious branch of industry. Armaments. Or the manufacture of pop records.'

'You don't really,' said Kate with tranquillity.

'You're happy to condemn me – us – to a lifetime of underpaid academic nitpicking? Anyway, there are no jobs.'

'You love it. And some people get jobs – quite a lot do.'

'Oh, you're all right, I know. All set up with a pension. That's what I'm marrying you for, I hope you realize.'

She worked in a museum, a civil servant, her responsibility to the past defined by grade and status. For the moment, she was in London, working on some vast new scheme of reclassification and reorganization, which she found tiresome. In the autumn, in their early courting period, she had been based at a provincial town in the process of setting up a refurbished County Museum; for Tom, now, love and lust would be for ever associated with plough-shares and sickles, with the machinery of the early glove industry, with brick moulds and stonemasons' tools, with hay wains and milk floats and early twentieth century tractors. In.this setting, he had waited patiently for her to finish her day's work; the sight of a threshing machine or butter churn would, for the rest of his life, bring an expectant lift of the heart.

There was something equine about her, he had thought fondly, as she trotted about with her labels and cards, a small, dark, muscular girl, energetic and ferociously scowling. She scowled as she worked, as she walked with him on the woodlands near the town, as she made love. He found this appealing. The happier you are, he said, the more bad-tempered you look, did you know? I like that, it makes you such a splendidly misleading person, only those who know you can have the faintest idea what's going on, have you always been like that?

She was twenty-four.

Do you want a ring? he said. All that stuff? Proof that my intentions are honourable – fairly honourable? And she had hugged him and glared from under those shaggy eyebrows and said that was the last thing she wanted, she wouldn't know what to do with it.

They had a weekend in France instead.

Her father had been Hugh Paxton, the archaeologist. It must be odd, Tom sometimes thought, to have been fathered by a man to

4

whom such a label was forever attached – 'The Hugh Paxton, you mean? The archaeologist.' How does it feel? he had asked her, early in their courting days, speaking as one whose father is Jim Rider, pure and simple. The corporation bus driver, if anyone. It doesn't feel anything, she said, it's just how it is, how it always was.

His was one of those names known even to those who know nothing of their field of work. Woolley, Childe, Piggott, Paxton, Wheeler – the names would have vague connotations where Ur, Mycenae, La Tène or Wessex might not. Hugh Paxton had missed, somehow, the age of the television archaeologist, though he had died only five years ago. Why? Tom asked, and Kate had shrugged and said, oh, he'd have hated it, it wasn't his kind of thing at all. Ma would have loved it, of course, she had added, a minute or so later.

There was a photo of him on Kate's dressing-table: a good-looking, slightly swarthy man (it was from him that her dark sturdiness came, her desirable springy body, that faint hairiness . . .). Tom had examined it with interest, felt mildly embarrassed sometimes at its scrutiny as he dressed and shaved, explained to it, apologetically, that he loved Kate and had the best possible intentions towards her. And Hugh Paxton looked the sort of man who would have known a bit of passion in his time, one way and another.

And now Tom sat beside Kate in the car (her car), headed for Danehurst along roads that soared across the Wiltshire downs, Kate hunched over the wheel in her usual unnerving position, nose too near the windscreen, taking the bends a little too fast.

'Aunt what?' he said.

'Aunt Nellie. Aunt Nellie is my mother's sister. They live together now because Aunt Nellie had a stroke two years ago and can't do much for herself.' She jinked sideways to miss an on-coming lorry.

Tom said, 'Watch it.' And then, 'That's very charitable of your mother.'

'Not really. Aunt Nellie has a bit of money of her own and Ma hasn't because my father left things in a muddle and there were a lot of death duties. It's a quid pro quo. Aunt Nellie subsidizes Danehurst – it's expensive to run.'

'Ah,' said Tom, adjusting his concept of Mrs Paxton.

'Aunt Nellie,' said Kate, in tones that would have sounded like fury to one unfamiliar with her way of disguising emotional revelation, 'is very nice.'

'Why have you never told me all this before?'

'I probably have, and you weren't listening. Anyway, you're marrying me, not my family.'

'People always say that. It's a common instance of self-delusion.'

Kate thought: I am wearing jeans and a jersey, so she will be dressed to kill and will say, Kate I do think you might make just a bit of an effort when you come home. She will say it where Tom can hear, and I will go red like I always have when she tells me off. But if I had worn my new dress and my boots she would have had gardening things on and said, oh dear, I'm afraid we can't live up to you London people, gracious Kate however much did you pay for that frock? Well, anyway, I'm glad you're earning such a lot now, how nice. And I would have felt quite differently uncomfortable.

I can't win, she thought angrily, and now already I am in a fuss and snapping at Tom and I love him and it is in no way his fault, no way at all.

They came out of Marlborough and drove beside the Kennet Valley, the trees and marshy gound making a darker green cleft between the wide flanks of the downs. Birds rolled in the wind above pale green fields and the flecked brown and white earth of chalk country. There was heavy traffic on the A4; the empty landscape at either side had an inaccessible serenity, as though behind glass. Kate said, 'We're there, all but,' and swung suddenly onto a side road, without signalling, bringing a yelp of indignation from the car behind.

An Edwardian house, not the beguiling affair of stone and thatch he had imagined. A large, faintly inappropriate house in a pleasant enough setting of hamlet, church, small schoolhouse, village pond. There was a big garden; beyond it, the downs opened up abruptly to a skyline swept by long skeins of cloud. He could see the green blister of a round barrow on the crest of the hill; round the corner, up the road, was Silbury. No wonder Paxton picked the place: his livelihood on the doorstep. He turned to ask Kate when they had bought the house, and saw her sitting at the wheel, knuckles clenched, the expression of rigid obstinacy on her face that indicated extreme anxiety. Thus, he had seen her stand waiting for him once at Green Park Underground station at the reunion after a tiff; she had thought he would not turn up: he had realized, with amused affection, that she minded. After that he had moved into her flat.

He said, 'Come on, you don't have to be that ashamed of me.'

She gave him a look that mixed rage and entreaty.

Laura Paxton sat in a faded chintz armchair beside a log fire and handled glasses on a table beside her. She said, 'Sherry, darling? And Tom? No gin or anything I'm afraid. Vermouth, I think.' She wore a silk dress that looked too thin for the weather, high-heeled shoes. She filled glasses, handed them, took a sip from her own and said, 'Well, so here's the famous fiancé at last.' She considered Tom, smiling.

He did not see how anyone could have so extraordinary a knack of instantly putting everyone else at a disadvantage. It is amazing, he thought, how is it done? You could go far, with a talent like that. He wanted to say to Kate: I see now, I do absolutely see, you need say no more. No wonder.

She was beautiful, he supposed. Her physical presence held the attention; when she was in the room you kept looking towards her, as towards a handsome piece of furniture, an intriguing picture. Her eyes, in an oval, rather flat face, were large and blue, with only a hint of wrinkling around them; she did not look her age. Her hair, fair and thin like a child's, worn in a straight school-girlish bob, showed no grey. She moved quickly. Her hands were long and thin; she used them in conversation, very deliberately, as though someone, once, had pointed out their charms and she had borne it in mind.

He was transfixed, not so much by her, as by the lurking, distorted Kate he saw in her. It was grotesque – the physical presence of Kate in this stranger. They were quite unalike – yet in that first half hour he was aware of Kate half a dozen times, so keenly that it seemed the recognition must be shared. As though, with incestuous knowledge, Mrs Paxton, pouring the sherry and offering it to him with, for a flash, Kate's glance, knew him in Kate's way: at all times, in all circumstances, naked, all reserves gone, all defences down.

With discomfort, he took the sherry and, in response to a question, began to talk about his work, his aspirations, in a tone and with a manner that were not his at all: brittle, self-conscious. It was as though his language were bewitched, like the girl in the fairy story, spewed forth as toads or diamonds, willy nilly. Laura Paxton laughed appreciatively; he suited her well enough, like that, it seemed. He saw Kate looking at him bleakly, as though to say: you too, one might have known. She sat hunched on a footstool, chewing a fingernail; the thought crossed his mind – surprising him – that he wished she would bother a bit more about what she wore. Not treat herself with such disregard; those jeans looked awful.

He thought this, and took a gulp of sherry that made him choke, and heard himself tell Laura Paxton in language that he did not recognize of opinions that he did not acknowledge. He was filled with self-disgust, as though tricked into laughter at a joke that

8

did not amuse. He did not know if she was very stupid or very clever.

Laura thought, he is better looking than Kate, really – they will look a bit odd, going up the aisle, if it gets that far. I shall splurge on something really good, and a hat – a Jaeger dress and coat, maybe. Nellie will be a problem, she will have to be there, Mrs Lucas can come and help. It will be a bit boring in the end, anyway, Kate will want to ask her friends I suppose and they are all too young to be interesting and Tom obviously doesn't have the kind of family who know people. And it will be very expensive, let's hope Nellie offers to help. 'What, darling?'

Kate said, 'Where is Aunt Nellie?'

'Oh, coming through for lunch, you can go and give her a hand in a few minutes. We've made the old dining room into a room for her now, you know, so much easier all on the ground floor.' She sighed. 'The outlook isn't very good, I'm afraid, things aren't getting much better, it's quite a problem, I can tell you. Though she's talking more easily now. Poor darling, she does sound a bit pickled all the time – which is specially hard when she's always been rather averse to drink. Oh, it's a wretched business.' She spread long thin hands to the fire, thought: I am bored, I have been bored for weeks, I must go up to London for a day or two, have lunch with someone, buy some things . . . There was a bumping sound in the passage outside the door. Laura said, 'Oh, here's Nellie making her own way. Open the door for her, one of you, could you?'

Tom, embarrassedly holding the door for the wheelchair, thought: well, *she* doesn't have anything of Kate, thank God, two of them making you feel creepily as though you might have been in bed with them would have been too much, and she's years older too. Christ, are people who've had a stroke deaf? I've no idea, is she *compos mentis* or not, how ignorant one is, it's appalling.

Nellie Peters gave the wheel an extra shove with her good hand to help it over the edge of the carpet where it always stuck. She looked across the room at her niece, with love, and thought: she has been having a frightful half-hour, she is just about at the end of her tether, poor dear, and it never gets any better for her, there is nothing to be done, there never was much, even when she was a child. Well, let's have a look at him, will he do? Is he going to help her, be the best thing that has ever happened for her, is there any hope of that? She began to say, in that slow, slurred voice that gave her a shock of detached indignation every time she heard it, 'It's lovely to see you, Kate, I . . .'

Laura chopped her off in mid-word. 'Nellie I told you not to struggle through on your own, absolutely no need for that, there's always someone to give you a hand.' She manoeuvred the wheelchair sharply into position beside the sofa, where it was awkwardly placed a little apart from the rest of them. 'All right? Yell if there's anything you want, darling. No sherry, I imagine.' She turned to Tom, 'Sorry – I'm being so rude. My sister Eleanor, of course – poor Nellie has had the most beastly luck, as I was saying, but there is a faint chance that things may improve with time' – this last in tones just very slightly lowered.

In the hall, a clock chimed and struck; a cat, hitherto unseen, strolled into the middle of the room, and stood swishing its tail before slumping down in a bar of sunlight on the carpet. Kate and her aunt kissed with the ineptitude of people who find it an embarrassment, but necessary.

And Tom, for whom the weekend stretched oppressively ahead, thought with sudden resolution that he was going to have to cope with this, not just now but for always, given Kate and the state of his feelings and also, dammit, that a woman like that cannot be allowed to do what she clearly does do.

He said to Kate, cutting suddenly into her reluctant answers to some probing by her mother, 'Are you going to take me for a walk this afternoon – I'm feeling energetic – a nice long instructive windy walk, how about that?'

'Oh dear,' said Laura, 'are you that kind of person? Outdoor and long walks and so forth. Hugh was, of course. It does rather run in the family.'

Kate said, 'Well, he could hardly have been an archaeologist and not been, could he, Ma?'

Laura turned to Tom. 'And by the way, do say Laura, won't you, not Mrs Paxton. I wish Kate would do the same but not a hope – she dropped Mummy for reasons best known to herself and now it's this horrid "Ma", I must say I do think that at this point in time Laura would be nicer, but there it is. She's a stubborn girl, my Kate.'

'Isn't calling parents by their Christian names rather out of date?' said Tom. 'I thought it was a thirties sort of thing. Like vegetarianism and progressive schools.'

Laura gave a him a look of dislike. 'Oh, I daresay one is very out of touch,' she said. 'It's just a matter of what one personally prefers. Is something wrong, Nellie?'

She was laughing, Tom realized, the aunt. You could be forgiven for thinking that odd strangled sound was one of distress, not pleasure. And Kate was grinning at her, a different, normal, relaxed Kate; his Kate, come to that.

'Well,' said Laura, 'let's eat. I've spent a lot of time making something rather nice. Kate, will you see to Aunt Nellie while I pop through to the kitchen – Tom my dear, perhaps you'd give me a hand with plates and whatnot.'

'Oh,' she said, at lunch, 'I quite forgot to tell you. I had a letter from some television man, a producer of something, Tony some-one – they want to do a programme about Hugh. Film it here, and at some of his old digs. Isn't that fan?'

Kate put her knife and fork down with a clatter. 'You never told me.'

'That's what I'm saying,' said Laura impatiently. 'It went out of my head – God knows why, it's not as though that much ever happens these days.'

'What did you say to him?'

'I said yes, of course. I'd help as much as I can and so forth. P'raps we'll all be in it, that would be amusing.'

Kate said nothing; her neck glowed. Tom said to Laura, 'What's the programme?'

'Oh, some cultural thing. It's a series they're doing on kind of intellectual people of the recent past – people who influenced the way different subjects are thought about. There's one on that economist person – what's his name?'

'Keynes?'

'I think so,' said Laura vaguely. 'And a poet – Auden, is it? Someone like that. And Hugh, and what's that person who taught English at Cambridge that nobody liked? Those kind of people.'

'Well, I wish they wouldn't,' said Kate with violence. 'Dad would have loathed it, anyway.'

Nellie had been silent for a lot of the meal, excluded often by the pace of conversation, though both Kate and Tom had made efforts to bring her in. Now she said, 'One wonders what it is they are trying to show – something about the man or something about the subject. Quite different things, possibly.'

There was a silence. Laura said, 'Oh well, anyway it's not that important but it will be a diversion, I daresay. Do you want coffee?'

It was a warm afternoon of late spring. Out of the house, with the great blowy bowl of the landscape around him, Tom felt exhilarated. He took Kate's hand and said, 'Where are we going, can you walk to Avebury from here? Let's go miles, I feel cooped up.' And then a look at her clamped, dejected face reminded him that this might be less than tactful, and he put an arm round her and hugged her. 'I don't mean lunch, and your mum, though I do see what you're on about now, love – I truly do. I just mean I want air – I've got deposits of B.M. grime in my lungs.' She thawed, and smiled, and they walked away up over the fields with arms round each other.

Avebury ran with school children, larking among the stones like puppies, chivvied by fretting teachers. Tom, standing beside a sarsen, picked idly at the skin of lichen, and thought of Stukeley. He said to Kate, 'He nearly got things right, you know, old William S. He was convinced Stonehenge was pre-Roman, he was sure Inigo Jones's stuff about it being a Roman temple was nonsense, he was onto the idea of there being a whole prehistoric sequence, with different types of site fitting into different periods. And then he mucked it all up with lunatic theories about the Druids. He got religion and spoilt everything by trying to fit the facts to the argument. He chucked out truth and a scientific approach to the past for the sake of a convenient theory – and an emotionally appealing one.'

Kate said, 'Lots of people do that. A woman came into the museum in the summer wanting a recipe for beeswax. To polish her furniture with.'

'What *are* you talking about?'

'What I said. She'd seen our section about nineteenth century household management and she wanted to make beeswax.'

'P'raps she kept bees.'

'No she didn't. It was just a fad. I felt like telling her to go out and buy a tin of Mansion polish from the supermarket next door.'

'You've got no respect for tradition. They'll be throwing you out of the museums department.'

'Museums are one thing,' said Kate, 'real life is a different matter altogether.' She ran slithering down the grassy rampart, saying, 'Let's go somewhere else, there are too many people here.'

He caught her up at the bottom, and she said suddenly, in an odd tone, almost shy, 'Shall I take you to one of Dad's old digs? His big site is just near here – Charlie's Tump. I was about six when they were working there, I can remember it vaguely . . .'

They climbed steeply, up a path creamy with thin chalk mud, leaving the road and the village behind, climbing into the wind, away from voices and cars, climbing it seemed upwards and back-wards into a quieter older place, where sarsens lay undisturbed like grey islands on the turf and sheep turned bland, enquiring faces as they passed. The wind was sharper up here; it plastered their hair to their heads and fringed Kate's ears with pink. She stumped up the path a yard or two ahead, like a tough little pony. Tom saw the green dome of the barrow on the skyline and called out, 'Why Charlie's Tump?' and she shouted back, 'Oh, it's just the local name – some nonsense about Charles I. There's a good view from the top. That's Windmill Hill, over there, and East Kennet the other side of the valley.'

He stood on top of the barrow and the green flanks of down-land swooped around him in a circle, windy and ancient, swept by moving bands of sunlight that lit now this section and now that, in a shaft of green and gold and rich light brown. Marvellous, he thought, I'm in the wrong racket, that's my trouble, I should have gone in for archaeology, a nice outdoor life instead of all this unhealthy bookwork. He turned, and saw Kate standing below him, staring towards a skinny copse at the edge of the field, a scatter of trees around a dip, furred over with the bright green of new leaves, and shouted, 'Come and tell me about this dig – what happened?'

I am digging, like Aunt Nellie and Daddy and Tony and Brenda and the one with the funny name. This is my dig, all my own, nobody else can dig here. This is my button that I have dug, and my bone and my bit of sharp black stuff and my bottle top.

There is hot sun on my back; if I poke this spider with a bit of grass it runs into a hole and watches me, inside; when I press my eyes with my fingers I can see red circles, then blue ones, then purple ones.

I can hear Daddy and Aunt Nellie talking. Daddy talks to Aunt Nellie in a special voice, it is not like the voice he talks to other people in.

It is not like the voice he talks to Mummy in.

I like Aunt Nellie. I like Daddy.

If I creep, like this, through the long grass at the edge of the field no one knows I am there, not even the sheep. I wriggle on my tummy and I can go quite fast, like a worm, and already I am at the end of the field and they do not know I have gone, I can't hear their voices any more, they can't see me.

There is someone in the trees, in there. Voices, whispering.

It's Mummy. Mummy with someone. If I go on creeping I can go through the bushes and jump on Mummy, make her laugh, make her see me, make her say 'Kate!' and hold her arms out.

I must be very quiet. There are things prickling me. I can nearly see them now. It is that man, the one with the funny name, who talks a funny way. The one Mummy likes. Now I can see them.

*What are they doing? Why are they down there? Why is he doing that to Mummy?*

# Chapter Two

Laura said, 'Gracious! She dragged you all the way up there – you must be exhausted. I haven't been there for years, there are some photos of that dig in the old albums, somewhere. I must get them out and show you – it was after he published that dig that Hugh got the Directorship, of course.' She went to rummage in the drawer of a tallboy.

They had had dinner. They sat now, all of them, by the fire in the drawing room; Kate read *The Times*, Nellie a book on the Tradescants, Laura talked. Tom's cheeks burned still with the wind; he looked across at Kate, scowling over Bernard Levin, and thought regretfully: silly girl, what got into her this afternoon, you'd have thought it was perversity of some kind I was suggesting.

I like this place, he had said, it's got something. And it's made me feel extremely randy all of a sudden. Come on.

And she stared at him in horror and said, in there! in the copse! don't be silly, Tom, you are joking, aren't you?

I'm not joking at all, he'd said. I want to make love. Now. In there.

Somebody might come, she argued in panic. And he said nobody's going to come, at the worst, you might sting your bum on a nettle, and that's a small price to pay, at least it ought to be. *I* wouldn't mind, he had added crossly, but never mind, if you don't want to.

I'm sorry, she had said, anguished, I'm sorry, Tom – but I couldn't, honestly, I really couldn't. Not out here.

'There,' said Laura, dumping an album on the table. 'This is the one. No, it isn't – this is our wedding, and just before. Never mind, have a look, Tom – they're rather amusing. And here's Kate as a baby, at the end.'

Kate as a baby has a strong suggestion of Kate now, which is beguiling. And here is Hugh Paxton, youngish, sitting in a deck chair reading a book in the garden of this house. And here is Laura, rather posed, on a beach somewhere, with what one has to concede is a very nice figure. And here . . .

'I'm sorry,' he said, shifting his chair to make room for Nellie at the table. 'Can you see all right? Is this you? No, it's Mrs Paxton, isn't it, Laura I mean.'

The photograph shows two people, standing side by side in front of – yes, in front of this house. The man has his head turned aside a little, as though perhaps evading the camera, he seems unwillingly there, in some way; the woman, on the other hand, smiles straight ahead and holds her skirt down against the wind, she looks confident and happy. There is a third person involved (naturally enough): the shadow of the taker, head and shoulders, protrudes in the right foreground of the picture.

Nellie's hand, now, her good hand, lies on the page to stop it flipping over.

They come towards me, walking side by side. There is a wind and it blows Hugh's hair upwards from his face, an inverted fringe. I start to say, 'Sorry to be so late, there was a . . .', and she slips her arm through his, through his crooked elbow, and calls out 'You're just in time, Mary's coming over for lunch, and the Sadlers, it's a celebration, Nellie, we've got something to tell you, we're going to get married, Nellie.'

He says nothing. They have stopped. He looks wooden, standing there beside her. He is wearing grey flannel trousers and a blazer. The trousers are baggy at the knee. I say nothing.

Laura said, 'Hugh and me. When can that be? Oh, I remember – you took it, Nellie. That old box Brownie you had. Not long after the war.'

★

17

Nellie gets out of the car; she is all blown about, she must have driven with the hood down, she looks a mess. Hugh's arm is round me; we walk together towards her; I say to him, 'Darling, you tell her.' I kiss her and say, 'You're just in time, it's a celebration, Nellie, Hugh's got something to tell you.' Hugh says, 'Well, Nellie, there's going to be a wedding, we want you to know first of all.'

I am wearing my New Look dress – long, long. I feel it brush my calves when I move. It has a petticoat that rustles.

Nellie says, 'I'm not entirely surprised. Congratulations. That's marvellous.' She takes her suitcase out of the car. She says, 'You'll have to learn how to get your hands dirty now, Laura.' She goes into the house; there are creases all across the back of her skirt.

'But it's that dig I was after, the Charlie's Tump dig. Ah, it's in this one. Goodness – who are all these people? There's me, and Hugh, and you, Nellie. And Kate, of course, in a dear little sunsuit or something, it must have been hot. And that's Brenda Carstairs, I think. But who on earth . . .'

Nellie's fumbling speech distorts words; it is hard to catch, sometimes, just what she has said.

'Oh,' said Laura, 'Carlos. Of course. Carlos Fuego – yes, he was there wasn't he, that summer. Don't bang the coffee cups down like that, Kate darling, you'll break them and they're the good ones. You're off to bed, are you? Use my bathroom, darling, and Tom can have the spare one to himself.'

Tom, waking in a strange room, experienced a fleeting moment of confusion and spiritual detachment. He lay in a void that had no certainties beyond the body, his body, between sheets that were unnaturally crisp and clean; he groped for time and place, for why and when, and heard the voice of his future mother-in-law outside the door. Facts flooded in, and with them a fond reaction to that good smell of coffee coming from somewhere, and a lingering sense of deprivation: Kate had been tiresomely standoffish last night. 'Honestly,' she had said, 'honestly you can't, not here, I really am sorry, I mean it's just as bad for me.' She had stood outside her bedroom door, in striped schoolgirl pyjamas dredged up from some forgotten drawer. '*Why* not?' 'The bed squeaks, and Ma's next door.' 'Oh, for goodness sake, Kate!' He had stumped off in discomfort to a solitary night.

Now he contemplated, in the morning light, the room, with its slightly bleak, stripped-for-action look of all guest rooms: flower prints on the wall, one or two second-best ornaments. His own parents did not have a guest room; Kate, last month, had slept in what was still, when he came home from college, his brother Kevin's room, with school photos pinned above the bed and foot-ball banners and old shoes tumbling from the cupboard. She had been perfectly happy. She had settled herself in like a dog turning round and round in an agreeable chair, eating greedily, in instant accord with his parents, avidly watching the television all evening. He had taken her to the pub, where she had hinted she would really rather get back. 'I thought you must be bored.'

'I haven't ever actually seen a colour telly before,' she had said. He had capitulated to the yearning in her face and taken her home again.

His mother had thought her a nice girl, no nonsense about her. His father had patted her on the arm at parting, indicating approval. Kate, on the way back to London, had said it's good there, let's go there often. How do you mean, *good?* he asked, and she replied, vaguely, oh, I don't know, just you feel anybody could overhear anything anyone else said and it wouldn't matter. Or thought, even.

He had felt obscurely flattered, and looked at his family with new eyes.

The thought of the eventual confrontation of his parents and Laura Paxton was so bizarre that he dismissed the whole thing and got out of bed, wondering if there would be Sunday papers and, more importantly, if the village rose to a pub: another lunchtime on those cut-glass thimbles of sherry would not do at all.

Nellie, negotiating the awkward turn in the passage outside her room, met him coming down the stairs, caught in his eye that flicker of embarrassment tempered with slight panic that she met in most eyes now and said, 'No help needed, thank you – Kate is already down, I think.' She trundled beside him to the kitchen and pushed from her, as she did half a dozen times a day, the remembrance of meeting people when you did not present, however well-meaning and sensitive the people might be, an instant problem. Tom held the kitchen door open for her and Laura, at the stove, turned and said, 'Oh Nellie dear, you are naughty, I keep telling you to stay put in the mornings, Kate would have brought you a tray. Egg and bacon, Tom?'

He said to Kate, later, 'I must say I can't see your mother trowelling away in the dirt – *did* she?'

'Not really. Well, she used to label sherds and that kind of thing, if the weather was nice, I can't ever remember her actually digging. Mostly she didn't come on digs. Aunt Nellie did, of course, unless she was busy with one of her own.'

He said in surprise, 'I hadn't realized she was an archaeologist herself, your aunt.'

'Oh yes. She worked with Dad way back, when he was starting out. That's how he met Ma – through Aunt Nellie.'

'I see.'

'And then all the time Dad was with the Council, after the war, she was at the Ministry of Works – but she still came on his digs sometimes. Like Charlie's Tump. But mostly she was off somewhere doing things for the Ministry.'

Ah. She looked different, Nellie Peters, with her past filled in like this. It enlarged and clarified. Tom thought with discomfort that he had been speaking to her in the wrong way, given that she was a person, who, like oneself . . . and then, with chagrin, that it was deplorable in the first place to adopt a particular tone according to whether you knew a person to be, like oneself, educated and informed, or not . . . And would Nellie Peters, educated and informed, observe and ponder upon his (instinctively) altered tone when next he addressed her?

He should, of course, have cottoned on earlier, during that business about the votive figure or whatever it was.

'You've *sold* it!' Kate had said, staring at her mother across the breakfast table.

'To a museum, darling. Nothing for you to be so disapproving about.'

'What, Aunt Nellie?'

'Nellie is saying,' Laura said with a sigh, 'that we had a little difference of opinion about it. The point is that new curtains were desperately needed for the drawing room – which you haven't even noticed I daresay – and frankly the only thing to do was to sell something. And this house is crammed with bits and pieces that really no one ever looks at, of enormous interest I know but Hugh gave all his best stuff to the B.M. or the county museum years ago and sentimental value is another matter and frankly again I'm not sure that's something I can afford. And John Barclay has said that little goddess thing must be worth a lot and there it was just sitting there . . .'

'Gathering dust?'

'Well, no actually, since it was in the glass-fronted case. But sitting there, and the drawing room crying out for new curtains . . .'

'Positively weeping.'

Laura got up. 'I think you're being just a tiny bit rude, Kate, if I may say so. And the fact remains that the things are mine to do what I like with, so please don't sit there with "And what would Daddy have said?" written all over your face, because the truth is I'm sure Hugh would have seen my point entirely and if he'd been just a mite more efficient about money, poor darling, this wouldn't be necessary.' She went out of the room, turning at the door to say, 'If anyone felt like getting on with the washing-up, that would be simply lovely.'

Kate started to slam dishes into the sink with dangerous fervour. Tom said to Nellie, 'What exactly was the thing that was sold?'

'It was a small votive object – chalk, a female fertility . . .' and then her treacherous speech had failed her and her voice had trailed off and in the pause he had said informatively, 'Oh yes – neolithic, I expect, like that thing from Grime's Graves in Norfolk, there are those flint-mines there, you know, where they found that curious little chalk figure in one of the shafts.'

It was surprising she had nodded with such tolerance. He sweated now at the recollection and decided that Kate's assertions of her aunt's niceness were quite correct.

The house *was* full of bits and pieces, it was true. He had wandered round, that morning, examining the monochrome detritus of prehistory – the uniformly beige display of pots and bowls and weapons – and had thought that it was perhaps this unrewarding front that had got the subject into trouble from the start. Laura had clearly had her way with the drawing room: there, shelves and cases held only the cheerful delicacy of some good eighteenth and nineteenth century china, and one or two pieces of modern pottery. But elsewhere Hugh Paxton's collections of pots in a state of collapse, of pots resurrected, of flints and axes and spears, of gangrenous metal pins and brooches, of bones and funerary urns, dominated the house. Just throwouts, really, Laura had said, the best stuff went to the museums, of course. And yes, indeed, it was like the random loot of some nineteenth century clerical antiquarian – a studyful of 'things of interest' unrelated to time and place. Or those mysterious objects passed from hand to hand by a panel of archaeologists in that old television game that he remembered as a child – chunks of pot or metal held up for assessment and definition.

And that, of course, he thought, is the basic problem – what, in the end, can you do with a subject that depends entirely on the survival of material objects? No wonder it's kept going off the rails, ever since the Saxons supposed the Roman towns were built by giants. Giants, gods, druids . . . A vehicle for every kind of expedient theory, the most malleable aspect of the past, prehistory. And the most treacherous. They get it all nicely sorted out into a chronological sequence, at last – the three ages – and then along come all sorts of disconcerting cultural overlaps that won't fit in, and cultural parallels in the eastern Mediterranean or wherever, and they have to work out a new explanation – the invasionist theory. And then someone dreams up radio-carbon dating and blows everything sky high – Stonehenge far older than Mycenae, northern megalithic tombs earlier than any other stone buildings, and everybody has to take a deep breath and start all over again. How do you feel – when it becomes irrefutably clear that your life's work has been based on a misapprehension? That you had been assembling the jigsaw puzzle all wrong and had better break it up and start again?

Not absolutely, of course. All that carefully collected evidence would still do – the product of all those wet or hot or windy weeks at Windmill Hill or Durrington Walls or Charlie's Tump or wherever. It was the interpretation of it that must be chucked out. Though at least for good rational scientific reasons – not abandoned as a sop to religious mania, like poor old Stukeley and his druids, no parallel there. All the same, though, one might be able to fit an elegant little note into the thesis somewhere about the inconsistency of prehistory as a subject all along the line . . .

Assuming, of course, that one got as far as actually writing it, and didn't just atrophy in a library first, turned to stone by apprehension and insidious doubt and guilty boredom, another petrified bust to join Voltaire and Dr Johnson and Plato – though less confident than they about the satisfactions of the life of the mind.

Tom thought of his friend Bob Taylor, his old friend-through-school-and-university, his colleague and rival from Sixth Form Prize to Finals, his mate and competitor, who would be starting his new job just about now.

'ICI?' he had said to Bob, incredulous – incredulous and furious.

'You mean it, do you? Well, well, well. What do they pay? A good whack, no doubt.'

Bob said, 'Look, the money is *not* the main thing, though I'm never going to convince you of that, I daresay. The main thing is that I'll *be doing* something, or so I fondly believe. One might actually be able to affect what happens somewhere, for better or for worse. I got to the state where I just couldn't any longer see myself for the next forty years or whatever, sitting around trying to . . .'

'Well, send us a food parcel from time to time, won't you, up here in the world of make-believe.'

'Oh, come off it, Tom, for Christ's sake.'

They glared at each other. This is my best friend, Tom had thought, this is my best friend, in whom I was well pleased.

He would drop Bob a line, he thought now – ask how things were going, tacitly say sorry, suggest they got together at some point.

And of course he was going to get as far as writing the thesis, just as he had always seen things through, be they O-levels or A-levels or the production of the school magazine or the assimilation of a library full of information about the course of British history over the statutory period of three years allotted by a generous government for the (higher) education of its (brighter) citizens. He would learn everything there was to be learned about William Stukeley, reflect upon the implications of his career, pronounce upon the matter, and hope something came of it all.

And, prowling around Danehurst with an interested eye upon the life-style suggested by its contents, the academic grind did not seem to Tom that bad. Plenty of books (not just archaeology either), nice pictures, tasteful comfort, and a particularly pleasant bit of England outside the windows. He admired some early engravings of Avebury and Stonehenge, laid an envious hand on a second edition of Fielding, and stood at the drawing room window where on a table beside him lay a cutting from a newspaper which he read (such is the instinctive response to print induced by a prolonged education): '. . . this valuable book fully bears out the now widely held belief of specialists that the improvement and ultimate recovery of stroke victims owes as much to environmental factors as to any kind of treatment, and above all to the encouragement and optimism of those around them. Convince the patient that he *can* recover the use of his faculties, and the greatest hurdle is overcome. Of invaluable practical use to the relatives of patients, Dr Samson's suggestions concerning the day-to-day . . .'

Hmn. Well, well. Suggestive, that, but in different ways, depending on who cut it out and left it there. And out there, moving slowly down the garden path, doing something to roses from her wheelchair, was Nellie, Aunt Nellie, reaching with slow frustration for an evasive stem. Should one offer to help? Or not?

The garden consisted of a large rectangular lawn, approached across the stone terrace onto which the french windows of the drawing room opened, and a further area beyond, screened by a high yew hedge with an opening in the middle. The lawn was walled on the other two sides, with herbaceous borders against the walls. In one corner was a decaying rustic summer house with thatched roof. Beyond the yew hedge was a further flower garden, a more arranged affair of paved paths and beds of low cushiony plants, a bright section of which was visible through the opening in the hedge. This, in turn, led via a low wooden gate to a vegetable garden, now almost completely uncultivated. The whole garden, indeed, suggested decline from better days: there was an uncontrolled air about trees and shrubs, a furriness of hedges and lawn, the flowerbeds were choked with growth. In photos in that album, the place had looked spick and span. Now, it seemed to have settled into a state of resigned recollection.

Like people, Tom thought, pleased by this piece of anthropomorphism, still watching Nellie, who was passing, now, through the opening in the yew hedge into the flower garden beyond. Very like people.

These two, her and Mrs P. – living on here like this – photo albums, cupboardsful of Hugh Paxton's stuff, Mrs P. – *Laura* – bored to tears. Why not go out and find a job? But of course ladies like that don't. The odd morning in the Oxfam shop; a bit of organized indignation about threats to the environment – those would be the only options open. Aunt Nellie, of course, seems to be a different kettle of fish, from what one hears.

And he set off now across the lawn, propelled by guilt and a heave of curiosity, to see if help mightn't be acceptable with this pruning or whatever it was she was up to.

And Nellie, intent on a battle with the suckers of a Madame Butterfly in which most advantages were held by the rose, and in her thoughts not present at all, but busy with the reconstruction of this same spot on an afternoon some thirty odd years ago, turned at the sound of movement and saw a man standing in the dark frame of the yew.

And there surges that exquisite tide of pleasure, of excitement, of fear.

And I say quickly, to cover my feelings because I am very unsure, as yet, what his might be, 'It's a lovely garden, Hugh – or at least it will be when you can get it going again, of course it's all in a dreadful mess now.'

It has been blighted by the war, as we all are . . . Five years older, gathering ourselves together, starting out again. Hugh does not look five years older; his hair is as thick and black as ever and he has the remains of a Far Eastern tan still: he is recently back from India.

I have not seen him since 1939, that Hampshire dig. Though one has thought – oh yes, thought a great deal, through long dreary hours at the Ministry, or firewatching, or sorting evacuees.

And the actuality is up to the expectation, and beyond, and here, now, am I with him on a visit to this house that he is almost certainly going to buy. And this afternoon we shall go up to West Kennet to take some measurements he needs and then back to

London, hours of time with him, hours and hours, and beyond that there stretches ahead the whole amazing unbelievable prospect of the Lillington dig. I shall see him, on and off, all summer.

Beyond the garden, the landscape blazes; it reflects my feelings; it glows and beams and all is right with the world. I should like to sing. Instead, I say in what comes out as a governessy voice, 'I suppose you would be wise to find out about main drainage – I believe cess pits can be an awful bother.'

Tom said, 'Hello. Can I give a hand?' and she looked startled, guilty even, as though caught out in something she shouldn't be at. 'Thank you,' she said. 'Could you – that bit there. . . .' And together they worked their way along the path, Tom grabbing at indicated growths of rose, and conversation took place, in mutual defiance of Nellie's difficulties, and assessment of one another. Nellie thought: yes, I like him, a bit over-confident maybe, but perceptive with it, a serious person. I think he will do very well for Kate. And he could be a match for Laura. I hope it all goes all right . . . And Tom thought: she's a nice old thing, sharp too, when she can get out what she means to say, it's a hellish way to try to talk to someone you'd really rather like to talk to, like trying to fight your way through some language you can't manage properly, French or whatever.

They came back across the lawn towards the house, to Laura on the terrace calling, 'Tea! Oh, there you are, Tom, Kate has been rushing round like a cat on hot bricks, I do believe she thought you might have walked out on her, poor darling! Come and have some tea, anyway.'

Seeing them into the car that evening, she kissed Kate and then turned to Tom, leaning forward so that, confused, he also proffered a cheek only to see her step back and hold out a hand, neatly wrong-footing him with a relegating smile. A remarkable performance; the most experienced actress would be impressed.

'Well, Tom,' she said, 'it's been lovely to see you at last – the myth made flesh as it were. Come again soon, both of you – next time I must see about laying on some social life for you. And Tom, thank you for being so awfully kind to Nellie – I saw you from the window, being sweet in the rose garden – it does mean a lot to her to have people take a bit of notice.'

Laura stood on the steps, waving, as Kate drove out of the gates and into the lane, abusing the gears in her agitation.

On the A4 headed for London, she said, 'Phew!' and Tom burst out laughing. 'Well, it's all very well for you . . .' Kate complained, and then laughed too, and in hilarity they drove into the rushing Wiltshire darkness, where the shafts of light from juggernaut container lorries blazed down the Old Bath road (from which Charles II made a detour, once, to visit Avebury and Silbury Hill in company with John Aubrey) and where Yamaha and Suzuki motorbikes buzzed between Stukeley's survey lines of the West Kennet Avenue.

And where, much more recently, Kate Paxton rode in a car behind the familiar, sustaining, enriching back of her father, a hairy tweed back, leaning forward to get the warm tweedy smell of it and to hear him properly.

He says he is going away to dig up something in Spain and I say can't I come too? and he says, sorry, Katie, I'm afraid not, not this time. And I say, is Mummy going? and he says nothing for a minute and then, no. And I say, is Aunt Nellie going? And he is busy with driving the car for a minute and then he says, I'm not sure yet. I want to go, I say, in a whiny voice, I don't want to stay here with Mummy.

And then he begins to tell me a story, a silly story about a dog that lived here a long time ago, a dog that belonged to the people then, the Stone people, the people he digs. The story makes me laugh, and I am happy suddenly; we fly through the dark and I smell his smell and listen to his voice and everything is all right, there is only now, there is no more what has happened or what is going to happen.

# Chapter Three

'I am going to Marlborough,' Laura said to Mrs Lucas. 'I have the library to do, and the supermarket, and – oh, and a thousand things, I shall be in a dreadful rush, I daresay I won't be back by lunch-time. So would you please be kind and see to something for my sister, there is a tart that could be heated.' She cashed a cheque, did the supermarket, bought expensive bath stuff from the chemist, looked in the window of the bookshop and met, in the doorway, a literary acquaintance who confided shyly that her book had found a publisher. Laura laid a hand on her arm, 'My dear, that is the most marvellous news! You must be so relieved!' She moved on to the library in company with this woman, meeting another mutual acquaintance on the way to whom she was able to say, quickly, to forestall her companion who would be too modest for further confidences, 'Mary has at last found a publisher for her book, isn't that lovely for her! It just shows what perseverance will do.' At the library she changed her books, and Nellie's, saw with sudden depression that it was only eleven-thirty, and the morning yawned ahead, looked round for Mary to suggest a cup of coffee, and found her unaccountably vanished. She went outside, and stood in fretful uncertainty, looking down the wide market street, that pleasant county town landscape of brick and timber-frame, of centuries juxtaposed, of the good and the vernacular and the deplorable in architectural confusion. Down the centre, a herring-bone formation of parked cars flashed in the sunshine, Marinas and Fiats and Volvos where, in the old days, and with greater ease, she had used to park the Ford.

She stood on the pavement, in her Jaeger wool suit (years old now, but cheered up with a new silk shirt) and the unspent morning hung on her like a weight. She looked at the street, and saw, not change or stability, not the new meters nor the faded nineteenth century lettering that advertised a Corn Chandler and Fuel Merchant on the side of a building, but the lamp-post against which, once, she had clipped the shining new wing of the Ford.

It is not my fault, of course, I am the most careful driver and it would never have happened if I had not been upset like this. I am trembling still, that is how it has happened.

It is their fault, they *made* me get in a state like that, lose my temper, make a scene, which is not like me, I am not that kind of person.

I am all on edge, I have been on edge all day. Am I pregnant, is that it? If I am pregnant then upsetting me like this will make me have a miscarriage, and that will be their fault.

I feel silly, that is the worst thing of all. I can see them still, all standing there with croquet mallets in their hands – ridiculous stupid game – staring at me. Hugh saying 'Laura, what the hell . . .' Nellie on the far side of the lawn, Hugh's dig notebook in her hand. Kate screaming. The Sadlers and the rest of them gawping.

All week it has gone on. They have been there in the study together, working on the Charlie's Tump stuff, by themselves, heads together over the desk, talking, not talking.

Oh, I know Nellie had a thing for Hugh, way back, before he met me, but that was over ages ago, and in any case Hugh . . .

He must not look at her like that. When he looks at her there is something in his face that only otherwise is there when he looks at Kate.

My head aches and I am on the edge of crying, and now the car is scratched, the new car.

She turned and walked briskly to the present car, a small Renault. She put her books and shopping into the back seat and re-locked it. Then, still purposefully, although she had not in fact decided what to do next, she continued down the length of the High Street, arriving eventually at St Mary's.

Here, she hesitated a moment and then went through the porch, past the notices inviting her prayers for the Third World, for the victims of the Indian floods, for the homeless and the starving. Inside the church, she stood for a moment in the nave, looking at the flower arrangements by the pulpit and on the window-ledges. They were the usual tasteless affairs of ill-assorted stuff sprouting in a fan from some rather nasty containers: Laura inspected them with contempt. In the village, she had started a few years ago to do the church flowers herself, now that she had more time, replacing the stiff jam-jar bouquets with pretty trailing arrangements, lots of silvery leaves and foliage effects and imaginative combinations. The church looked heaps better now, though admittedly there had been a bit of resentment, one sensed, from the Vicar's wife and old Mrs Binns and the people who had been doing the flowers for years. One had had to be tactful – explaining how one had after all done a Constance Spry course years ago, had a bit of an eye for interior decoration and so forth.

She stepped into a pew and sank to her knees, giving the dusty hassock a little shake first. She did not know, really, how it was that she had come more and more to religion. Of course, they had been raised in a Christian home, she and Nellie, and on and off, over the years, she had been a church goer, but infrequently. Hugh, of course, never was. Nor Nellie. Now, though – quite apart from the flower arranging – she found herself regularly in the village church. She had her special seat, out of the draught from the door, no one else now would dream of sitting there. And she had got into the habit of praying in privacy, most days, just a few words as she went to bed, it was a nice ritual, in some way settling.

She bent her head and murmured the Lord's Prayer. Then she looked up at the light shafting dustily down on the altar and considered. Help the unfortunate, she prayed, the sick and the poor and the old. Please may the motorway plans come to nothing, the ones that might affect the Kennet Valley. May that tiresome sinus trouble I've been getting go away.

She raised her eyes, noticing a particularly barbaric arrangement of purple anemones on the altar. Overhead, the church clock hummed and struck twelve; the building crouched emptily around her; outside, cars bustled by. And please, she prayed, make something happen, make things more interesting. She got up, and tugged her skirt straight again. And as she did so it occurred to her that she could call on that new couple who had bought a house in West Overton, on the way home, on the pretext of suggesting membership of the Wiltshire Historical Association: people said he was something rather high up in the civil service, and one would probably be offered a sherry . . .

It was nearly two before she got home. As she made herself a snack for lunch the telephone rang. 'Mrs Paxton?' – a man's voice, an agreeable voice, its tone suggesting a desire to please, an expectation of further relationship – 'This is Tony Greenway, from the BBC. Thank you so much for your letter, I can't tell you how delighted I was to hear that you feel enthusiastic about our plans for the programme on your husband – that really was the most encouraging news. Now, the thing is, would there be any chance of my coming down to see you in the near future?'

'Well, yes,' Laura said. 'Yes, I think I could manage that, I . . .'

'What I thought was, could I take you for lunch some day soon? I expect you'll know the local restaurants to suggest somewhere, and then perhaps I could give you a general picture of the project and see what your feelings are?'

Laura said she thought that sounded a nice idea. The Ailsford Arms in Marlborough, she suggested, wasn't too bad.

'Lovely,' said Tony Greenway. 'Now, let's see . . . Is there any possibility of next Thursday?'

Laura said, 'Just let me check my diary – next week *is* a bit hectic, I seem to remember.' She stared out of the window for a few moments and then said, 'No – isn't that lucky, Thursday as it happens is clear.'

'Super. Can I come and pick you up about twelve-thirty, then, would that be all right?'

Tony Greenway put the receiver down and scrawled across a pad: 'Paxton widow 12.30. Locations. Colleagues and relations. Slant on personality. Check career details, background data. Photos, private collection, papers?'

Laura, humming, went back to her scrambled eggs and added a pinch of herbs.

Tom, as a child, had been taken once by his parents to some stately home. Which it was, he no longer remembered: the day had compacted in the mind to a series of sensations and incidents – a long car ride, Kevin being sick, a picnic by a road roaring with traffic, an interminable tree-lined avenue like an exercise in perspective with, at the end, a doll's house mansion. And, with great clarity, the portrait of an armoured, probably seventeenth century, gentleman posed besides a marble-pillared fireplace – the same fireplace, as the hectoring guide pointed out, before which the conducted tour now stood. And Tom, confronted with this simple piece of information, this juxtaposition of the vanished and the extant, had looked at the strong-featured face in the portrait and seen, suddenly, a real man, albeit no longer here but none the less real for that. The past, he had realized, is true.

It was probably that moment that had committed him to what he was now doing, he thought, running his finger down a page of the B.M. catalogue, noting with irritation another sequence of titles that would have to be looked at. He glanced at the clock and saw with relief that it was twelve-forty, a not too unrespectable knocking-off time to meet Kate at one, given that it was a nice day for a leisurely walk to the pub and a browse maybe in the bookshop on the way.

She was late. He ordered two Ploughman's Lunches, pleased

by the inappropriateness of this in Gower Street, and sat waiting for her below a display of pre-war railway advertisements, the delights of Devon and Cornwall as promised by the G.W.R. Disorderly files of schoolchildren, headed for the Museum, flowed past the windows. Kate herself was currently engaged on the organization of a new project whereby an assortment of choice objects from a number of a different museums were to be arranged into a permanent travelling exhibition available to provincial museums and educational establishments: it was carefully devised to interest people of about fourteen and called 'Our Island Heritage'. It was bedevilled with administrative problems and causing Kate much bother.

She arrived, and said gloomily, 'Ma rang.'

'She's well, I hope?'

She shot him a suspicious look. 'Why shouldn't she be? She always has been. Or are you being satirical or something? I never know for sure. Sometimes you're making fun and I don't absolutely know, it's off-putting.'

'I thought it was interesting,' said Tom. 'Isn't that interesting – not instantly being sure what people mean?'

'No. It's unsettling. And I wish she wouldn't ring the Museum, I've asked her not to. She just says but darling I always used to ring Hugh at the Council nobody minded at all. And when I say well that was different, he was the head of it after all, I'm just a Grade II Assistant and it annoys people to have to come chasing up to Archives to find me she says well Kate I expect if you work hard you'll do quite well in the end.'

Tom laughed.

'She says why don't we go down this weekend.'

'Why don't we, then?'

'She's got this person from the BBC coming, the one who's doing the programme on Dad.'

'Ah.'

'And people for lunch on Sunday.'

'What sort of people?'

'People who live in Wiltshire and find things to do,' said Kate morosely.

'Where I come from,' said Tom, 'they go to a lot of trouble not to do anything they haven't got to.'

He had discovered with surprise, on his arrival in the southern white-collar counties, the furious busyness of the professional classes. You could not hold your head up in society, it seemed, if you were unable to claim intolerable pressures, both inside an occupation and, even more, outside it. At a sherry party in his supervisor's house, he had listened with interest to a group of (he gathered) unemployed women vying with one another in their accounts of lives with never a spare moment, dizzy in the service of Parent Teacher Associations, Conservation Societies, adult literacy campaigns and ornithology. Going home again, he found himself taking a new view of his parents' untroubled appreciation of the eight hour day and the five day week. If he had asked his father if he was busy, he would have stared in incomprehension: if you were at work, you were at work, and if you were at home you were at home, and that was all there was to it. He said to Kate, 'Well, all I can say is they don't have this problem with leisure in Rotherham. They aren't even ashamed of it.'

She left him at the tube station, and he walked back to the Museum alone and sat down again in front of his pile of books, his loose-leaf files, his card index box. Two and half centuries away, William Stukeley, out of doors in the fresh air of May 1721, stumped around the Wiltshire downs, measuring lumps and bumps in the turf and doing his bit to free the landscape of fantasy.

Kate did the shopping on her way back to the museum: meat for a goulash, a nice chunk of cheese, some household bits and pieces. She had said to Tom 'Don't be late, the thing I'm going to cook won't keep' – meaning, don't skive off for a drink with some crony when the Reading Room shuts – and he had replied in that light way of his that might or might not conceal crossness, do you *have* to keep taking the magic out of living in sin, Kate? And this had preyed on her mind ill afternoon. Do I nag? she had thought, am I going to be that kind of wife? Am I possessive? Ought we to be living together, or have we spoilt things? Does he love me as much as I love him?

She fretted and analysed, while scouring reference books and inventories, telephoning that unhelpful man at the V and A, comparing glossy photographs of Viking shields. And, flicking through back numbers of *Antiquity* in search of a reference to the stuff from that Orkney hoard, she found an article by her father, and read it, hunched over the trestle table with a dozen other things she ought to be doing and the afternoon half gone already: '. . . the vexed question of the British faience beads and whether or not they are of local provenance, my personal belief being that . . .'

Beads. Not faience beads from the Bronze Age that may or may not be a Mediterranean importation and hence a worry to archaeologists for many years, but glass beads from Woolworths, bright reds and blues and greens and orange like gum-drops. My beads that I am making into a necklace for Mummy, threading them on a string with a big needle, sitting here on the hall floor with my tongue sticking out a bit because I have to think hard what I am doing, the beads are slippy and I keep dropping them, and I am making a pattern with them too so I have to be careful which one I put next.

It is a beautiful necklace.

And I take it to her in her bedroom, where she is getting ready, sitting at the dressing-table with her face things in front of her, pots and bottles that I musn't ever touch. 'Lovely, Kate,' she says. 'Isn't that pretty.' And she puts it down on the table beside her and goes on doing things to her hair. And I say 'Aren't you going to *wear* it, aren't you going to put it on?' and she laughs and says,

'But sweetie it doesn't go with my frock, does it? Look, the colours simply swear at each other,' and she holds it up against her neck, against the green-blue frock she is wearing, and laughs again. And I stand there. I say I think it looks nice. I see our faces side by side in the mirror. She sees our faces too and she says don't talk in that whiny voice, Kate, and don't stick your lip out like that, that's not pretty at all, you'll grow up with a face like that if you go on doing it and no one will ever want to marry you. She is making her hair into curls with her finger, and then she puts the comb down and powders her nose and looks at herself very carefully in the little mirror with the silver handle. 'Run and play now, darling,' she says, 'I'm in a hurry, I'm going out to lunch.'

I go downstairs. I sit on the terrace at the place where there is an ants' nest between the stones, and watch the ants. Presently, I poke the ants with a twig and they all run about in a fuss; I squash some of them; it is unkind but I go on doing it.

Aunt Nellie is in the study, writing things. I go in and say, 'I've made a necklace for you, Aunt Nellie.' Aunt Nellie says it is a lovely necklace. She puts it on over her brown jersey and she gives me a bit of paper and a pencil and goes on with her writing, and I write too, I make lists like Aunt Nellie.

I look at the necklace, round Aunt Nellie's neck. It looks funny; it looks wrong. Aunt Nellie is not a necklace kind of person.

Laura said, 'And this is my daughter Kate, and her young man Tom Rider. Tony Greenway, from the BBC. Tom is writing about somebody frightfully obscure for his thesis, and then he is hoping to be a lecturer somewhere or other, is that right, Tom?'

Tony Greenway, Tom thought, had a beautifully perfected line in deference combined with professional confidence kept discreetly in check. He stood at the fireplace in his brown velvet jacket and spectacles that made him look a little like Mahler, and said all the right things to Laura. He turned to Kate and made sensible, well-informed conversation about the museum scene. He said to Tom, with a nice warm smile 'We can't have missed each other by too much at Oxford, I imagine. I must say I envy you – I'd have liked to do post-graduate stuff but no way, I didn't get a respectable enough degree.'

Laura was thinking that Tony Greenway improved on acquaintance. She had been disappointed at first meeting. To begin with, he was much younger than she had expected. Somehow, she had imagined a more imposing, more distinguished-looking person – someone like Huw Weldon or Lord Clark – and instead here was this thin shortish young man in these rather informal clothes, not a lot older than Kate's Tom. She had sat opposite him at one of the window tables in the Ailsford Arms, fretfully crumbled her roll and tried to conceal her feelings of anti-climax. He was, at any rate, satisfyingly deferential and obviously frightfully impressed by Hugh and everything and the kind of life one had led. 'Well, no,' she said, 'I didn't in fact go with Hugh on excavations all that often. I mean, a lot of it is very routine you know, the exciting part is often sorting things out afterwards and of course one did a lot of that. I suppose my part was more seeing to it that things ran smoothly, I've always been a sociable sort of person' – she beamed at him over the pâté, warming as she talked – 'more so than Hugh, really, and of course one knew all sorts of fascinating people then, Danehurst was always full of visitors, one entertained, well, rather more than one does nowadays, and . . .'

Now, over Saturday night dinner, Tony Greenway was outlining his plans for the programme. He turned frequently to Laura, to say things like 'If, of course you feel that that is the kind of thing we should do . . .', 'But what I do terribly want is suggestions from yourself. . . .'

Laura progressed through graciousness to girlish conspiracy. She opened a second bottle of wine. Kate looked glum. Nellie said little and appeared watchful.

'Tom and Kate will take you up to Charlie's Tump tomorrow,'

said Laura. 'I always find it frightfully windy up there, it's not really my cup of tea. And any other of the sites you might want for filming, Kate knows where everything is. And I'll look through the old photos to see what might be useful – there are some rather super ones of us all on the Brittany dig, in, goodness it must be nineteen forty something.'

'What would be marvellous,' said Tony, 'would be if there was anything we could use to give a personal slant – diaries, letters. Did he keep a diary on excavations?'

'Oh, goodness,' said Laura, 'I've really no idea, I . . .',

Nellie said sharply, 'No, he didn't.'

Alone with Tom in the drawing room after dinner, while the women cleared up, Tony dropped suddenly his role of deferential guest. He stretched out in an armchair and said, 'What's so fascinating about this kind of assignment is that you never know what you're going to dig up. Smoke?'

'Not perhaps the most felicitous word, in this instance.'

Tony laughed. 'I don't mean, of course, past scandals or anything like that – just that if things work out you can get a kind of unexpected twist on a person, show him from various angles, that kind of thing. I want to talk to more of Paxton's old colleagues, students – the family is only a part of it. I've had a word with one or two people already and one's beginning to get a picture. I say, Mrs P must have been a bit dashing, when young, from the look of her.'

Tom said, 'Mmn. I daresay,' and then, 'Do you know much about archaeology?'

'Absolutely not,' said Tony, with attractive candour. 'But one picks things up fairly quickly, you know, that's what this job's all about. I'm an information man, through and through. Now obviously what's interesting about the Paxton career structure is radio-carbon dating and its implications. By the way, you're not an archaeologist, are you? Who is this obscure bloke you're doing a thesis on?'

'He isn't particularly obscure, as it happens. He's called Stukeley.'

'Tell me,' said Tony Greenway, propping a cushion behind his head.

For some reason hard to pin-point, he was not altogether unlikeable. In fact, he wasn't really unlikeable at all, which was odd, given practically everything he said and, apparently, thought. There was a kind of deep residual self-deprecation about him: when he said 'God, I envy you, doing something really serious,' he meant it, even if, with the next breath, he was offering all sorts of half-baked but obviously deeply-felt opinions about anything and everything.

'Well,' said Tom, 'he was a doctor originally, but his first interest was always antiquarianism. . . .' He outlined Stukeley's career, noting that Tony's listening had a professional quality to it, the listening of someone for whom anything may be grist to a mill '. . . he was actually, bar John Aubrey, the first efficient field-archaeologist, his surveys of Avebury and Stonehenge are excellent, and a lot of his conjectures about things are very nearly right – he grasped the idea of a long sequence of prehistoric cultures, and the probability of continental invasions, and he thought about visible remains in groups – barrows or hill-forts or whatever – and tried to interpret them in the light of the actual historical evidence available at the time. But *then* – what's interesting is that then he was ordained, and he went off his rocker – at least went off his scientific rocker – and produced wild fantasies about the Druids. That Stonehenge was a Druidical creation and that the Druids themselves were a priestly sect who came to England from Phoenicia after the Flood and set up a kind of patriarchal religion closely allied to Christianity – in other words that they were the true ancestors of the eighteenth century Church of England. It all fitted in very nicely, you see – then you could claim the most renowned site of antiquity for the Church. It's all illustrative of the shift from the rational to the romantic and the decline of the seventeenth century scientific approach – but I s'pose what intrigues me most is someone manipulating the past for his own intellectual ends. Rather grubby intellectual ends – shoring up the status of the C of E.'

Tony said, 'Fascinating.' He went on, thoughtfully, 'You know, I'm wondering if I couldn't use him in some way, this chap. Once the twentieth century gurus series is in the can I'm going to be involved in something rather big about religious sects. I can't help wondering if . . .'

'Stukeley? Oh, no, I don't think he'd make good television at all,' said Tom decidedly.

'Druids . . .' Tony went on, warming to the idea. 'I like it. I like it a lot.'

'I can't see it working,' said Tom desperately. Whatever Stukeley's own transgressions, the idea of him being mauled around in this way was somehow outrageous. 'It would be bookish,' he added with cunning. 'Very difficult to present it without being bookish.'

Tony nodded reflectively. 'I daresay you're right,' he said after a moment or two.

Was it possessiveness, or natural good taste, that made the idea of a televised Stukeley so repellent? Either way, Tom felt a surge of relief at having, apparently, scotched the project. It occurred to him that there was an interesting parallel in Tony's instinctive need to 'use' Stukeley and the utilitarianism of the early antiquaries – the determination to make intellectual, or other capital out of our ancestors. He would have liked to share this perception with Tony, but decided it might be unwise: that, too, might spark something off. In any case, Tony had now turned to other matters and was talking enthusiastically about possible locations for filming.

Kate was at her stiffest. She sat beside Tony in the passenger seat of the car and gave wooden explanations of interesting landscape features. They drove south to Stonehenge and joined several hundred other people busily eroding the Wiltshire topsoil. 'Those are the Aubrey holes,' said Kate. 'And that is the Mycenean dagger, only of course it isn't really, and that's the Heel Stone.' Tony looked despondent and said he doubted if one would ever get anything very effective here. They went back to the car park where Tony suggested ice creams all round. Kate asked for a Neapolitan Nut Bonanza. 'It's twenty-five pence,' she said. 'Is that all right? I'll pay.' 'Look,' said Tony, 'you can have half a dozen if you like. It's all on the BBC.' Kate suddenly grinned, and Tom remembered why he loved her.

Back in the car, headed for Avebury, Tony said, 'I gather he was a bit of a colourful figure, your father? I've been talking to a few people and that's the impression one gets.'

'I don't think so,' said Kate, 'I wouldn't have thought so. I don't know really.'

'People speak very warmly of him.'

Kate, her neck mottled, appeared much taken with some distant aspect of the scenery.

'I wondered,' Tony went on, 'if you'd like to come on the programme for a few minutes – just talk about him quite informally. You know – how you remember him, that kind of thing.'

'I'd be hopeless,' said Kate, in a choked voice. 'No, really, I'd rather not.' To one who did not know her, she might have been suffering from reborn grief rather than outrage.

'I quite understand,' said Tony respectfully. They drove on in silence.

It was late afternoon when they got back to Avebury, and dusk by the time they had finished there. Kate said, 'We really ought to be going soon – I don't want to be too late back in London. Perhaps we should leave Charlie's Tump for another time.'

'Oh come on,' said Tom. 'He's got to see it, it was your father's big dig after all.' Kate allowed herself to be led back to the car.

By the time they reached the end of the track and left the car in a gateway, to walk the last quarter mile, the light had almost drained away. The landscape was a uniform grey-blue, spiced here and there in the valleys with the lights of a village; the hills lay in long dark curves against a sky that was barely lighter; to the west, an orange ball of a sun hung just above the black copse. The wind poured over the hilltop, making the trees creak; otherwise there was nothing to be heard except the crying of lambs. Tony Greenway said, 'It's a barrow, I take it?' He stood, staring round, hunched into his anorak. Kate explained the dig and its significance. Tony nodded and listened and asked several quite perceptive questions. Tom climbed to the top of the hillock and stood there, looking out over the fields, the valley, the grey soft hills. The place seemed very old, almost un-inhabited, and inexpressibly sad. Under his feet was the tumbled stone chamber in which people of impenetrable beliefs had buried their dead; down there in the valley lorries twinkled their way along the A4. This landscape had been exploited by countless people in countless different ways and yet its endurance was absolute: the same sun hangs above the same cleft in the hills; the same uncaring wind bites hands and face. And I know everything, and nothing, Tom thought; I stand here, full of learning, I could give you a pretty good run-down on the last two thousand years, and I know nothing, I am constantly amazed by the world, I am as surprised by life as whoever it was Hugh Paxton dug out of this barrow. I have cost the state several thousand pounds, my head is full of expensive information, and my judgement is probably no better than the last man's or the one before. Of course, I have scepticism, and rationality, and unbelief, which I suppose is better than bigotry and superstition and credulity. I am not likely to kill anyone else, except under great provocation, neither am I likely to take violent exception to people not feeling the same way as I do about things, and I probably won't trample on those less able to look after their own interests. All of which adds up to quite a lot, on reflection. But . . . but the fact remains that I stand here, knowing everything that I know about what has been, and I know very little about what is. I live in a mysterious world.

Tony Greenway appeared beside him. It's rather a super place, I must say.'

'Mmn.'

'I'll certainly want a sequence here. What I shall never get across, alas, is the atmosphere.'

'You think it's got an atmosphere?'

'Oh, Lord, yes. I mean, one has this feeling of immense antiquity, of so much having happened up here.'

'Actually,' said Tom, 'this isn't Charlie's Tump at all. Kate's frightfully short-sighted, as you've probably noticed, and with the light being so bad she directed you up the wrong track. This is just what's left of a gun emplacement from the last war.'

There was a silence. Tom said, 'Sorry, I'm pulling your leg, of course – I couldn't resist it.'

Tony laughed. 'Point taken. All atmosphere is in the eye of the beholder. Romanticism.'

'Quite. Which isn't to say that I'm not all for it. I think we could do with more of it – projection of feelings. It's not doing it that's dangerous.'

Tony said earnestly, 'You know, I do so agree with you, Tom.'

'Well, we've got you one location, anyway. It makes me think of *Urn Burial*, this place. "The treasures of time lie high, in Urnes, Coynes, and Monuments, scarce below the roots of some vegetables".'

'Hold it a minute. Say that again.'

'"The treasures of time lie high . . ."'

'I like it,' said Tony. 'We've got a tide, too. The Treasures of Time. Great. What is it, did you say?'

'*Urn Burial*. Browne.'

'Ah.'

'What's happened to Kate?'

'She thought that lamb had got its head stuck through the fence – she went to investigate.'

It was almost dark now, the definition of shapes – trees, hills, hedges – fading every minute. Tom, filled with sudden high spirits said, 'Wait here a moment.' He slithered down the side of the barrow, crept round to the clump of bushes at the far end, watched Kate groping her way back along the fence, leapt out and grabbed her by the waist as she passed.

Kate's shriek brought Tony scrambling down. 'It's all right,' said Tom. 'I was just testing Kate's powers of imagination – they seem to be in good order.'

Kate said, 'You gave me the fright of my life, what on earth are you on about?' but she slid her arm cosily through his.

'I've just been lecturing Tony about the value of imagination.'

'Imagination isn't jumping when people behave like five-year olds.'

'True, but it's having some apprehension of the unknown.'

'The unknown in other people,' said Kate. 'That being what my ma is so bad at,' she added, more quietly. Tony, shuttered off by the twilight, stood a yard or two away, watching them politely.

Tom said, 'I'd say it's more that she's barely aware of other people. A bit un-nerving, really. But lack of imagination comes into it, certainly. Tony's problem was with the landscape, though – does it have qualities of its own, or is it entirely what we think it is?'

Tony said, a little peevishly, 'You're getting too philosophical for me. All this arose, if you remember, from how we get the best out of this place as a location. Was this where that drinking-cup was found, and a shield, or something?'

'That's right,' said Kate. 'It was a burial with particularly fine grave goods – one of the best Wessex finds. It hadn't been robbed earlier, like so many, and everything was pretty well intact. There were grooved daggers, and the gold cup, and a lot of other stuff, rather spectacular really. They did two seasons on it, and it fitted in with anti-invasionist theory, which Dad was always very much in favour of, even before radio-carbon, really, as a display of wealth by prosperous local chieftains.'

'The original Wiltshire squirearchy?' said Tony. 'And it was after that your father got the Directorship of the Council for Prehistoric Studies?'

'Yes.'

They came down from the hill in near-darkness, stumbling along a track become unreliable, full of stones and invisible holes. Kate clung to Tom's arm; Tony, a yard or two behind, slithered on the mud once or twice and swore.

'One thing,' he said. 'One can't complain of being desk-bound in this job. I'll push off as soon as I've dropped you back and said my farewells – maybe we could meet up for a drink in London sometime?'

# Chapter Four

There were things that were within one's powers and things that were not. There were small, private triumphs when something else became possible, or nearly possible. When one discovered that, using the invaluable little tong-device that Kate had found, one could pull up one's stockings unassisted. That, by careful manipulation of the wheelchair and a judicious prior arrangement of cushions and chairs, one could get in and out of bed on one's own. But there mocked and challenged, daily, those unattainable goals – the bathroom shelf, the switch on the standard lamp in the drawing room, Hugh's study.

Clarity of speech.

If one could devise some way of getting the chair down those two steps, the study would be within bounds. A ramp? A couple of boards, securely placed; that old door that used to be in the garden shed . . .

And Laura, staring, says 'Why, for goodness' sake, Nellie? If there's something you want out of the study I can get it for you, you've only got to say. Do some work? But darling that's the last thing you should be doing, you have to take things very very quietly, there is no need to force yourself to do anything. What work, anyway?'

Sort out Hugh's papers. Always wanted to see if that unfinished work on pottery sequences could be made publishable. Catalogue his dig notes.

And Laura says, 'Well, darling, I do think it's quite unnecessary, and actually I've been thinking anyway of sending all the papers to the Council, the study needs a good clear-out. Do you,' she goes on, 'want anything from Marlborough this morning, I am going in to shop.'

Laura has been in better spirits lately, better-tempered. She has these new friends, the Hamiltons, who have come to live in West Overton, a near-retirement Treasury official and his sleek ageless wife, very busy about the place, full of creditable enthusiasms and energies. Laura and Barbara Hamilton are wondering about opening up a little place to sell really nice lithographs and prints, Barbara knows a lot of people in the art world, she has an eye for that kind of thing. A percentage of the profits would go to the Nature Conservancy; the prints, though, will not be Peter Scott ducks, that was not thought amusing when one suggested it

Playing at shops.

A long time ago, when we were children, we were given a toy shop. It had a wooden counter, and wooden shelves and drawers behind. There were tiny packets (empty) of tea and sugar, with proper writing – Lyons, Tate and Lyle – and packets of semolina and sultanas and candied peel and biscuits and little blue paper bags for rice and flour. And a real pair of scales. And pretend fruit, made of plaster: oranges and lemons and bananas. And cardboard money. And a pad of paper headed Toytown Stores to write bills on.

Laura was nearly always the shopkeeper, because of being the youngest and because the shop was for some reason more hers than mine, though given to us jointly I think by an aunt. Laura was five or six, as pretty as a picture or so everyone said, her hair so fair as to be almost white, as it will be again one day, around a face that is not so very different, that is recognizably the Laura of today.

She weighs and counts and arranges, and I buy and order and pay. We both love the shop, it is fantasy made manifest; perhaps Laura loves it slightly more, and I get irritated because I am so seldom the shopkeeper, and after a while I refuse to play any more.

Later, when Laura is somewhere else, I play with the shop by myself. I arrange it with great care, to my liking, and I do very complicated sums, I present myself with bills and pay them and take real flour and sugar from the kitchen and weigh it and put it in the blue bags. I have a whale of a time.

And suddenly there is Laura, standing over me. She is so enraged she is speechless, her face is quite scarlet, she looks as though she might explode. And she does: she flies not at me but at the shop; she hurls herself at it and the wooden counter splinters and the shelves and the drawers, the cardboard packets are squashed, the money sent flying in all directions, the imitation fruit pulped to white powder under her shoes.

The shop is ruined. We stare in horror at the ruins. Laura tramps through it, tears streaming down her face, and says, 'I didn't want it anyway, it wasn't real. I don't care.'

Nellie ate her breakfast alone in the kitchen, Laura having gone to Marlborough. She made tea, and toast, and achieved with the help of a walking stick handle the packet of cornflakes in the corner cupboard that had hitherto eluded her, and enjoyed that small triumph. She read *The Times* from front to back, sat thinking for a while about what she had read, trundled back to her room to fetch the handy bag in which she kept her immediate needs – books, notepad and pen – and then wheeled herself through the drawing room window and onto the terrace, it being a nice day.

A lovely day, indeed. Ten o'clock, and the sun lying warmly on face and arms and hands, the birds clamorous, the garden crackling with spring growth. And, sitting there, abandoning for the moment the matter in hand of writing to an old colleague, she was filled with pleasure, all else for the moment driven out: time and fate and what might come. Pleasure in the senses, in what lay before her eyes, simply in being. She had always liked to be out of doors, had resented the incarceration of the winter, had been thankful for work that was carried on as much in the open air as out of it. So that, although in all her life there can hardly have been a day when she would not have been at work by ten o'clock in the morning, there had been many days when she had been, as now, outside.

She would have worked, if she had been permitted, until there was nothing she could usefully do. Inactivity had always annoyed her. When, from time to time, she had had jobs that seemed to her inadequate in their requirements, she had found herself more to do. She had never had high aspirations – Directorships, Chairs, were not for her. She had taken what was offered, been out of a job quite often, given her services on many digs for nothing, worked on necessary projects for a pittance. The small capital sum left her by her parents had made this possible; that, and the lack of dependants. Laura, similarly endowed, had got through the lot long ago.

Things are not so bad, she thought, there is worse, there is far worse. And she began once more to write to the old colleague, a cheerful, chatty letter, relating what was of interest or amusing, omitting much.

Laura said, 'We adored each other, of course.' She had had two glasses of sherry; she felt confidential, and melancholy in a rather agreeable way. 'I was awfully young when we were married, just a girl really, Hugh was quite a bit older than me.'

Barbara Hamilton nodded understandingly. 'I *do* so wish we'd known him. I just have that feeling we'd have got on so well.'

Laura hesitated. 'Well, yes. Of course, Hugh had that impatient streak to him, it came of being half Welsh. I must admit he could be rude to people.'

Barbara said, 'I think really clever men, really exceptional people, are allowed that, don't you? They just are on a slightly different plane. We knew Willie Maugham rather well and one always felt that about him.'

One slightly tiresome thing about Barbara was the way she would keep mentioning important or interesting people she knew or had known, who were often as, if not more, important and interesting than the people one knew or had known oneself. Laura said, 'Mmn, I s'pose so.' Barbara's husband was probably going to be made a Sir before he retired, it was hinted. Laura finished her third sherry and went on, 'Of course, being with someone like that all one's life one comes to feel that it's nothing unusual.'

Barbara said, 'And with him doing such a fascinating subject you must have been awfully tempted to get involved yourself.'

'I always felt strongly,' said Laura, 'that he needed a background where he could be quite private, detach himself from work when he wanted to, get away from it all. I don't think it would have helped at all for me to be involved too. Unfortunately, my sister rather . . . Hugh always felt it was a very good thing I wasn't *all* that involved in archaeology, I mean, quite interested enough to know what was going on, but not immersed, if you see what I mean.'

'Oh, quite,' said Barbara.


He is being quite unreasonable, he is in one of his beastly Welsh tempers, I won't stand for it, why should I? It is always what he is doing that has to come first, I am never thought of, I can be left at Danehurst for weeks on end while he is off somewhere.

We shout at each other. I shout about being left on my own at Danehurst and about going always by myself to dinners and things that he says bore him. I shout about not having holidays abroad like other people. I shout about money.

And he shouts back, horrid unfair things that I don't want to remember. I can only hear his voice, with that hard angry edge to it, and see his face, looking at me as though I were someone he did not know. I feel sick to my stomach; it is like being afraid; is it that I am afraid?

I do care about his work. I do take the trouble to find out what he is doing. I know I could have gone to Spain with him.

All right, then, I shout, what did you ask me to marry you for, then? You should have married Nellie, if that's the sort of wife you wanted.

He turns his back on me and goes out of the room.

I sit there and look at the shut door and I feel scared. And lonely. Perhaps I should not have said that. But it is true, and in any case . . .

Presently the scared feeling goes away. In any case, I know why he married me, and why he did not marry Nellie, never would have done. And later, in bed, I will be able to make it all right again, like I always can when I want to. Maybe in the end I will even be able to make him come to the Sadlers' dinner with me.

Tom said, 'You were pretty short with Tony Greenway.'

'I didn't like him.'

'That was apparent.'

'Oh dear,' said Kate, stricken, 'do you think he realized?'

'No. And if he did, I should imagine he's a pretty resilient fellow. I didn't think he was all that bad. He makes a change, anyway.'

He was gripped with restlessness, clutched by it so that during the day he shuffled his papers, watched the clock, made frequent sorties for a smoke, a drink, a wander through the streets. In the evenings he dragged Kate, who would have preferred to stay in, to cinemas and pubs. He was doing the thing he wanted to do, in the place he found most stimulating, spent his time with the person he preferred, and he felt discontented. He heard his mother's voice – 'Never satisfied, that's your trouble . . .' When Tony Greenway rang one evening to suggest meeting for a drink, he accepted with enthusiasm; Kate said she thought she wouldn't bother, if nobody minded. He left her in the flat, reading, a sullen-child expression on her face.

Tony looked tired. There was strain behind the sprightliness of his greeting. After a few minutes' chat he began to relax and said, 'Sorry, it's been a hideous day, I'm knackered. I'll be O.K. after a drink. Anyway, I'm out of the studio tomorrow, I've got to take a trip up north, that'll set me up again.'

Later, dropping Tom back at the flat, he said suddenly 'I suppose you wouldn't like to join me on this jaunt tomorrow?'

'Where is it you're going?'

'I've got to go and see this old dear up in Yorkshire. Someone we used on a programme. There's been a bit of trouble about her fee – the contract people boobed somehow – and also she didn't absolutely like the way we slanted her bit. It's the sort of thing that *could* be done by letter, but can be smoothed out much more satisfactorily in a face-to-face situation. It won't take too long. She lives near Fountains Abbey so you can have a look round that while I chat her up. And I've got one or two more chores to do while we're up there.'

'Yorkshire and back in one day?'

'It's no distance,' said Tony, surprised. 'What's the problem? A quick run up the M1, that's all. Fancy it?'

'Yes. I rather think I do. Thanks.'

Tony's car crouched above the road. It was long and low and sleek, with two seats into which you lowered yourself and were at once lapped in squashy leather: there were token concessions only to back seat passengers and luggage. Travelling, there was an awareness of faintly whistling tarmac only a few inches beneath. The map that Tony pulled from the leather pocket at his side showed an England held in a network of lines snaking out from London, probing out to the far west, up to the far north, shooting a bolt into East Anglia, tying up the Midlands. There were no county boundaries marked, no physical features, no places other than those snared by the motorway system, In the margin were scribbled names and numbers: Brm 1¼, Manch 2½, N'Castle 4½, Exeter 3. Tony spread the thing out for a moment over the wheel, ran a finger upwards, and said 'Something under three should do it. You turn off soon after the Leeds road.' He began to weave, with opportunist skill, through the early morning London traffic.

Tom said, 'What exactly was this series?'

'The series?' There was a fractional hesitation. 'Oh, I'm not sure it would be your cup of tea, Tom, truth to tell. It was a thing we did on way-out theories to do with places, with the landscape. Nutty stuff, I suppose, most of it, but you know people have the most tremendous taste for that kind of thing. These lines linking churches and prehistoric things and whatnot – leys – that may have some sort of mysterious force. And the powers that are supposed to be held by particular places, we had some people down in Somerset who do some funny stuff with a big stone down there, a kind of healing ceremony, there was a bloke who swore blind he'd been cured of cancer. And some straight ghost stuff, a rather good sequence at Kenilworth at night, there was something very weird on the film but I must say I'm not convinced the cameraman didn't fake it up a bit. It was a natural for the cameramen – we got some very elegant film – and frankly it was very popular too. The letters are still coming in.' He shot a sideways glance at Tom. 'People really are awfully keen on this kind of thing, you know. It seems to fulfil a need of some kind.'

'You shouldn't encourage them.'

'It was a piece of detached journalism,' said Tony reprovingly. 'We made our own position quite clear: uncommitted.'

'Which particular brand of nut is this lady we're going to see now?'

'Well, it was astrology of a kind, but not quite that. She has this theory that in some parts of England the signs of the zodiac are sort of stamped on the landscape, outlined by old tracks and field boundaries and the edges of woods and roads and so forth.'

'Ah,' said Tom, 'what for?'

'That's not made absolutely clear, of course. At Glastonbury, apparently you get the lot – Pisces and Aquarius and so on – and it's all something to do with Arthur, she isn't too explicit about that.'

'I daresay she isn't.'

'It's all frightfully far-fetched of course, but you can more or less see what she means when she shows you her maps and things. We tied it in with all the rest of the Glastonbury stuff. She used to live there, but I gather she ran into some kind of trouble with the authorities, she does push her views rather and of course not everyone has much time for it.'

'I'm not surprised, if she was going round claiming that Somerset County Council is guided by unseen forces.'

'Oh, it's all quite cranky,' said Tony. 'One's perfectly well aware of that, of course. You don't find it just a bit intriguing all the same?'

'No.'

There was a pause. They were on the motorway now, gliding up the fast lane, the car a private capsule of tinted glass. Tom went on, 'Sorry – it's just that personally I don't have any time for people attributing psychic energy to bits of Somerset or Wiltshire or wherever.'

'Oh, I take your point. But it goes on, that you can't deny. Always has. After all, that place with the peculiar name we went to . . .'

'Charlie's Tump?'

'That's right. I mean, Kate was saying it's called that because of some dotty local belief that Charles I hid there, when in fact he can't ever have gone near the place.'

'Oh yes, true enough. People have always needed to explain the inexplicable – the physical world and the past both fall into that category. That's why the place is littered with Devils' Dykes and Giants' Causeways and suchlike . . .' – Tony nodded sagely – 'but we're supposed to know better now. We shouldn't still be inventing the past. Or using it as a convenience.' Except, of course, he thought, that we all do that all the time, in our separate ways. He felt with guilt that perhaps he had been a bit dogmatic: Tony, after all, meant well. But Tony did not seem offended, and indeed after driving for a while in silence was now talking about something quite different. 'Sorry – what?'

'I said ever thought of crossing the Atlantic? Seeing as how things aren't too good here, job wise.'

'No,' said Tom. After a moment, he added 'It's not that I think this place owes me a living. More I'd feel it something of a defeat if it couldn't find a use for me. Also, it so happens I like it here.'

Tony nodded. He flicked the radio control. '. . . black school-leavers' said a news-reading voice. 'A spokesman for the Department of Employment and Industry said the latest figures showed little improvement in the overall situation . . .'

'Sorry,' said Tony, stabbing another button: the car was filled with Brahms. 'That do?' 'Grand' said Tom, staring out at a scenic countryside, pleasantly decorated with grazing animals, its dirt or damp or smells eliminated by a layer of tinted, laminated glass. 'I approve of this kind of jaunt,' said Tony. 'It unwinds me. We'll lunch at Pontefract I think, I don't go for motorway caffs and there's a rather nice pub there.' They sped north, amid convoys of traffic; Tom sat in a pleasurable torpor, listening to the music, looking out from time to time at fields and villages and distant church spires, that desert England ignored by Tony's map.

Over lunch, Tom had been amazed at the calm and familiarity with which, evidently, Tony sped about the place. He had been here only last week, *en route* for Scotland. Bristol the day before yesterday; Wales next week; Carlisle on Thursday. Oh, he said, that's one of the things I like about my line of work, you're out and about a lot, you see the world all right. He treated the country like an enlarged Underground system, popping without consideration from station to station: he knew hotels and eating-places from Edinburgh to Southampton, traffic-dodging short cuts in every city centre. He was perplexed by Tom's interest. 'It's just,' Tom explained, 'that I was brought up to treat travel with deference, not to be undertaken lightly or without a great deal of forward planning and the habit has stuck. Also, I've never had enough money to move around. And I can't drive. And I haven't got a car.'

They reached their destination, a village near Fountains Abbey, in the early afternoon. Tom, in response to Tony's suggestion that he look in for a few minutes and meet this Mrs Harbottle, said he thought he might do that – 'If you don't think she'll spot my aura of scepticism?' 'Shouldn't think so,' said Tony. 'She's used to it, I imagine. You might find it amusing anyway – and you can slope off after a bit and leave me to talk business.'

The bungalow was set back from the lane in a lush and leafy countryside; it seemed to wallow in greenery. Mrs Harbottle, opening the door, said 'Ah. Mr Greenway. As good as your word. Come along in with you.' Her voice was loud, and of confident gentility. Tony said, 'This is my colleague, Tom Rider.' They were ushered down a passage that smelled of cat, and into a sitting room overlooking tipping fields in which black and white cows grazed like cardboard cut-outs, all pointing the same way.

Mrs Harbottle was a stout woman of sixty odd. She wore a tweed jacket over a jersey that showed the outline of corsetry beneath; thick stockings hung in reptilian wrinkles on her legs; her hair escaped in wisps from a perfunctory arrangement of netting and hair pins at the back. She said, 'Had a good drive up? By the way if either of you need the doings it's first right at the end of the passage.' She began to talk to Tony, with enthusiasm, about letters that had been forwarded to her after the programme. 'Put me in touch with all sorts of fellow spirits,' she said. 'Really smashing.'

Tom looked round the room. There was a lot of brass and chintz. A pile of parish magazines and the *Church Times* on a table suggested religious involvement of some kind. On the wall were framed coloured photographs of pleasing views.

The door burst open and a labrador bounded into the room, wagging its tail furiously. It rushed at each of them in turn and then proceeded to make a sexual assault on Tony's leg. Mrs Harbottle dragged it away, saying, 'Naughty boy. Mr Greenway doesn't like that.' She pushed the dog down beside her chair. 'Did you see my programme, Mr er –, there's a few things I'm not happy about but on the whole I think it gave quite a good picture of our work.'

Tom said, 'I didn't, I'm afraid. Tony's been telling me something about it.'

'I'd like you to take a copy of my book. It's written in collaboration with my colleague Alfred Binns, of Bath.' She reached out to the table beside her and took from a pile a thin volume, wearing the imprint of a private press, and entitled *The Green Fuse*. It bore the signs of the zodiac on the cover, super-imposed on a colour photograph of a bit of rural England. 'Five pounds ninety' said Mrs Harbottle. 'The title comes from a poem by the Welsh poet Dylan Thomas. If Mr Greenway has been telling you about my work you may recognize the reference. "The force that through the green fuse drives . . ."'

'Thank you,' said Tom, putting the book back on the table. 'I haven't got six pounds, I'm afraid. It's an interesting use of the quotation, I must say.'

Mrs Harbottle heaved herself out of her chair. 'In that case,' she said, 'I must find you a copy of our monthly magazine. You may like to take out a sub – four fifty a year.' She went out of the room.

'Christ,' said Tom. The labrador had also got up and was approaching Tony's leg with renewed interest. Tony put out a foot and shoved it away vigorously. Mrs Harbottle returned with a pile of magazines which she dumped on Tom's knee. 'Just have a look through the latest issue, it'll give you an idea. I can let you have that number for fifty pence, since we've a few left over.'

The magazine, in format, looked much like the *Church Times*. In a central spread, someone had been taking appalling liberties with the Ordnance Survey map of part of Herefordshire. The correspondence column was kicking around the idea that the road-system of inner London, if properly interpreted, reveals the outline of Sagittarius. Some fellow-traveller, in a lengthy article, was discussing the properties of rays emanating from a pattern of bird-shapes, eyes and the letter S detectable in the contour-lines of the Pyrenees. Tom was reminded of one of Stukeley's wilder fancies: the notion that the ground plan of Avebury and its avenues represent a circle penetrated by a snake – 'an hieroglyphic or symbol of highest note and antiquity'. Putting the pile down firmly on the table he said, 'No, thank you, Mrs Harbottle. I don't really go in for this kind of thing.'

Mrs Harbottle, apparently undisturbed, said, 'What's your job, Mr – er . . . ?'

'Rider,' said Tony. 'Tom Rider. Tom's a historian.'

'Then you should be ashamed of yourself,' said Mrs Harbottle with energy. 'You ought to know we don't know all the answers. I can see you're one of those people who refuse to be open-minded.' She leaned towards him, so that he could see more clearly the ginger hairs that lurked in the folds of her chin and gave her a faint peppery moustache; she wagged a finger at him, 'There is more to heaven and earth than is dreamed of in all thy philosophy, O Hamlet.'

Tony cleared his throat. 'You know,' he said, with a glance at his watch, 'I really think perhaps Mrs Harbottle and I had better have our little talk.'

'Right,' said Tom quickly, getting to his feet. Mrs Harbottle shook him warmly by the hand and said if he was going along to the Abbey he must climb the hill and look down on the complex of buildings and he would see the outline of the Wheel of Fortune pointing to the north-east. 'The cosmic forces are clearly to be felt,' she added, 'if you only let yourself be receptive.' The labrador followed Tom to the garden gate, sniffing at his trousers.

He went down the lane, walking quickly, in sunlight quivering through beech leaves – round a corner, and there, straddling the narrow valley, were those golden ruins. He paid his entrance fee and went across the grass, Mrs Harbottle quite forgotten, and Tony; enjoying himself, enjoying the place.

He found it difficult to define what he felt, confronted by somewhere like this. Or rather, to sort out what he felt: pleasure in the beauty of it; an exasperating uprush of sentiment that had eerie connections with the most despised manifestations of chauvinism and soft-centred Englishry; a springing to attention of the intellect – now what have we here? Who built this, why? How? When? Outrage at the insensitivities of change – car park, appalling twenties housing nearby, quacking transistors all around. Amazement that the thing should be here at all. A confusion of responses – the only certainty being that none were relevant to the original intentions of the place.

He wandered, for the next hour, guide-book and plan in hand, intent upon windows and cloisters and vaulting. The Abbey was doing good business: tourists dotted the grass precincts like people attending a garden party; plenty of dollars, marks, yen and so forth had clearly been earned; the building's skilfully arrested decline was a testimony to twentieth century enlightenment. Henry VIII ought to be properly ashamed of himself. The agreeably empty surrounding countryside, of course, was a reminder of the economic basis of monastic life, and a suitable correction to other, more romantic, less realistic feelings that the scenery might inspire. Places are what we know them to be, not what we feel they might be, Tom told himself sternly, and thought again of Tony at Charlie's Tump, and thence of Kate (who, he realized with a certain guilt, had not crossed his mind all day). He sat down on the grass beside the river, pictured her trotting around her museum, brow furrowed, busy with this and that, thought that it would have been nice to have her here with him now, and fell asleep in the sun.

He woke to find Tony standing over him, saying with a tinge of irritation, 'So there you are.'

'Sorry. Too much beer at lunch.'

'We'd better be off, I suppose. Mrs H is all sorted out quite amicably – it didn't take as long as I'd expected. Sorry she battened onto you like that.'

'Not at all. It was an edifying experience.'

'You come across all sorts of weird types,' said Tony, as they walked back to the car park, 'in my business. You get a bit inured, I suppose.' Back in the car, he glanced at his watch, ran a finger down the map again. 'We'll go back via Coventry, if you don't mind, I want to look in at a factory on the outskirts – it's a possible for a feature I'm doing later this year, an industrial relations thing. O.K. by you? We'll be lateish back in London, but I thought we might have dinner somewhere on the way.'

Somewhere in the Midlands, Tony peeled off the motorway, sped down dual carriage-ways, glanced once or twice at some type-written notes he took from his pocket, fetched up at a factory entrance where he wound the car window down for a brief, purpose-ful exchange with the man at the gate. He said to Tom, 'This should take ten–fifteen minutes.'

'I'll wait in the car.'

One could not but be impressed at the dexterity of Tony's approach to life: confident, unflappable, deflected neither by doubts nor diffidence, free-wheeling about the place, moving on, leaving behind. Here am I, thought Tom, with discontent, untravelled, unlessoned, frequently uneasy. Certainly unsure. Prone to guilt. Infirm of purpose. Inconsistent.

Ten minutes passed. He surveyed what was to be seen of the landscape – the tarmac, wire-enclosed industrial estate, the factory buildings, the parking lots. Boredom was setting in. What did they make here? Car components, presumably, from the familiar name at the entrance. Which, though? A shift came out, and cars and bicycles eddied around him, quite a few black faces, people talking in accents that were of everywhere and nowhere. I don't know about places like this, he thought, even though I grew up among them, even though most of my friends' fathers worked in them. You didn't listen to what the grown-ups were saying, it wasn't that interesting. Since then, I've not been there. Still, where I come from at least you'd know where you were from the way people spoke.

He sat there, half listening to the flat, unrevealing voices around him, half reading a two-day-old newspaper from the back seat of Tony's car.

Tony said, 'Sorry to be so long. Couldn't find the chap I'd phoned.'

'Satisfactory?'

'Not really. There are some snags I don't think we'd be able to get round.' He didn't expatiate. Back on the dual carriage-way he said, 'You know – I think if you don't mind I'll pop into the shopping precinct for a moment – there's just time before the shops shut. I've remembered this is where I left a jacket to be cleaned weeks ago – we were on an overnight stop here, another industrial thing, and some idiot poured half a bottle of wine over me at dinner. I put it in for two-hour cleaning and then the bloody thing wasn't ready by the time we left. I wouldn't mind getting it back, it was a good jacket.'

Dual carriage-ways and roundabouts swept them in a gentle curve above the suburbs: acre upon acre of dinky housing estates, spruce in the sunlight, indicated with pleasant rural-sounding names – Tile Hill, Broad Lane, Stivichall. Tony swung from lane to lane: City Centre, Ring Road, North, South, East, West. Buildings grew; traffic slowed and thickened; pedestrians appeared. They plunged into the maw of a multi-storey car park, swung up ramps, down ramps, slotted the car away, clattered down concrete stairs, emerged into a concourse of plate-glass windows and flocking people. 'Hang on,' said Tony, 'just let me get my bearings. Somewhere by Marks and Spencer, I think it was.' They walked a half mile or so, past Boots, Dolcis, the British Home Stores, Dorothy Perkins, W. H. Smith, Sainsbury's. 'Funny,' said Tony, 'I could have sworn . . .' They retraced their steps: Curry's, Lloyds Bank, Halifax Building Society, John Collier, Woolworth's. Tony halted, bathed in muzak from the Wimpy Bar. 'You know, I've made an idiotic mistake,' he said. 'It was Nottingham, not Coventry. I was beginning to feel there was something not quite right. Sorry about that.'

'Not at all,' said Tom. 'Nice to see a place one doesn't know.' They hurried back, along the wide, peopled boulevards, up steps, along ramps. 'Odd,' Tony said, 'my memory's usually pretty good.

Nottingham, that "Women at Work" series must have been. Here we are . . .' Up more steps, along another ramp, more steps. Floor C, Deck 2: no car. 'Christ,' said Tony, 'wrong bloody car park.'

'It's funny,' he said, half an hour later, gliding back onto the motorway, 'You do lose your bearings a bit, working at this sort of pace. I don't just mean fetching up in the wrong shopping centre – sorry about that – I mean there's never a chance to, well, sit down and take stock. I envy you, Tom, I really do.'

'I was just wondering if I didn't rather envy you.'

In Hertfordshire, Tony turned off the motorway once more. 'I hope I'll be able to find this place,' he said. 'It's a year or more since I was here. Village called Hevenham.' It was dusk, and raining. They splashed down narrowing roads. 'Hmnn,' said Tony. 'Bit tricky.' 'Map?' 'There's a road-map in the pocket beside you.' Tom turned up the appropriate page in a book reassuringly spattered with place-names.

There was a crunch and a pop from under the bonnet. The engine died. Tony said, 'Bloody hell'. He steered the car into a field-entrance. Tom said, 'Oh dear.'

Tony got out, and opened the bonnet. He stared down. After a minute he came back. 'I don't suppose you know about the insides of cars? Well, the only thing to do is walk to the nearest house, I suppose.'

'Actually,' Tom said, 'we're only about a mile from this village.' Tony brightened. 'Well, providing we can rustle up a garage, and it's nothing too serious, all is not lost. We can eat while they fix it and push on after. Can you just chuck me my jacket.'

'Tony,' said Tom after a moment, 'I'm afraid you must have . . .'

Tony peered frantically into the back of the car. 'Christ. That place we stopped for petrol. I took it out to pay. I must have left it at their cash desk.' There was a silence. Tom said, 'Well, you do seem to have bad luck with jackets, I must say.' Tony was trying to restrain his agitation. 'Wallet, cheque book, credit cards, the lot,' he said. 'Look, 'I'm most awfully sorry. Can we put this down to you and settle up later? I must say, I hope I can get my stuff back or it's going to be a hell of a hassle.'

Tom said cheerfully, 'Sure. It'll have to be a cheap dinner, though. I've got about two fifty on me.' Tony looked shaken. 'Oh, I see. And you haven't got. . .' ''Fraid not. My credit's not that good anyway.'

They set off. Tony, jacketless, in jeans and a sweater, the rain spotting his Mahler spectacles so that he had to keep taking them off to wipe them, looked less well-adjusted than usual; in fact, the stuffing seemed to have been knocked out of him. Tom noticed for the first time that he walked with a slight stoop. He said, 'I'm afraid you're getting soaked.' 'Mmn. What I'll have to try to do, is get them to put it down to the BBC.' 'Do you think they'll have heard of it?' said Tom. 'It looks pretty rustic round here.' Tony laughed without conviction.

The village, at last attained, offered little but a pub of dauntingly functional appearance, a small garage, and the hotel-restaurant for which Tony had been heading. The garage was shut. The restaurant looked interestingly expensive. Tony said, 'I suppose I'd better try the garage first.' He hesitated, and then walked towards the bungalow at the back of the forecourt.

After a few minutes he returned, looking even more depleted than before. 'They were unenthusiastic, to put it mildly. Eventually they said they'd send a chap out to have a look.' Tom said, 'I expect your stock'll go up a bit after that – they'll know an expensive car when they see one.' Tony, clearly ruffled by his experience with the garage, was staring gloomily at the pub. 'Look,' he said, 'let's go into The Gay Adventure and see if we can't fix something up.' Tom followed him into the restaurant; it was ill-lit and thickly carpeted. Tony perked up.

The warm welcome cooled rapidly. Tony talked. Tom withdrew and studied some tasteful prints of old fire engines on the wall. Tony's back view, glanced at from time to time, had an air

64

of quiet desperation about it; a thin shoulder blade stuck out, moving up and down as he talked. Once, he laughed – a brief, self-deprecating, ingratiating laugh. It was not possible to see the restaurateur's response. At last, the man lifted the telephone. Tom saw that agitated shoulder-blade slump in relief. There were diallings, brief exchanges, then Tony's rather high voice saying 'Mike? Tony here – thank God there's someone around. Look, I've got a problem. . . .'

He joined Tom. 'Well, all's well. We can eat. In fact, we can do ourselves proud after that little nightmare. They're getting onto the garage too. What'll you have to drink?' He led the way into the bar.

Tom said, 'And here was I thinking it was going to be the evening of the common man. You won't be wanting my two fifty, then?'

Tony was reinflated. He scanned the menu, ordered Martinis, supervised Tom's selection of a meal. The waiter came with a message from the garage. 'It's some nonsense with the electricals,' said Tony. 'Apparently it'll take them a couple of hours at least, so we might as well take our time. Another drink?'

After a while Tom said, 'I think I'd better ring Kate.' He felt fairly high; lunch had been a long time ago; in the phone booth, the digits on the dial were not as clear as he would have liked. 'Kate?' 'Where on earth are you? I thought you'd be back hours ago.' 'Well,' he said, 'it's like this, actually it's a long story, the fact is . . .' 'You're in a pub,' said Kate crossly. 'Well, yes and no.' 'What do you mean, yes and no?' Tom looked through the glass into the red-leather-and-tropical-plant reception hall: 'Well, rather more yes than no, I suppose.' 'Are you with Tony thing still?' 'Sort of.' 'I can't hear you properly, when are you coming back? Tom, are you there . . .'

He said confidingly to Tony, 'You know, I think she thinks I'm with a girl.'

'I hope you told her she had no cause for alarm. They want us to go through and eat.' At the table, he went on 'I have a feeling

65

your Kate is a wee bit hostile where I'm concerned'. Tom made good-gracious-no faces; there was a nice big bottle of wine on the table.

It occurred to him that he would have no idea if Tony liked girls or not. Or what. He stared reflectively at Tony, who was talking about his time at Oxford, and his time wondering what he wanted to do, and his time beginning to do it.

Some while later, he thought of Kate again. He said to Tony, 'I think I'll just . . .'

Kate sounded muffled. 'You what?' 'Just thought I'd see you're all right.' 'What else could I be, sitting here? What are you *doing*, Tom? What do you mean, what's my zodiac sign, how would I know? Tom?' The lady at the reception desk, seen with intriguing distortion through the glass panel of the phone booth, appeared to have two sets of bosoms, one above the other; they undulated as she wrote in a ledger. 'Gemini,' he said, 'I should think you'd be Gemini, whatever that may be.' Somewhere a long way away, Kate crackled indignantly. This won't do, he thought, this won't do at all, this will all end in tears, this will.

She wasn't best pleased, he said to Tony, she was a bit stroppy in fact, and Tony was laughing, and filling up their glasses. You know, Tom said, you know I'll tell you something, nothing is what you think it is, that nut lady of yours has a point though of course her particular point is right off target. But nothing is what it seems to be, not people nor places nor nothing. Now take Kate's Aunt Nellie, that you met the other day, now you might think though you would be quite mistaken in thinking.

And presently, Tony for some reason was very kindly giving him a hand into that inconstant car, and the motorway was humming again a few inches below. And his head was full of some very effective orchestra on Tony's radio. And . . .

# Chapter Five

Laura said, 'And how is Tom?' She looked at Kate across the restaurant table and thought, she is pasty, she doesn't have the lovely complexion I did at her age, she looks much more like Hugh.

'He's fine. How's Aunt Nellie?'

Laura inspected her salad: the dressing looked doubtful. 'Well, darling, one goes on hoping for miracles, but I don't know . . . Poor Nellie, it is dreadfully hard for someone used to being active, and of course she will keep trying the impossible. She is going to be very dependent on me in the future, I'm afraid.'

'Do you mind?'

'Mind?' said Laura, startled. 'It's not a question of mind or not mind, it's the way things have turned out.'

She doesn't, in a funny way, Kate thought. She quite likes the idea. What is it like to have a sister? I can't imagine it. I don't think I'm very good at imagining. 'What an unusual necklace, darling. That's new, isn't it?'

'Tom gave it to me. We found it in a junk shop.'

It is quite nice, but it doesn't go at all with that shirt, not that one must say so, of course. She has no colour sense, she never has been clever about clothes. I used to get her pretty things when she was a little girl and then she made a fuss about wearing them, it was all very tiresome. I can see her now.

. . . Standing beside me at my dressing-table, I can see both our faces in the mirror, mine and hers, she is not much like me which is a pity. And she has got grass stains all down the front of her frock, it is really too bad. I scold her, I say I *told* you not to roll on the lawn in that frock, go and take it off and ask Mrs Lucas to put it to soak; she sticks her lip out, pulls a face, really she can look plain when she wants to.

She has been threading beads. She wants me to wear this necklace she has made. She puts it round my neck, and I feel her sticky, hot fingers against me. I never like people to touch me, except – well except in the obvious ways. Children touch you all the time, they pat and paw and poke, it is something I have never much liked. I can't help it, it is the way I am.

I am tactful. I say what a lovely necklace it is, but it is a pity it doesn't go with my frock – look, I say, look at the colours. I want Katie to learn to have nice taste, to have an eye for things. I say *I* know, why don't you go and see if Aunt Nellie would like it, I expect she'd love it, Aunt Nellie hasn't got as many necklaces as I have.

'In a junk shop near the flat,' said Kate.

'Which of course I've never seen.'

'Oh, Ma, it's awfully grotty. It isn't your kind of place at all.'

'I offered, ages ago, to come and make it nice for you.'

'Thanks, Ma, but honestly, it suits me fine as it is.'

'Well, it's up to you,' said Laura graciously. She was wearing a new coat, and had stowed a couple of shopping bags under her chair. 'I have had quite a successful morning,' she went on.

'Oh, good.'

'And this afternoon I am meeting Barbara Hamilton. We are going to an art exhibition together.'

'You ought to come to London more often.'

Laura sighed. 'Perhaps eventually, when one is less tied. Of course I sometimes think, eventually, of selling Danehurst. It will get too big. And if I hadn't Mrs Lucas. Barbara and I have toyed with the idea of turning it into an Arts Centre of some kind. An Arts Centre for the county. The government would have to give us money, of course, and we would run it jointly, it would take time to get off the ground, but one imagines it in ten or fifteen years' time being a sort of second Chichester. For art, though, not plays.'

'Yes,' said Kate.

'There would have to be tremendous alterations, of course. We would get in some really top architect.'

'In ten or fifteen years' time you'll be over seventy, ma.'

There was a silence. 'Possibly,' said Laura coldly. She studied the bill. 'I don't remember having soup. I suppose we did. Tony Greenway has been on to me again. He is coming down at some point to have a look through Hugh's papers, to see if there is anything that might be of any use for this programme. Nellie is very disapproving for some reason.'

'I'm not surprised. I don't like the idea of someone poking around in Dad's stuff, either.'

'Not private things. Not letters. Just his work things. Dig notes and so on.'

'Hmnn.'

'I should imagine he's queer, wouldn't you?' said Laura.

'Who?'

'Tony Greenway.'

'I've not the slightest idea. What does it matter, anyway?'

'Oh, it doesn't *matter*,' said Laura. 'It's just that I notice that kind of thing about people. Nothing to look so prim about, darling, I thought your generation was so outspoken . . .'

In ten minutes, Kate thought, I shall be back in the museum. I shall work terribly hard all afternoon. This evening I shall see Tom again. I haven't seen him now for – for five and a half hours.

'. . . partly of course because one has always rather kept up with things, as a matter of fact I never really feel *of* any particular time in the way one is supposed to be *of* the time when one was young, whereas some people very much are, take Barbara Hamilton for instance not that she'd care to have it said but her I do see very much as a thirties person. Or your Tom.'

'What about Tom?'

'Oh, Tom is very much of now, isn't he?' said Laura with a laugh.

'He really couldn't be anything else. And now I don't know about you darling but I have a lot to do, I shall have to rush.'

One of William Stukeley's contemporaries claimed to have had revelations of life before birth; the account was somewhat mystical and while including a convincing description of being suspended in a 'sea of greenish liquid' referred also to angelic hosts and divine choirs. Tom's earliest memory was dull: he was walking with his father along the tow-path of a canal near his home; squatting down to inspect something on the bank, he slipped and plunged one foot deep into the soft mud below; the mud sucked and clung, he shrieked, his father hauled him up and wiped him down. How old he had been, he did not know; judging by the remembered height of a concrete bollard at the spot, which was still there, he must have been about three – the bollard had towered above him.

Other memories were equally insignificant – and personal. Which led him to suspect that those autobiographies which so impressively tether the subject's youth to the course of history are often either reconstructed or invented. If you grew up during a war, of course, or were in some other way inescapably linked to public events, then things would be simpler; you would indeed have shared some kind of collective experience and have bombs or loneliness or the proximity of famous people to prove it. But if you have the good fortune – or misfortune – to spend your childhood in peacetime in a politically stable country in modest, but not deprived circumstances, then memory has a certain timeless quality. One's own life seems to run parallel to what is happening on the public stage, rather than being involved with it. Which, of course, is not the case. The winds of change blow on us all, conditioning a great deal more than how we dress or what we eat.

Which made it unsatisfactory that the sharpest recollections were in that sense mundane. When was it that his schoolboy self had hurtled down a hill, freewheeling on a bicycle, the senses ablaze at the sight of a female thigh rising and falling alongside?

Not just any female thigh, either, but that of his first girl, Lorna Blackstock, and what has become of her, goodness only knows. The bike is still in the shed at home; a more durable relationship. And when was it, sometime before, that he had sat in the kitchen, on a static summer afternoon, hot, suspended in time – forever three o'clock, forever twelve, or thirteen, or fourteen – reading a novel in which a larger world is suggested. On the fringes of consciousness, unexperienced emotions and preoccupations lurk; flies sizzle against the window; Mum comes in and fills a saucepan at the sink.

Only in the more accessible past does history rear its head; one begins to read newspapers, hold opinions, take note. A Tom more ancestral to the Tom of today sprawls in a chair, listens to a bloke on the telly holding forth about the Americans in Vietnam, does not agree, argues subsequently with his father. And another Tom listens with a critical ear to discussion of incomes policy, of who gets how much for doing what, and sees that this is not a matter of abstract or academic interest, that one is going to be in there with the rest, and pretty soon too.

All of which has led, somehow, to the Tom of today, of now, who would probably be surprised by Laura's claim, and possibly affronted. Few of us, after all, feel obliged to accept an affinity with – or take responsibility for – our own day and age.

Tom, walking down Tottenham Court Road, was thinking that Stukeley's world – despite its physical discomforts – had a lot to offer a certain kind of person. His kind of person, he suspected. Given, of course, the right educational and social opportunities. A small cultural and intellectual elite largely known to one another; diversity of job opportunity. Of course, there was a lot that would not have done at all, but that could be said of any time. Undiscriminating acceptance of what you know will not do either.

He had decided to go down to Oxford for a few days; there was stuff in the Bodleian he needed to look at. He could get a bed off

Martin and Beth Laker, out at whatever that village they lived in was called. Kate could come at the weekend and join him.

One would have to conspire with Mrs Lucas. Mrs Lucas would have to be asked – at some point when Laura was out – to investigate the garden shed to see if that old door was still there. And if it was, then Mrs Lucas would have to be persuaded to enlist her husband to give a hand with bringing it in and seeing if it could be transformed into a ramp to cover those pernicious steps down to the study. And if it could, then . . . Well, then the deed would have to be done – again in Laura's absence – and one would have to face the consequences as best one could. The cold wind of Laura's wrath would be mitigated by the pleasure of having got in there, of having by then gathered together at least the best part of what one wanted.

'Next week, then,' said Tony. 'If that's really all right with you, Mrs Paxton.'

'Laura, please.'

'Laura. That really is most awfully kind. I can't tell you what a help it is on this kind of project to have so much co-operation. And I do want this to be a rather special programme. By the way, I had a nice outing the other day with your future son-in-law.'

'Oh yes. Tom.'

'Tom. I do think he's such an interesting person. He's very clever, isn't he?'

'Is he? Well, I suppose he has done rather well considering. I'll see you next week, then, Tony.'

Tom said, 'I've not ridden one for quite a while. How far is it?'

'About seven miles.'

'Christ! I hope I'll make it.'

The bike, apart from being of the wrong sex, had chain trouble, and broke down somewhere outside Oxford. But Martin, of course, could fix that. He squatted by the side of the main road, cars and lorries flashing windily past, his black beard threatening to get tangled with the pedals, and sorted things out. Tom, watching, trying to stow his unsuitable briefcase more satisfactorily into the bike basket, thought with affection that of all his old friends, Martin was about the most stable. At twenty-five, he was a pre-dictable extension of what he had been at eighteen. He had spent much of his spare time, as a student, fishing with a local angling club. Very coarse fishing. And going for long walks. And learning woodwork and welding and, as far as one could make out, some light engineering at evening classes at Oxford Tech. Reading English had been rather by the way. He was always tranquil, always contented, completely kind.

They turned off onto less frequented roads. Martin said, 'By the way, we've got a new baby, I probably forgot to tell you. A girl.'

'That's three?'

'Yes. Jessie goes to the primary now. Beth's very much into vegetable dying at the moment. I'm building an extension at the back of the cottage that we can both use as a workshop.' The Lakers' visible means of support, it seemed, was ornamental ironwork, augmented by what Martin earned from craftsmanly assignments about the place; he was returning home now from a day spent on the restoration of some fifteenth century panelling in the hall of one of the Oxford colleges. He was building up quite an extensive word-of-mouth reputation as the chap to call in for anything requiring the kind of meticulous, solicitous, custom-built attention not available from the average builder. Tom said, 'What are they paying you?'

Martin named a figure.

'That's ridiculous. It's not nearly enough. Do you realize that place owns half north Oxford? And vast tracts of agricultural England?'

'That's not the point,' said Martin. 'Anyway, I like doing it.'

The cottage was in one of the aeroplane villages. Its original small centre of triangular green enclosed by a dozen or so stone cottages and farmhouses, church and school, was held now in the amoeba-like clutch of two or three extremely functional housing estates for the aerodrome personnel. The aerodrome itself, enclosed in wire fencing, glittered all around, its long low silver buildings catching the sun. Aircraft went about their business all the time, roaring low over the rooftops, vanishing with plumes of vapour into the Oxfordshire skies. They made Tom feel anxious but the Lakers seemed to have become impervious. Beth greeted him with a hug. She wore a long brown woollen skirt, blouse pinned at the neck with a Victorian brooch, and a black shawl; she might, he thought, have been an extra on the set of a lavish production of a Hardy novel; he had always liked Beth. They ate a large meal, drank the bottle of wine Tom had brought and ended up in the pub, with Martin and Beth taking it in turns to pop back across the road to see that the children were all right.

Beth said, 'We want to meet Kate.'

'I thought if it was O.K. by you she could come down at the weekend.'

In the morning, he woke on the couch in the cottage's only downstairs room to find Jessie, in vest and pants, contemplating him.

'Why have you got your coat on over the sleeping-bag?'

'Because I was cold.'

'I'm not cold.'

'I can't think why not.'

Jessie sat down on the floor and set about laboriously getting into a pair of greyish socks; her bony knees jutted above her bent head in attitudes of physical improbability, like a cat cleaning itself. She said, 'We do numbers sometimes. I do it with Susie.'

'Ah.'

'When we do dancing we take our shoes and socks off and leave them by the apparatus. Aren't you going to get up?'

'In a minute.'

'Matthew wets his bed.'

'I daresay it's because he's young.'

'He's two and a half,' said Jessie after a pause. Tom thought: it's funny, but I believe I like children.

'Have you got pyjamas on?'

'No.'

'Can I see?'

'I suppose you'll have to, if I'm going to get up.'

'Once I went swimming in the river, and boats came.' She rolled onto her back, thin legs waving in the air, arching down over her head.

'Can you do that?'

'I shouldn't think so.'

'Neither can Martin. I'm best at running out of me and Susie.'

She sat watching in appreciative silence while he dressed. Overhead, he could hear Beth and Martin moving about, and the pigeon noises of the baby. Beth came down and made breakfast. Nobody talked except the children. Jessie said to Tom, 'Where are you going?' 'To read some books.' 'Why?' 'Ah,' he said. 'Now that's difficult. Because I feel I ought to, I suppose.'

He came back to the village early, and they all went down to the river. They sat on the bank, beside a creek muddied by drinking cattle, and ate the food Beth had put in a basket. The children played on the grass. The river wound in erratic bends through the wide, flat field, fringed with willows and teazles; on the far bank, a cluster of calves stared and snorted; Martin, lying propped on one elbow, explained about the formation of glacial boulder valleys such as this. He was a man who throve on technical knowledge, on explanations, on the analysis of how a thing is made or done; ideas did not interest him at all. He gesticulated at the river and the low encircling hills; over the fields a church clock chimed and struck; from time to time the quiet was blasted by aircraft arriving or departing. Martin talked about glacial deposits and boulder clay; Beth made a Victorian posy of wild flowers and stuck it in the waist of her skirt; Tom lay on his back, stared at the white scrawls of aircraft in the sky. He had declined the bicycle that morning and taken the bus into Oxford. Walking the streets, sitting in the library, he had been aware not of nostalgia but of a kindly detachment towards the place – there it was still, but personally one had moved on; the same feeling, he realized, that he experienced meeting his parents' neighbours when he went home.

That evening, he sat in the lean-to shed beside the cottage that served as a workshop, watching Martin at his furnace and anvil. Sparks showered into the dusk. Martin, leather-aproned, his face red in the firelight, was a Wagnerian figure. There was a smell of bread baking; presently, Beth brought them rolls hot from the oven. She sat beside Tom on the bench and said, 'What will you do when you've finished your thesis?'

'Ah, now that's a good point.'

'You'll be married by then.'

'Yes, I suppose I will.'

On the far side of the green, there was a continuous coming and going of motor-bikes, crashing into the peace of the place like raiders from another planet. Beth sighed. 'It's a bother, the Fox has become the pub where all the young go. It won't last, though, they'll take off somewhere else in a few weeks, it's always the way.'

'Never mind,' said Tom. 'You're doing a grand job over this side. William Morris would be proud of you.'

'You're laughing at us,' she said amiably.

'I wouldn't have the gall.'

On Saturday, when Kate was due to come down, he realized with mild surprise how much he had enjoyed the week – the chance meetings with one or two old acquaintances, the placidity of the Lakers, the *laissez-faire* quality of their friendship. On one evening Martin's sister Cherry had turned up, with whom Tom had had a rewarding frolic in a Lake District cottage, years ago. They drank a lot of beer and played a wild card game; Tom felt exuberant and lecherous and, in the morning, guilty. He had imagined sternly that love cured one of susceptibility to one's sexual past.

Kate was startled by the Lakers. She stepped into the cottage with her defences up, Tom could see. She was uneasy, and acted possessively with him to compensate. Matthew, leaning against her knee, dribbled lovingly on her hand and he saw her expression of distaste, and quick furtive wiping against the chair. Why, he wondered in exasperation, is it that the easier people are, the more difficult she finds it to respond? She thought, he knew, that she was being disliked; she was misinterpreting every glance or remark. The Lakers had probably never disliked anybody in their lives; they suffered, if suffer was the word, from indiscriminate indulgence. They would have found excuses for Ghenghis Khan. 'Come and see Beth's mangle,' he said, looking for a distraction. 'I told her you'd probably know how old it is.'

It was a nineteenth century iron mangle on a stand. Kate said, 'We had one pretty well exactly like that at Lincoln. It's about eighteen sixty to seventy, I should imagine. What are you going to do with it?'

Beth said, 'I use it.'

'What for?'

'To mangle with.'

There was a tin bucket on the floor beside it, full of washing. Kate said, 'Wouldn't a spin dryer be more effective?'

'I don't imagine we could afford one.'

'You could sell the mangle to an antique shop and get quite enough for a spin dryer.'

There was a pause. Beth laughed. 'I hadn't thought of that,' she said. 'But do you know, quite frankly I don't think I want to. I've got fond of it.' She ran her hand affectionately over the ironwork. 'It was in an awful state, Martin did it up for me.'

Martin said to Kate, 'You look a bit shocked. Don't you like to see things like that still being used?'

'Well, I suppose so. It's just – just that I can't really see the point if there's an easier way to do things.'

Tom said, 'Kate is sternly practical in her approach to the past – that's what museum training does to you. It's the rest of us who go in for misplaced romanticism.'

Jessie, swinging from the handle of the mangle, was staring at Kate. 'Why has she got a pink face?'

Martin said, 'Get off that, or I'll put you through it with the nappies.'

'Go on then.'

'Just watch it, or I will.'

'Go on. I want to come out all squashed.'

Beth said, 'Oh dear, you won't approve of my old kitchen range, then.'

Kate said stiffly, 'It's rather handsome, I was noticing it just now, but no, I wouldn't want it myself. I mean, it seems to me if you *can* have something you can just switch on and off, then why go to all that trouble of coke and stoking and whatnot. I mean, that's why new things get invented . . .' She moved closer to Tom. The Lakers stood looking at her with friendly concern. Martin said, 'Well, yes, of course. But if a thing is nice to look at *and* reasonably functional – *and* old – then isn't it worth sacrificing a bit of convenience?'

'I suppose it might be,' said Kate, without conviction. There was a trapped look about her – both trapped and faintly aggressive. She went on, 'I mean, if everyone thought like that you wouldn't get any innovation at all.'

Martin said, 'Fair enough. But it seems to me getting better at things technologically doesn't always leave you better off.'

'Ah,' said Tom, 'people have spent a lot of time arguing about that.'

'*I* don't feel well off with glossy cookers and hoovers and whatnot,' said Beth. 'Not that I've ever had them, really.' She shifted the baby onto the other hip and wiped its nose.

'It depends what you want, I suppose,' said Kate. She sounded curt; her blotched neck betrayed, to Tom, her anguish. He thought, in irritation and in pity, she stands there, dedicated to the belief that you can put the past safely away in a glass case and have a look at it when you feel like. And all the time she wears her own like an albatross. I've never known anyone so branded by upbringing. He said to the Lakers, 'Well, are we going down to that nice river of yours?'

She had tried, he later supposed. To the best of her ability. Awkwardly, she had played with the children. She had read Jessie a story, embarrassed by the text, reading too fast. They had slept, that night, on the sitting room couch together, rather cramped. He had woken once to feel Kate staring into the darkness and guessed, despite her denials, that she had spent a more or less sleepless night. Jessie, in the morning, had arrived to inspect them. She said cosily, to Kate, 'I saw him with nothing on. Almost nothing on. Just his pants.' Kate said, 'Oh.'

'Do you want to see me stand on my hands?'

'Yes, I'd love to.'

'I don't really want to,' said Jessie. She added reprovingly, 'Anyway you shouldn't ask me to when I've just had my breakfast, it might make me be sick.' She squatted on the floor, sucking her knee, and watched them speculatively until Kate, clutching her coat around her, went upstairs to wash.

And, driving back to London that Sunday evening, they had said little. Kate had driven too fast, hunched forward to peer through the dark fan made by the windscreen wiper. 'Good thing the rain kept off till now,' Tom said. 'We wouldn't have got that walk in. Nice place, isn't it – bar the aeroplanes?' 'Yes, very nice. By the way I forgot – did you find the stuff you wanted in the Bodleian?'

I love you, she thought, I do love you so. And I am so frightened of what might happen.

# Chapter Six

'I am thinking,' Laura said to Nellie, 'of running a little Arts Festival with Barbara Hamilton later this year. Or next.'

'I see.'

'Centred on the three villages, we thought. Exhibitions in the churches, and some musical evenings – Barbara knows Yehudi Menuhin quite well and she thinks she might be able to persuade him to come.'

'The villages will enjoy Yehudi Menuhin,' said Nellie.

'Well, yes – but it will be mainly for visitors, of course, we feel sure we could draw quite a lot of people. It may mean marquees and things, the village halls mightn't be able to cope. And then on the painting side I thought of doing a Paul Nash exhibition, one could try to borrow some of the wartime paintings, make it a sort of little retrospective show.'

'Well, that will keep you very busy.'

'Oh, I shall be terribly busy. But we feel it would be such a worthwhile thing to do.'

They were driving to Swindon, for Nellie's check-up at the hospital. The wheelchair, folded, rattled from time to time in the back of the Renault. Laura drove fast, but competently; she drove better than Kate; it often surprised Nellie that Laura drove well. You would not have expected it. She also was unmoved by domestic disaster, such as floods or blown fuses, and would be practical and efficient. Blood and guts did not worry her, either; once, years ago, she had done the necessary, immediate things at the scene of an unpleasant road accident, while Hugh had sat white-faced with his head between his knees. Afterwards, she had been annoyed because it had made them late for an engagement.

Nellie, sitting beside her now, longed suddenly to drive herself; she had liked driving; one was always popping about the place, time was, in the old Ford Popular and then the Morris and finally the Volkswagen. This won't do, she told herself, what is driving, after all?

Look at those trees against the skyline. I had forgotten how, on this particular stretch of road, the downs fold into themselves, on and on, green against fawn against gold; the fields apple-green, looking as though they had been combed; cottages tucked down into the ground; everything growing. The smell of it.

Laura said, 'We should be just about right for time. I hope he doesn't keep us hanging about again, Dr Williams. I'll get one of the porters to come and give us a hand when we get there.'

'No need.'

'It's what they're there for,' said Laura crossly. I wish Nellie would be private, she thought, not the beastly National Health. I'm sure she could afford it, really, she just is so obstinate about it. That waiting room place is loathsome, all those people bundled in coats smelling of rain, children tripping over your feet. Awful torn magazines about car racing and cookery.

I don't mind being kept waiting, Nellie thought, in fact I have to admit that I hope we are. I like looking at people. Listening. I had no idea one would ever come to find the comings and goings of a hospital waiting room enthralling. As good as the telly. Better, being real life.

And, at the entrance to the hospital, as Laura turns to go into the visitors' car park, their thoughts, up to a point, run parallel.

Hugh died here. I came in and out, every day, those last horrid weeks, with that sick feeling inside me all the time. I didn't care what I looked like; I used to catch sight of myself in mirrors and shop windows and it was a person I didn't know, clothes put on all anyhow, hair stringy and no make-up. I couldn't believe it was happening; I thought that kind of thing only happened to other people. It was like a bad dream, but one had always woken up from bad dreams.

The nurses all liked him; he was jokey with them, even when he was so ill; sometimes I was jealous, he seemed almost to prefer them to me. I used to sit by him, hour after hour, reading the paper to him, doing nothing, often, just sitting. I wanted to say things to him. I wanted to say I'm sorry, I can't help it, I am like this, there is nothing I can do. I wanted to say I know, you think I don't know, but I do, I always have. Sometimes I have seen myself, like another person, and hated it.

I used to hold his hand. Once, I fell asleep, and when I woke, he had taken his hand away and was staring out of the window.


Hugh died here. I only came twice, those last weeks. It wasn't for me to intrude, they should have that time alone. I sent things to him with Laura – books and flowers from the garden and newspaper articles he would be interested in.

He was sixty; no great age. My age now.

Laura did not know he was going to die. The doctors told her, but in such a way that she did not have to hear if she did not want to. Every day, she was bright. She said, he is really much better, he sat up for a long time today, they are so pleased with how he is getting on, he will be out by the end of the month, with any luck.

The last time I saw him, we talked about a dig, and about Kate. He used to worry about Kate. He said, 'What a long time we've known each other, Nellie, what years and years. Oh, well . . .' We were there together in that narrow hospital room, with sun falling across a blue blanket on his bed. I knew he was going to die. I knew, and yet it was quite all right, quite calm. He was more important to me than anyone else, in all my life.

After he died Laura came to me. She stayed for weeks and months. I used to see her eyes looking out of her face, scared, like a child waking up in the dark, and I could not bear it.

★

The porter said, 'Upsy daisy now, lady, easy does it. Will she want the rug round her knees?'

'I do not want the rug round my knees,' said Nellie. 'Thank you all the same.'

Laura said, 'Thank you *very* much. I'll be able to manage on my own now.' She gave him a nice smile. A tip would be out of place, she decided. A hospital is not like a hotel, or a taxi. She pushed the chair down the long corridors, though Nellie would have preferred to propel herself. In the waiting room, she found a battered and mature number *of Country Life* and sat reading it, her chair shunted a little apart from the other attendant relatives. Nellie struck up a conversation with an acquaintance made during her time as an in-patient. When her turn was called Laura rose to go into the doctor's room with her, but was turned back by a nurse: 'I think not, dear. I expect if you want to Dr Williams would have a word with you after.' Laura, nettled, returned to *Country Life*.

When at last Nellie re-emerged she rose. 'All set, darling? I'll just pop in and see him myself for a moment.'

She found him tiresome, in fact, Dr Williams. One of those dapper, sexless, pink and white men. He had been a bit too inclined to tell one what was what when Nellie was in hospital. She sat down, without waiting for him to speak, and said, 'Well, how do you find her? Very little change, I'm afraid.'

'On the contrary, Miss Peters isn't doing badly at all. There is a considerable improvement.'

Laura sighed, 'She can do so little for herself, poor darling.'

The doctor smoothed out the papers on the desk in front of them, tapped them with a pencil. 'The more that she does, the better, Mrs Paxton. She must be encouraged. I can't stress that enough. She needs an atmosphere of optimism and encouragement.'

Such a brisk man, Laura thought. Horrid to have around if you were ill. 'Really?' she murmured.

'A complete recovery is perfectly possible. But it depends very much on day-to-day progress, and that in turn depends on the people around her. You are managing all right, I take it, with such nursing as has to be done?'

'Oh,' said Laura, 'one is managing, I suppose, yes, as best one can.' She sighed again.

'The physiotherapist is coming regularly, of course?'

That clumpy girl with the Birmingham accent – it was hard to understand how Nellie could stand being closeted with her once a week, but Nellie didn't seem to mind. One heard them laughing together, though what there was to laugh about, with all those gruesome exercises to be done, it was hard to see. 'Yes,' she said, 'she comes.'

He was going on and on, in his rather hectoring way. I hate the smell of hospitals, she thought, and the noises, the way nurses' shoes squeak on the lino, trolleys raiding around all the time. It makes me think of Hugh's illness, that I don't want to think of. She stared coldly at the doctor. He was off on another tack. 'Recurrence?' she said, sharply now.

'I did warn when your sister was first ill that a stroke is very often followed by another. That is not to say that it will be, in her case, we can't tell, but it is always a possibility.'

'Oh, I think that's most unlikely,' said Laura energetically. What an absurdly pessimistic thing to say, she thought, doctors are supposed to cheer you up, not spread gloom and despondency. 'No, there's absolutely no sign of that, I can assure you.' She got up. What nonsense, of course that is nonsense, Nellie may not be that much better, but she's not going to die or anything. 'Well, it's been so kind of you to talk to me, Dr Williams, and it's reassuring to hear that Nellie's improving, though I'm afraid that all the same she is going to be rather dependent on one for a long time to come.' She walked quickly out of the room, gathered up Nellie, hurried to the car. She felt a bit sick, her stomach heaved; it is rushing off so soon after breakfast, she thought, it upsets me, next time we must get the appointment for later on.

She talked, feverishly, all the way home. And what has got into *her,* Nellie thought, I know that voice, that look, it is when something has rattled her, when she is anxious. When the chasms yawn.

All my life, she thought, I have been exasperated by my sister. And unendurably sorry for her.

'That's all right,' said Tony. 'You didn't get too much of a roasting from Kate, I hope. You do get pissed rather easily, don't you? Look, what I was phoning about is, I'm going down to Danehurst on Friday to have a look through these papers of Hugh Paxton's – Laura said something about bringing you and Kate down, I gather Kate's car's in dock, is that right? Fine. Right. Well now look, I'm in the studio till six at the earliest so it might save a bit of time if you came along there, and then we can get straight off. Good. Just wait in reception and I'll be with you as quickly as I can.'

But in the event, there was a message awaiting them that Mr Greenway was delayed, and would they go through to the studio. A girl conducted them there and Tony broke free from a knot of shirt-sleeved figures to greet them. 'Look, I'm so sorry, it's been one of those days when not one bloody thing goes right. I thought, rather than kick your heels out there you might as well see what goes on here. We're not actually recording, but I'm tied up for another twenty minutes or so. Marni will fill you in.' He was breathing heavily, as though he had just taken vigorous exercise; his face shone with sweat.

It was amazing, Tom thought, that so many people should be required for whatever it was they were about (some discussion programme, as far as he could see). So many people walking around or standing in groups apparently locked in furious argument, or perched up in little seats behind cameras or squatting on the ground with earphones on, muttering away to no one. There was, indeed, an atmosphere of exhausted frenzy, bearing out Tony's claim. A thin, handsome girl wearing a boiler suit of manifestly fashionable cut walked quickly past them, her knuckles ground into her temples. 'Jesus,' she said, 'just sweet Jesus, that's all.' A man holding a clip-board shouted after her, 'Look darling, either we chuck the lot or we think again. No way do I compromise.' Up in the shadowy heights of the roof, a voice was shouting in some purely technical language. Cables hung around like lianas. Spotlights swivelled, and hit you savagely in the eye. Everyone smelled of sweat.

Tom thought of the nation, at the receiving end, slumped before its television set in torpid contemplation, teacup in hand.

'O.K.,' said Tony, joining them, 'we're packing it in now. Terribly sorry to have kept you. Lovely to see you, Kate.' They went out to the car. Kate asked questions, politely; she had not, Tom knew, been at all interested. He said to Tony, 'That all seemed an amazing amount of hassle. I shall bear it in mind when next I'm watching something.' Tony said, 'What?'; he was clearly stupid with exhaustion.

On the outskirts of London they stopped for a drink. Tony, picking up, said, 'It's awfully good of Laura to lay on this dinner tonight. Meeting Paul Summers will be a great help to me.'

Kate said sharply, 'Dinner? I thought it was just us?'

'Oh no. I gather she has Summers coming, and some people called Hammond, is it? Hammond, Hamilton. And someone else, I think.'

Typical, thought Kate. Not saying. So we arrive in the wrong clothes, and she can say, probably in front of every one, Kate darling I do think just a little bit of an effort might have been made. And later, to me, and Kate dear I wonder if you could ever so tactfully sometime hint to Tom that when people are coming in . . . I know it's tricky for him, to know what's what, as it were.

'Ah,' said Tom, 'fifteen love to Laura. Neat. And who's Paul Summers?'

Kate took a gulp at her drink. 'Paul Summers was Dad's right-hand man, sort of. He was Field Officer at the Council for years and years. He's something quite grand now, himself.'

'Ministry of the Environment,' said Tony.

'Can I have another drink? It's going to be an awful evening – so don't say I didn't warn you.'

'There you all are,' said Laura. 'At last. Kate darling there's just time for you to pop up and change, I can't think you'll feel comfy like that.'

'I'll be all right, Ma, thanks.'

'What a very dashing shirt, Tom. You're happy as you are too, are you? Well, come and meet people, then.'

Old and young and mid-way, thought Nellie, watchful from the fireplace. A funny mixture, by and large. Interesting, though perhaps not quite in the way Laura thinks. Paul Summers has aged a lot. The television man looks in need of fresh air. The Hamiltons have so perfected the art of self-preservation they appear to be embalmed: those pink and white faces, that neatly waved grey hair. Kate is off her guard and must beware. Tom is a very rapid consumer of gin and tonic. This friend who is something in the National Trust I do not think I care for.

Laura thought, of course people like Tom and Tony thing may turn out to be someone in the end, you never know, one forgets they have hardly even begun. Once, James Hamilton wasn't any-one in particular. Or John Barclay. She patted the sofa beside her and said, 'John, do come and sit here and tell me all about your book, when is it coming out?' I have always rather liked queers, she thought, there is something about the way they look at you: cosy and a bit suggestive too. Paul has got fat; he is quite high up now, Nellie says; I used to find him rather sticky, in the old days.

Does a man like this well-fed well-barbered well-spoken civil servant, Tom wondered, does he end up thus because he has so chosen and to that purpose dexterously steered his life, or has he become like that because of what has happened to him? I never saw a man with such clean finger nails. And the bloke who goes round country houses making lists of Grinling Gibbons fireplaces, does he wear a spotted bow tie and suggest a slight but well-controlled touch of the Augustus Johns by inclination or association? Do we choose, or are we chosen? I should rather like to know, being at the point of one or the other. At least Laura seems to be being free with the drink tonight, anyway.

Tony, leaning confidingly towards Paul Summers, talked of the programme on Hugh Paxton. Presently, diaries were brought out, an arrangement pencilled in.

Laura led them through to dinner, disposed them round the table.

'Tell me,' said James Hamilton to Tom, 'how is Oxford?'

'What you will have to watch out for,' Paul Summers was telling Kate, 'is getting trapped in the museum treadmill. Keep an eye out for other openings.'

'. . . always marginally prefer Wilton,' said Barbara Hamilton, 'though Stourhead is unforgettable.'

'Of course I dine in All Souls once or twice a year.'

'. . . the Royal Commission on Ancient Monuments.'

'. . . know the Pagets rather well, at Hornby Castle.'

Once, Nellie thought, I ate a meal at this table, time out of mind ago, and my younger sister Laura sat over there, with her back to the window, looking, I thought, a bit bored because Hugh and I were talking shop, on and off. She came, I think, because she was at a loose end and it was a nice day and she was curious, perhaps. She called Hugh Mr Paxton and tried to ask intelligent questions about the dig. And in the middle of saying something I saw his eyes on her, and how they were, and all of a sudden the day wasn't so nice after all. It had gone cold. Time out of mind ago, that was. Or should be.

That mark on the dresser, Kate thought, that little gash you wouldn't notice if you didn't know about it, is where once Ma slammed down a big flowery jug and it broke. They had been shouting at each other; he stood over there by the window and she stood there by the dresser and I watched from the hall, where they didn't know I was. '. . . only doing what you do yourself Laura,' he said. 'I know, you know. I always have.' I swung on the bannister, watching; they were like people in a pretend thing, I thought, a cinema or the pantomime. 'Know, you know,' I hummed to myself. 'Know, you know. Doing what you do. Know you do.' And Ma's face was all red and angry and she banged the jug down and it broke into great big flowery pieces.

People were having quite a lot to drink. Some people. Tom was filling up his glass and saying that no, he didn't in fact dine much in All Souls. He had had lunch in St Peter's last year, he offered helpfully, in the Buttery. James Hamilton had turned now to Laura and was wondering what quirk of fate it was that led one so often to make the right, fortunate decision – talking to Tom here about Oxford reminds me that it was simply my housemaster having a brother at Wadham that took me there rather than elsewhere, for which thanks be, because there was Barbara, the Dean's pretty daughter (he raised his glass to Barbara, who raised hers prettily back) and . . .

'Oh,' said Laura, 'I think one is always making the wrong decisions. I could have gone to art college, but I didn't.'

'Do you think you'd be different, Ma?'

'Goodness, I don't know.'

'Of course,' said Tony, 'choices are only random up to a point, aren't they? Shall I do this or shall I do that. Most of them get thrust on us by social circumstance, or economic.'

'You young,' said Barbara, 'didn't have the war, of course, and all that that implied.'

'Quite. But I was thinking less of being shaped by history than vaguer sort of processes like what is available at a particular time, by way of education or jobs or simply convention, what sort of things your sort of person does. Which is history of a kind, I suppose.'

'Nowadays,' said Laura, 'as far as I can see you get all sorts of people doing all sorts of things.'

'Confusing, isn't it?' said Tom. He met Laura's blue stare across a vase of what looked to him like carefully-arranged weeds and bent his head hastily to his plate again.

James Hamilton suggested that the problem posed by a more fluid society might be that diversity of choice and raised expectations lead not so much to *more* rational decisions, but to *less* rational ones; in other words if more people both are able and expect to do more things they . . .

'Get in a muddle,' said Laura, 'and most of them don't know what they want anyway. Mrs Lucas's sister's boy has got a job at Harwell. Let's hope he doesn't blow us all up. Mrs Lucas only has to look at the washing-machine for it to go wrong.'

Take my own particular pond, James went on smoothly, now frankly one of the pleasures of impending retirement is to leave the Service with a sense of how very much its recruitment has changed since my own youth. We are broader based. I like it.

I don't, thought Laura, and I bet you don't really either, only it doesn't do to say. 'Gooseberry fool?' she said. 'Tom? Paul?'

'Thanks,' said Tom. He squinted at the bowl in front of him. The little green bits are hemlock, I should imagine, last resort of the socially threatened. I expect it grows wild in these parts. He picked up his glass, and put it down again, feeling Kate's eye upon him.

'Thanks, Laura,' said Paul Summers. 'Lovely. I remember your gooseberry fool from the old days. You know, following on what was being said I can't help thinking of Hugh and remembering the way he came to the Council, to the Directorship, which had a smack of the random about it, I suppose. His application came in late – in fact there was a bit of bother about whether it could be allowed – and then just the week or so before the appointing committee met, the article on Charlie's Tump was in *Antiquity*, and everyone was talking about it, and I suppose that swung the balance. A lot of people had thought Matlock would get the job.'

'That cup from Charlie's Tump is quite lovely,' said Barbara. 'The gold one. One would adore to have a modern replica.'

James Hamilton swilled his wine-glass, thoughtfully. 'Interesting. Good timing – that particular dig came at the right moment for him. Did he *know* what would be there, Laura?'

'No, of course not. Because the barrow was much older, anyway. They weren't expecting to find that kind of thing at all. They nearly dug quite a different one, miles from here. And it *was* a rush getting that article out, that I do remember.'

'Whose grave was it?'

'One can't possibly know,' said Paul Summers. 'Some Bronze Age man of substance. Anyway, an unknown benefactor to Hugh – he gave him a good reference, just in time for the Directorship.'

The effect of alcohol, Tom thought, is not so much to hinder the perception or cloud the vision as to render same more acute. So long as not too much is required of you by way of saying or doing things, all is well. The mind fairly ticks away. The blue-rinsed up-market hotel receptionist on my right is not quite as at her ease as one might think; she is frightened of old Tony there, which is interesting, because old Tony is as harmless as they come. Disconcerted by the unfamiliar, I suppose. And her husband is a right so-and-so. And this chap who worked with Hugh Paxton didn't in fact like him overmuch, though he thinks no one knows.

And Hugh Paxton, like Stukeley up to a point, cashed in on the national past, though not wittingly or with calculation, as we all do who earn our keep at this particular trade. Stukeley, of course, distorted in order to get the results he wanted; Hugh Paxton presumably didn't do that. Except in the way that convenient evidence for a theory always seems to come to hand more readily than inconvenient evidence. Convenient Wessex man, in this case.

Laura is an attractive woman. One can be aware of that, with perfect detachment and without prejudice. Or, at least, with a good deal of prejudice, but in all fairness.

What is odd, what I find odd, is that earlier archaeologists should have been so anxious to attribute everything to continental influence. You'd have thought it would have fitted in with good old imperialist chauvinist days to claim the culture that produced Avebury and Stonehenge and the Charlie's Tump grave-goods for Britain. But not a bit of it – it all had to have come from the Mediterranean, via other nice civilized places like France. And that, of course, is to do with the conditioning of a classical education: anything that is culturally worth having comes from Greece or Rome. Very odd that not until the humdrum superseded retracted Britain of the nineteen sixties do we start thinking that maybe that part of it at least began here, with a bunch of home-grown Wiltshire farmers.

'Of course,' he said, 'you could say that there isn't anything all that culturally spectacular about mobilizing an admittedly startling amount of man-power in order to stand a lot of stones on their ends for superstitious reasons. You could say that, quite properly.' They were all staring rather, at this not particularly sensational remark. James Hamilton, wearing an interrupted look, had his mouth open; he had very dapper teeth for a man of his age. 'But of course,' Tom went on, 'the whole point is aspirations, in whatever direction. New Guinea tribesmen have never built anything; most of them haven't even learnt how to make pottery. Primitive societies either stand still or they don't. Wessex very much didn't which is why in the fullness of time people like Stukeley and Hugh Paxton come along and spend their lives trying to work out what it was all about, and making a name for themselves in the process, and either getting it wrong or right, or somewhere in between, and confusing the issue with a whole lot of prejudices and assumptions of their own . . .'

'Gracious, Tom,' said Laura coldly, 'what a diatribe! Well now, let's go through for some coffee?'

And Nellie, silent on the side-lines, thought, this is better than the hospital waiting room, thank God I am not robbed of hearing nor the powers of observation. Poor Tom, put in his place, though of course in fact it is not poor Tom at all, because Tom's day is yet to come and is going to be a rather satisfactory one, I suspect. And he is not, as it happens, much alarmed by Laura. But it is poor Kate, chewing her fingernails there just as she used to do at sixteen, and ten, and six. And as for the rest of them, it is interesting to note people all somewhat set in their ways – and the young can be that, too – doing their best to look as though they are not. Laura's evening could be said to be a success, on the whole, though just at the moment that is not what she is thinking.

# Chapter Seven

'My sister is extraordinary,' said Laura to Tony. 'She had an obsession about getting in here to go through some papers of Hugh's, and nothing would stop her, she even enlisted Ted Lucas who is slow on the uptake to say the least of it, and they heaved some sort of old door over the steps . . . Well anyway, she has had what she calls a sort-out.' Laura surveyed the neat and dusted desk with disapproval. 'The dig notes are in these boxes here, so I'll leave you to it, shall I?'

And Tony sits at this desk of a man he never met, and reads, and blinks through his Mahler spectacles at difficult handwriting, and takes notes. He is quite absorbed; he puzzles over technical details and wonders who various people referred to are (and lists them, for his secretary to check) and wishes not for the first time in his career that one could dally further but it is no good, his year is mapped out already with schedules and dead-lines and studio dates; there is so long for Hugh Paxton and no more. Once or twice he feels intrusive; a scrawled note in another hand falls from between the pages of an exercise book – 'Have gone up to the dig, can you bring the cameras when you come, also water and lunch things on table, see you later J.' J must remain an unknown quantity in Hugh Paxton's life, and he puts the note tidily back, as also a sepia photograph showing two people, with eyes screwed up against the sun, amid a dusty landscape, Paxton himself and the sister, what is she called? her in the wheel chair, who is also irrelevant, so far as Tony is concerned. It is remarkable, he thinks, how comprehensive a picture one builds up, I have a pretty good idea what sort of a man Hugh Paxton was, if I met him I would know what approach to take, what his foibles are, his prejudices, that he didn't stand fools lightly, went straight to the point, worked hard and expected others to. But relaxed hard too, drank quite a bit, had an eye for the girls. One gets a composite picture, talking to people, reading this stuff, the man fills out . . .

While Nellie, in her room, sits, equally absorbed, before her own extracted evidence. Here are all the notes on pottery sequences, and yes, she thinks with gathering energy that it might well be possible to work up something publishable. She too reads and makes notes, but for her the job is dramatized by recollection with all its shifty tricks: what was and what one thought was and what may have been.

Tom, also, sits at a desk. I am almost ready to start writing, he thinks. Another few weeks. He contemplates his card-index boxes and his tidy piles of notes, clipped together in a Boots file that he has had since sixth form days. William Stukeley and his contemporaries: a study . . . I am almost ready to pronounce judgement. I have read everything that ought to have been read and given proper thought to all that should properly be thought of. Now I must sit down and write history.

'Warriner Park. Some vast comprehensive.'
  'I'll come with you.'
  'Whatever for?'
  'Help you heave all that stuff around.'
  'Well,' said Kate doubtfully, 'if you like, but . . .'
  'All right, all right. I know when I'm not wanted.'
  'Oh, don't be *silly*, Tom. It's just you'll be bored stiff. Birmingham's not the most attractive place in the world. There'll probably be no end of bother finding the right teachers and getting it all set up.'
  'All the more reason for giving you a hand.'
  Kate's 'Island Heritage' travelling exhibition was now complete and ready for release. Its debut was to take place in a Birmingham

school which had been among the first to express interest, and Kate, anxious about the security and proper display of this valuable and painstakingly assembled collection, had decided to take it herself to the school and supervise its initial arrangement. An official from Birmingham Museum, who was to be responsible for its transfer to the next school on the list, was to meet her there.

They drove up the motorway in pouring rain, the back of the Fiat crammed full of the boxes housing Roman lamps, coins and tiles, and facsimiles of pages from Bede's *Ecclesiastical History*, the Caxton Bible, the Lindisfarne Gospel, the earliest edition of Chaucer, a First Folio Shakespeare and selected passages of the Paston letters. A specially constructed case, lined with plastic foam, held some Celtic metalware and a Viking shield, buckle and sword: these were the real thing and causing Kate much anguish. 'Just the job for a bit of aggro on the football terraces,' said Tom cheerfully. 'You're going to have to make sure they put double padlocks on this lot.' Kate groaned. There was also an assortment of more homely articles of domestic use, ranging from prehistoric to medieval, some costumes and a fourteenth century tapestry, some very fine blown-up photographs illustrating early vernacular architecture, with explanatory notes, and a huge wall-chart explaining the provenance of cultural influences from the Iron Age to the end of the sixteenth century, by means of maps, differently coloured arrows, simplified chronological tables and diagrammatic symbols. Kate and various colleagues had devised this and agonized over it for months. It had come out aesthetically satisfactory but perhaps rather confusing. 'The trouble is,' said Kate, 'it *is* confusing. There's no two ways about it.' This enormous scroll now stuck into the middle of Tom's back, as they approached Birmingham. Above him, swathed in plastic sheeting and tied to the roof-rack, was a full-size replica of the Bewcastle Cross in expanded polystyrene of quite astonishing lightness. Periodically the wind would catch its protruding end, causing the car to rock alarmingly.

The school, when at last they ran it to ground amid Birmingham's proliferation of ring-roads and fly-overs and dual carriage-ways, turned out to be spread out over a large area, and of fairly recent construction. It was light and bright, set down in blocks of sage green and dull orange amid playing fields and its own internal road-system of tarmac tracks with sign-posts about Language Blocks and Sixth Form Units and Remedial Teaching Centres. A satellite colony of terrapin buildings suggested a staged expansion. The windows snapped in the sunlight and children drifted about the place, many of them West Indian and Pakistani. There were motor-bikes and scooters among the push-bikes in the sheds along-side the car park. They went into what appeared to be the main building, in search of the teacher who was supposed to be expect-ing them. When he appeared – young, bearded and jeaned, looking, Tom thought, more like an actor than anyone's stereotype of a schoolmaster – they followed him to the room set aside for the display of the 'Island Heritage'. Kate inspected the doors and windows. 'Can it be locked? Sorry, Mr – er – Mr Sanderson, but some of the exhibits are real, you see, and quite irreplaceable.'

'Ron. It'll be bolted and barred, yes, don't worry.' Kate relaxed a little, and entered into a discussion about trestle tables and pin-boards. Tom volunteered to start bringing the boxes in.

He left the Bewcastle Cross until the final journey. It was awkward to carry, and he set off across the car park with it aslant his shoulders at first until it struck him that his appearance was perhaps in rather bad taste, so he shifted it to an irritating position under one arm from which it banged into each of the many swing doors that had to be negotiated *en route* to the exhibition room, where Kate and Ron were now busy setting up the display. With relief, he leaned it up against the wall. Ron said, 'What on earth's that?' Kate explained. Children, curious, clustered at the door, also asking questions. 'Buzz off,' said Ron. 'You'll find out, all in good time. It's a super exhibition,' he went on, 'we're awfully grateful to have had first crack at it, as it were. Knowing it was in the offing, of course, we've tried as much as possible to tie it in with ordinary class teaching. Even so, I'm afraid it's going to seem baffling and maybe a bit irrelevant to a lot of our children.' 'Irrelevant?' said Kate, wrestling with drawing-pins and the cultural scroll. 'We have a large immigrant quota.' 'Oh,' she said, smoothing down a corner that showed Angles, Saxons and Jutes, pink-arrowed, emanating from northern Europe; under her left elbow, Normans, blue, surged out of Cherbourg. 'Yes, I suppose so.' 'What would be marvellous,' Ron continued, 'would be if one could get together the same sort of thing but pertinent to their own cultural groupings – you know, on the West Indies, say, or India.' 'Mmn,' said Kate, turning her attention to Roman coins. 'I suppose it could be done. Not my province, though, I'm afraid, you'd have to talk to someone in that field at the B.M.' 'Some of us feel strongly that they don't have nearly enough in the curriculum that's geared to their own cultures – we'd like to see classes in Urdu and that kind of thing, options on Indian history and art. But it's not popular with the educational establishment. Not sufficiently exam-oriented. Not vocational.' 'This isn't very vocational either,' said Kate, positioning the Viking sword and shield on a display board. 'Well, maybe I don't mean vocational, quite. Mainstream.' Outside, faces – pink, brown, yellow and whitish, bobbed against the glass of the door; feet rushed in the corridor; a bell rang. 'But,' said Tom, 'they live here now, that's a plain fact. They live here and they're going to work here and probably die here. So it is relevant, it has to be. Maybe they were better at this in America.' 'Oh dear,' said Ron, 'saluting the flag and all that. I think not.' 'I wasn't going to propose that. Just that you can't suggest that this is irrelevant and propose classes in Urdu one moment and then wonder why people don't adapt themselves better the next.' 'Ever lived in Birmingham?' said Ron. 'No, but I don't need . . .' 'Just chuck me that ball of string, will you,' said Kate. 'Or taught?' 'No, nor that neither, and I daresay you're in the thick of it and I'm not, but the simple fact remains that . . .' 'Sorry,' said Kate, 'can I just get at the scissors? Thanks.' 'I'm not,' Tom went on, 'proposing some kind of identity massacre, it's just common sense dictates that you must . . .'

The door, which Ron had closed against the intruding children, now opened.

'Can I have a preview?' said Cherry Laker. And then, 'Good Lord! Tom! Whatever brings you here?'

'Cherry! Well I'm blowed!'

'Didn't you know I taught here?'

'No, I swear. Oh, this is Kate – Kate Paxton. Cherry Laker. Martin's sister, you know.' Kate said, 'Hello,' stiffly.

'Of course,' said Cherry, 'now I get why you're here – the "Island Heritage" exhibition. What fun. Let's all go and have some lunch somewhere – you won't be wanting school dinner.' She looked extremely fetching and, like Ron, rather far removed from one's concept of a school teacher. Kate had turned back to her display board and was saying something in a very offhand tone about having to stay here until Mr Wilmot from the City Museum arrived.

'Actually,' said Ron, 'I'll have to push off now. I've got a class. Here's the key. Would you drop it in at the school office when you go?'

'I can help,' Cherry offered, 'I've got a free period. I say, what a splendid diagram. Even I can understand it, so the kids should be all right.' She giggled. Tom said, 'Cherry teaches Art.' He saw Kate's suspicious glance swerve from the Viking shield to Cherry's full, red cotton skirt and tight, black T-shirt; she nodded and pointed at a pot of glue. He handed it to her; Cherry was admiring the Celtic pins and brooches. 'Look, he's awfully late, this Wilmot bloke. Why don't we leave a message in case he comes, and go and have something to eat, like Cherry says, I'm starving.' 'You go, if you want,' said Kate, in a cool, distant voice. 'I'd rather wait for him.'

When, after another ten minutes, Wilmot had still not come, Cherry said, 'Well, I don't know about you, but if I don't have something to eat I shan't get through the afternoon. Couldn't we leave a . . .' 'You two go,' said Kate. 'Go on.' She scowled at the pin-board, aligning the architectural photographs. 'No,' Tom began, 'I tell you what, we'll . . .' 'Go *on*.' Cherry said, 'I'm just going to get my purse, I'll pop back and see who's coming, if anyone.' She went.

'Look,' said Tom, 'he's presumably made a mistake about the time. He'll show up this afternoon. Let's . . .'

'Now I know why you wanted to come.'

'What?'

'I said, now I know. So much for all that let me help you heave the boxes around stuff.'

'Look, what exactly are you getting at?'

'You *knew* she worked here.'

'I damn well didn't. At least yes I knew she worked in some Birmingham school, she said something about it at Martin and Beth's, but there are dozens of schools in Birmingham. Don't be ridiculous, Kate. And anyway, what the hell makes you think . . .'

'At Martin and Beth's. You didn't tell me she'd been there.'

'Well, why should I? It wasn't worth mentioning.'

'I thought you hadn't seen her for years.'

'I hadn't.'

'Not since you were – involved with her.'

'What a stupid prissy word. I wish I'd never mentioned it. Too bloody honest, that's my trouble. Look, Cherry is the kind of girl who frequently gets – involved – as you so quaintly put it. She's just an old friend, now, neither more nor less. So stop being so silly. And I hadn't the faintest idea she taught here.'

Kate snorted. 'Friend! Now who's being prissy.' They glared at each other.

Cherry put her head round the door. 'Anyone for beer and a banger? There's quite a nice pub down the road.'

Kate said, 'Tom's going' at the same moment as Tom said, 'Neither of us, I'm afraid.' There was a silence. Tom picked up his jacket. 'Right you are. I'll bring you back a sandwich.' Kate did not reply. He walked put of the room.

'Oh,' said Cherry, 'I quite like it really. I mean, yes, it's awful in some ways, Birmingham, but there's a fair bit going on, and anyway, you can always find something, or make it yourself.' She had had a pint and a half of beer and was very slightly tipsy; she had, Tom remembered, a weak head, a fact of which, in the past, he had taken advantage on more than one occasion. He said, 'I bet.'

'This is fun. Little did I think, this morning . . . It *is* nice to see you.'

He put his hand on her arm. 'It's pretty good to see you, Cherry.'

'We don't see each other for five years, and then twice in a month.'

'Predestination.'

They laughed. Tom said, 'Another half?'

'Oh,' she said. 'You. Up to your old tricks. Oh no, of course you're not, you're engaged, aren't you? Oh God, do you know, for the moment I'd quite forgotten! She didn't mind us going off like this, did she?'

'No, of course not.'

'Oh, good. Martin and Beth said she's awfully nice. I wish someone would engage me, isn't she lucky. All *I* get is improper suggestions.'

'Come off it. Beth was telling me a tale or two. Some love-lorn musician in hot pursuit. Blokes being cast aside like old gloves.'

Cherry grinned. 'Oh well, I suppose I'm not the settling-down type, that's all there is to it. I say, isn't this just about the most revolting pork pie you've ever met? It's a pity you're not going to be here long – I could have shown you the jollier aspects of Birmingham. How's this thing you're writing going – are you going to get some terribly grand job when you've finished it?'

'No,' said Tom. He bought himself another beer, listened to Cherry chattering on, looked at her with appreciation. He thought what a nice girl she was, what a warm easy undemanding girl, and how appropriate her looks were to her personality, all that tousled dark brown hair and those expansive inviting breasts and that soft round brown forearm lying on the bar in such a way that you wanted to put a hand on it. He thought, with guilt and irritation, of Kate; he told himself with defiance that he had certainly *not* known at which blessed Birmingham school Cherry was to be found, and even if he had . . . Why, he didn't even know its name. Oh well, yes, maybe Kate had said something. But even if it had been mentioned that time at Martin and Beth's he had most certainly forgotten, or been too pickled to take notice. Hadn't he? Nobody's subconscious is that efficient, least of all mine.

'Hey!' said Cherry, 'where have you gone? I've lost you. You look like someone who's suddenly remembered they left the gas on. Are you worried about Kate? We'd better get back.'

'I suppose we had.'

When they got back to the school the exhibition room was locked. There was no sign of Kate. They were on their way to the car park to see if the car was still there when Ron met them. 'Oh, there you are. Look, she said to tell you she's gone to the Museum to find this Mr Wilmot – he never showed up. She said she'll meet you back here at three-thirty.'

'There,' said Cherry, 'stop worrying. And now I've got you on my hands for another hour and a half. What am I going to do with you?'

'Don't you have to teach?'

'No, as it happens. I should be tidying the art room . . . Oh, blow that, I know what we're going to do – I'm going to show you how the West Indians are making sure part of nineteenth century Brum goes out with a bang. Come on – that's my car, that ruin there.'

She drove him to an area of meanly terraced streets, scheduled for demolition, a superseded world of red brick and outside privies and corner shops long since closed down. Half a mile away, the tower blocks reared out of the rooftops, the shape of things to come. 'There,' she said, 'isn't it fun!'

The houses were painted; sometimes half a dozen of them in a row, sometimes just two or three out of a street. The bricks had been painted in thick, glossy violently-coloured paint: pillar-box red, lilac, orange, bright green, vermilion. And the lines of the mortar picked out in black, or sometimes white. The effect was startling – a joke, a gesture, something both sophisticated and child-like, gay, pathetic, defiant, indifferent. There was nobody at all about; once, a woman came to a door and shook out a mat – otherwise the streets seemed abandoned. And yet, were clearly not.

Tom said, 'How extraordinary.'

'Don't you like it?'

'Yes. I don't know. Yes, I do.'

'It'll all be gone,' said Cherry, 'in a year or two.'

It was fine now. The tower blocks glittered in the sunshine, pearly glass, pale opalescent colours reflecting the sky, the sun, the slate and brick below. They floated, insubstantial, above the city. And Tom, looking along the bizarrely distorted street in which he stood with Cherry, kept seeing in the mind's eye Doré-like images of these same streets, and the now quiescent chimneys of red brick factories and warehouses beyond: the shawled figures of mill-workers huddled in doorways, blackened shapes against blackened brick with smoke or maybe fog swirling at knee-height, the sky lit by the glare of a furnace. A cliché image, itself another kind of distortion. And the houses, meanwhile, had weathered it all, and stood to fight another day, or a few more, in their exotic fancy-dress. He studied the one nearest – two up and two down done up in glossy pink, each header and stretcher neatly outlined in black, the doorstep treacly brown. He said, 'There's been a lot of trouble taken. And a lot of paint.'

'Yes. It seems a shame they're coming down.'

'Now where are you taking me.'

'The canal.'

They walked along the tow-path. Black water rainbowed with oil slicks; grass-filled barges; derelict factory chimneys, puny alongside their bright new successors. Gutted car bodies; a little boy fishing; Thos. Samuels & Son. Coal Merchant Est. 1806, in ghost-lettering on a tumbled warehouse. 'I like all this,' said Cherry. 'I come and sketch down here. I've got a thing about lock-gates. Shall we go on a bit?'

After a while she asked what the time was. 'Ought we to be going back?'

Tom looked at his watch. 'We're fine, it's only just past three.'

They walked until the tow-path petered out, obliterated by the tarmac of a new factory car park; ahead, the canal vanished into the black hole of a tunnel. They explored the muddy carcass of a narrow-boat; admired the repellent, primeval fish caught by another small boy; sat on a lock-gate in the sunshine while Cherry sketched. Tom said, 'Well, I *am* glad I came, not the sort of day I expected at all . . .' 'It's a pity Kate had to hang around for her museum man.' 'Mmn.' 'Oughtn't we to be getting back?' 'I suppose so. Yes.'

There was a disquieting air of desertion about the school, when they arrived there. Cherry said, 'Tom, are you sure your watch is O.K.? It must be later than we thought – everybody's gone.'

'Blast! It's stopped.'

It was five past four according to the cleaners. 'Oh dear,' said Cherry. 'How awful – she'll have been hanging about up there. I'll come with you, and explain.'

The exhibition room was locked and empty. On the door was pinned an envelope addressed to T.R. Tom opened it. 'Have gone', said a single sheet of paper, 'Kate'. He showed it to Cherry.

They looked at each other. 'Oh dear oh dear oh dear,' said Cherry. 'Now you've been and gone and done it.' After a moment she added, 'She might have hung on just a bit longer, I suppose.'

'Yes, she might have.'

'Is it me, partly?'

'I should imagine so.'

'Ah.' She eyed him thoughtfully. 'All the same, if I'd been her, I wouldn't have given up like that. I'd have stayed and fought it out. You're worth that much.'

'Thanks.'

'Tell her,' she said, 'when you make it up.'

'Hmmn. I'll see.'

'And now I suppose we'd better see about finding you a train.'

Tom said, 'I don't think I feel like finding a train. Not just yet, anyway.'


She said, 'This is really very wicked of us.'

'Yes, isn't it.'

'Nice, though.'

'Mmn. Great. You know, one of the appealing things about you I'd forgotten is that your pubic hair doesn't match the rest of your hair. It's ginger. Distinctly ginger.'

'Is it?' said Cherry with interest. She sat up and stared. 'I'd never really looked. Yes, so it is. Our grandmother had red hair, there must be a recessive gene in the family. I wonder if Martin's is.'

'I do *like* you, Cherry.'

'I like you, too.'

'I'm staying the night, by the way. I've lost interest in trains altogether.'

'Oh you are, are you?'

'If you've got any lovers coming round you'll have to tell them to push off.'

'I've been chaste, I'll have you know, for the last seven months. No, eight.'

'Whatever for?'

'No one I specially fancy, I suppose. Hey, that's rude, now I come to think of it. You're implying I . . .'

'I'm not implying anything.'

'Have you ever been back to the Lakes?'

'No. Have you?'

'Once with Martin and Beth. Same cottage. I thought of you.'

'Only then?'

'Don't be silly. I often have.' She put a hand on his thigh.

'Don't do that. You'll get me all over-excited again.'

'So I see.'

'I may stay here for days,' he said, climbing on top of her, 'So be warned.'

And the window, defined by the early morning light, is wrong somehow, as also is the warm naked body alongside, so that for a moment or two there is a panicky plunging of the senses, until the mind takes over and sorts things out. Which does not, actually, improve matters much. I have done that which I ought not to have done, and there is no health in me. At least the trouble is, there is rather too much health. I have trespassed against others, namely Kate, notwithstanding that in a way she trespassed against me first by storming out in a temper, but Kate is vulnerable in ways that I am not, through no fault of her own, and a compassionate man would accept that, and concede. The trouble is, how far, and for how long, can I be compassionate?

# Chapter Eight

In dreams, one was always young; one was the real Laura, pretty and admired and sought-after, in the thick of things. Sometimes Hugh was there, but more often he was not. More often one was not attached to anyone in particular, with everything to come; sometimes quite fictional men featured, most explicitly. Kate was never there. From time to time, in the dreams, one was buying clothes: flowery girlish clothes, clear in every detail so that, on waking (lying in bed still sleep-ridden but with disillusion creeping in like the ticking of the dressing-table clock) one could see them still with perfect clarity. Pattern and colour and style – the set of a sleeve, gathering of a skirt, placing of a tuck. The shop from which they came, the price ticket. Except that the prices were all out of step: five or six pounds for a pure silk shirt-waister, shillings and pence instead of decimals. And always in the dream one had found exactly what one wanted, none of that exhausting frustrating search of real life, ending the day sore-footed and empty-handed.

Money had gone mad, Laura thought, nowadays. Bills came, and you looked at them, incredulous, and frequently sent them back to the electricity board or whoever with an angry letter because surely the stupid people must have made a mistake, added on an extra nought or something, it couldn't be as much as that. But always, it turned out, it was. Oh, one knew about inflation and everything, but even so. And nice Mr Sidley at the bank had been replaced by a not at all nice young man with a horrid cockney accent who had written an unpleasant letter about the overdraft.

'I shall have to go to Ashley Lister's memorial service,' she said to Nellie. 'In London. It is a bother, but people would notice if one didn't.' And there would be one of those announcements in *The Times*, with a long list of names; Mrs Laura Paxton, she would say, not Mrs Hugh Paxton. She liked the sound of it: Mrs Laura Paxton. It was a name you would notice yourself, in a list, and wonder about its bearer. She would wear the navy coat and dress, not black, people don't wear black nowadays, with a new hat if she could find something nice in Marlborough, and a silk scarf, not too bright, but not dismal either. No point in being dismal, Ashley was very old, he'd been ill for ages, his death was expected. And there would be lots of people one had lost touch with, old friends, and people who worked with Hugh at one time or another.

'I am going to London,' she said to Mrs Lucas, pausing at the hall mirror for a last check: yes, the hat was really rather nice. 'A memorial service. A dear old friend who died recently. Sir Ashley Lister. He was Director of the Council of Archaeology in London before Mr Paxton, an old old friend of ours.' Mrs Lucas, on her hands and knees dusting the skirting-board, made a non-committal noise that might, or might not be, an expression of interest and sympathy and Laura went on, 'So sad. And while I think of it, could you be very sweet and peel us some potatoes for tonight, and the carrots. I shall be late back, and very tired I expect, it is a strain, this sort of day.'

In the train, she read the paper (the long-range weather forecast promised some hot weather; an acquaintance had died, and the daughter of someone Barbara Hamilton kept talking about was engaged; it sounded as though the electricity people might be striking again, which would be a nuisance) and then sat in her corner and watched Wiltshire give way to Berkshire and finally to the outskirts of London. Back gardens flowed by, long and thin with asphalted paths and blown washing and little glittering greenhouses and Laura, staring idly down, wondered how on earth people could live like that, cheek by jowl and with the trains hammering past. Once, the train slowed almost to a stop, and a small girl with short wiry dark hair, rather like Kate had been at that age, climbed onto a fence and waved. Laura, not waving back, thought that children looked dreadfully scruffy nowadays, all dressed alike in jeans and those anorak things, even quite nice children, the children of people one knew; she thought of a little tweed coat with a velvet collar that Kate had had from Harrods, and thence, for a while, of Kate herself, to whom she had spoken last night on the phone. Kate had been terse and unforthcoming and sounded as though she might have a cold. 'Why are you sniffing?' Laura had said, 'have you got a cold?' and Kate had said mmn, she supposed she might have, and actually she had a bit of a headache and maybe she'd go to bed early. 'Nellie has had a touch of 'flu,' Laura had said with reproof. 'But she's better now, and luckily neither Mrs Lucas nor I seem to have caught it. I should take some aspirin.' She is a bit wrapped up in herself, she thought, like all the young. As though *they* had problems; then, there are no problems, if only one knew it.

At Paddington, she took a taxi; extravagant, since she had plenty of time, but so much nicer. Then, of course, she was early at the church and had to stroll in the nearby park until there was a respectable flow of people going up the steps. Inside, she looked around with interest, and exchanged smiles – appropriately muted smiles – with one or two people she knew. There was old Lady Lister, very doddery poor thing, with what must be the son and daughter-in-law, and the grandchildren. And there was Paul Summers and the Sadlers and any number of other people from the archaeological world. There was a big congregation; a long life, many connections. Men in dark suits, looking not quite comfortable; women in hats and coats or suits they did not often wear. More women than men, oddly.

The service began. They were invited to pray for the soul of the departed. Laura sank gracefully to her knees (the woman next to her flumped down awkwardly, missing the hassock and scraping her chair on the stone floor; you can always tell the regular from the ceremonial church-goer) and recommended her old friend –

no, acquaintance really, one hadn't actually known him all that well – to God. 'May he rest in peace' she prayed. She did not really know what was meant by that, and would not have wanted to enquire too far. Religion, after all, was meant to be a matter of comfort and solace, not something that raised awkward questions. She had always thought it very silly, the way people torment themselves about having faith or not having it, or worry away at what is implied by this, that or the other, or make a great fuss about switching churches. In fact, Laura had often thought that she would have liked to be a Catholic; she had always felt an affinity with those big busy cool churches abroad, the smell of incense, obsequious priests, candles. Even with the ghastly statues and pictures. But one had been brought up Anglican, and the processes of change would have been a great bother, and anyway one didn't feel all that strongly about it.

'Look after him,' she prayed, 'because he was a nice old man and actually he was very helpful to Hugh, years ago, he was on the appointing Board for the Directorship and Hugh always said he must have spoken out for him because David Spears and Russell Twining were both against him, and he mightn't have got it if Ashley hadn't been on his side. May he not have suffered much; may he have departed in peace. David Spears is dead now too, of course; Russell Twining is a Professor somewhere or other, one sees his name sometimes, he had a beastly overbearing wife . . .' She opened her eyes and observed, for a moment, the officiating clergyman, his profile to the congregation, working his way now through the ramifications of Ashley Lister's career. A glorious vase of lilies by the pulpit, not arums either, but the nice ones, madonnas and regale and turk's cap. 'Thank You,' said Laura, 'for the long and useful life of Thy servant Ashley Lister.' She rose to her feet, and at the same time unobtrusively shifted her chair a couple of inches to the left; her neighbour on the other side, a rather fat man, had been sticking one hip into her for the last five minutes, and there was a good deal of the service yet to go.

She sang a hymn; she sat and listened to Lessons read by various people selected to represent the different staging-posts in Ashley Lister's life. Somebody spoke about Ashley as a person and somebody else about him as an archaeologist. A choir sang. A string quartet played some Brahms: a secular touch that aroused Laura's mistrust in the first place, though after a minute or two she decided it was a rather nice idea. Along with the rest of the congregation, she relaxed a little for the duration of the piece and looked around her, noting more familiar faces. Once, she caught her neighbour, the stout man, glancing covertly sideways at her, staring almost; he was very dark, the hand that lay on his knee sunburnt, the knee itself trousered in a style that Laura, also covertly inspecting, decided was definitely not English. Someone foreign. Ashley would have known quite a lot of foreigners, of course. She looked firmly ahead, to dismiss the sideways gaze (not that it wasn't just a bit flattering), assuming a musically appreciative expression.

The quartet ended. A further prayer, another offering from the choir, and the service was over. With a little outbreak of rustling and murmuring, the congregation prepared to leave. Laura's female neighbour, she of the uncertain kneeling technique, put on her gloves and said, 'Really very nice, just what Ashley would have liked, I'm sure.' Laura smiled agreement. They moved sideways into the aisle, caught now in the general slow-moving exit. Laura found herself alongside her other neighbour. Propelled by the crowd, he accidentally jostled her. 'Pardon,' he said, and now she looked him full in the face. A rather jowly face, with unshaven look (constitutional, probably); swarthy (yes, certainly foreign); a tie that offended Laura's fastidious eye.

Something vaguely, distantly, disconcertingly reminiscent.

And now he too was alerted. Puzzled. Confusion bloomed into recognition.

'Lola!'

'Laura,' she said, thrown off her guard, 'Laura Paxton. I'm sorry, I can't quite . . .'

'Laura – of course! Carlos. Carlos Fuego.' He took her hand in his, in both his, she thought for an embarrassed moment he was going to kiss her. 'So many years! So many, many years! And as beautiful as ever, Laura.'

Larks singing, above Charlie's Tump; a very pleasurable gush of something or other every time one set eyes on him; boredom, Hugh wrapped up in the dig, blind and deaf to anything else; brown Spanish eyes – admiring, proposing; twigs and bits of stone under one's back; the thing oddly enhanced by panicky anticipation of discovery.

Oh God, she thought. Him. She forced a smile. Made noises of surprise and pleasure. They moved together up the aisle. Gracious, Laura was thinking, how ever could one have . . . So overweight now, and looking years older than . . . well, than one does oneself. Yes, she.said, at Danehurst still, with my sister, you remember my sister I expect. And he was saying the right, tactful things about Hugh, standing aside now, as they reached the door, to shepherd her solicitously through the crowd, through the porch, out into the sunlight. Had he always spoken such perfect English? He was very high up now in Spain, it would seem from what he said, had done well. His eyes were not suggestive and brown any more, but black and sharp. They were a little disconcerting, turned full on you.

No, she found herself saying, no actually as it happens I'm not doing anything for lunch, what a nice idea . . .

'Well,' he said, raising his glass. 'Here's to a most agreeable reunion, Laura.'

He had talked about his wife (rather pointedly, one felt), produced coloured photos of his children (something a bit vulgar about *coloured* snaps), asked after Kate. He had taken her to a very nice restaurant. He had talked entertainingly of this and that, plied her with wine, been a charming host. Of course there was no question of one feeling at all, well, at all attracted any more, but there was no denying he was pleasant company. Laura, graciously, mellowed.

'I suppose you knew Ashley well, Carlos. I thought the service was awfully well done. More women than men there – odd. Why should Ashley have known more women than men?'

'I shouldn't think he did. It is merely that women have a longer expectation of life.'

'I didn't know that,' said Laura. 'How peculiar. Are you sure?'

'Not peculiar at all, my dear Laura. A fact, that's all. You are tougher.' He grinned at her; there was a wink of gold tooth, rather too much gold tooth. What nonsense, Laura thought, I bet he's just made that up on the spur of the moment.

'Well,' she said, 'I don't feel tough at all, personally.'

'Nor do you look it. You are a very handsome woman, Laura.'

'Thank you,' said Laura primly. She looked down at her plate; Carlos's eyes were very penetrating, and they were at this point making undoubted reference, which she thought unfair. That wasn't done.

No one else ever had. But of course they had been English, the others. The three others; let's not exaggerate. One had bumped into them, from time to time, over the years, and there had always been the most gentlemanly discretion. Not a word or glance capable of misinterpretation. Of course, one had always had very good taste in friends and in . . . well, in people one knew well.

'You had excellent breasts,' said Carlos. 'Very English. Like apples.'

Laura choked. She took a gulp of wine, hunted feverishly for her napkin and dabbed her lips.

'One wanted to take a bite,' Carlos went on. 'Scr – r – r – runch. Like – what is that very good apple that is for Christmas time? Firm and juicy.'

'Cox,' said Laura. 'Cox's Orange Pippin, I expect you mean.' She looked round nervously; his voice was much too loud. 'It *is* a nice apple. We grow Laxtons rather more at Danehurst, and Worcesters, Cox's don't seem to like us, they . . .'

'I've embarrassed you,' said Carlos.

'Well, I . . . No, not at all, Carlos, it's just I . . .' She drank some more wine.

'Don't you like to recall? It is good, as one gets older.'

'Yes, of course.'

'It was sad for you, that summer at Charlie's Tump.'

'Sad?' She stared at him, startled.

'You weren't happy, Laura. So beautiful, and not happy at all.'

'I was perfectly happy,' she said indignantly.

Carlos shook his head. 'You laughed and talked and all the time your eyes were looking out like a little girl that nobody loves.'

'Nonsense.'

'I am impertinent?'

'No,' said Laura. 'Just wrong.'

'Well, it was how it seemed to me. And I thought, such a pretty woman, somebody should do something. So I did.' He patted her hand. 'Very good memories, Laura. Tell me, how has it been for you, since that time – you have been happy, things have been good for you?'

Laura withdrew her hand under the pretext of buttering a roll. She felt, now, not so much disconcerted at the turn the conversation had taken as offended at the implication of his remarks. 'Well,' she said, 'it was very sweet of you to be so concerned about me, Carlos, but you really needn't have bothered. Actually,' she gave a little laugh, 'I was a bit worried about you, I remember. I thought you were a bit out of things on the dig, being, well being the only person who wasn't English, and all the others knowing each other so well.'

'You tried to make me feel at home?'

'Well,' said Laura, evading his eye, 'naturally one wanted to see that everyone was settling in, Hugh always left the domestic side of things very much to me.' With irritation, she felt her face burn; really, this is getting worse and worse, I'm saying the stupidest things. 'I can't remember now where you all stayed – at the pub in Avebury, was it?'

'I forget. I remember better those nice English apples.' He patted her hand again. 'Some more wine, Laura? No? Then I finish it. And the dig, of course, the dig that made your husband famous, one was proud to be associated. I had it in mind to come to Wiltshire while I am over on this trip, and see again, for nostalgia.'

'Yes,' said Laura. 'And you must come to Danehurst, of course, if you do. The only thing is just this next week or two I'm awfully tied up with one thing and another. Some people are making a television film about Hugh.'

'Ah.'

'I am inevitably a bit involved.'

'Hamlet without the Prince of Denmark.'

'What?'

'This film. Sorry, that is perhaps not well put.'

'Oh, yes, it's very good English.'

'Forgive me. I meant just, to make a film of the work of such a – such a strong person, and he himself is absent, is curious. Curious for those who remember him. Hollow.'

'Perhaps a bit,' said Laura. 'Anyway, there it is.'

'A brilliant man. Archaeology owes much. Myself, I remember principally a person always talking, always energetic, always busy, and behind it somehow melancholy. Complicated – how do you say? – complex.'

'Melancholy? Oh no, Hugh was always awfully easy going and cheerful. You're quite wrong there, Carlos.'

Carlos made a gesture of concession. 'You know better than I, of course, much much better.'

'Not melancholy at all,' said Laura firmly. 'A bit up and down, I suppose, but we're all that, aren't we? Gracious, look at the time – I'll really have to be going, Carlos. Thank you so much for the most delicious lunch.'

★

I sit in the drawing room and the rain rattles against the window like spears; it is only three o'clock in the afternoon, but almost as dark as evening. Hugh sits in the other chair. Nobody speaks. At last Hugh says, 'Would you like us to separate? Is that what you would like?' He looks tired, there are dark grooves under his eyes; but I am tired too, just as tired, I hardly slept a wink last night. I shake my head: that is not what I want, I have a sick feeling if I even think of that. I cannot be alone, he must not leave me alone, that I couldn't endure. Hugh says, 'All right. Not that then. We'll go on as we are.' He sighs, 'I don't know what you want, I wonder sometimes if you know yourself.' He looks across the dark room at me, 'Laura, have you ever loved *anyone*?'

An exhausting day, she said to Nellie. Lovely flowers and singing, at the service. Lots of people asked after you. I got the material for the new cushion covers. Oh, and I ran into Carlos Fuego – do you remember him? – we had lunch. He's very high up in the Madrid museum now, but dreadfully fat, I wouldn't have known him at all.

# Chapter Nine

'Sure,' said Tony. 'Feel free. I'm hardly ever in, anyway. There's a sofa in what's laughingly called my study. The porter has a key. No trouble, Tom, no trouble at all – as long as you like. What? Oh come, you'll patch it up in due course, surely. I'll be seeing you, then.'

Tony's flat was full of carpet and glass-topped chrome-legged tables and small signs of affluence to which one was unaccustomed such as avocado stones in the sink tidy, full rather than empty bottles and lots of newspapers and periodicals. It was a place that invited parasitism and Tom settled in without compunction. In the evenings he watched Tony's very large coloured television and thought about ringing Kate or went with Tony and friends of Tony's to the pub round the corner and thought about ringing Kate. During the day he attended to Stukeley, ate Ploughman's Lunches with B.M. cronies in Gower Street, and thought about ringing Kate.

The year, as everything conspired to remind him, was rolling on. June, and before long it would be autumn which academically is a beginning and not an end. He turned, daily, to the Appointments page of *The Times*. He read that the University of East Anglia wanted a Lecturer in Social Change; the University of Warwick, an Assistant Lecturer in Business Studies; Bradford, a Fellow in Issues. No vacancies in History today; nor on many other days, come to that. On the other hand, looking at the opposite page, Tom noted that were he differently (and presumably less arduously and expensively) qualified he could earn £4,000 p. a. as P.A. / Sec to a dynamic Belgravia-based executive: rather more than East Anglia proposed for their Lecturer in Social Change. Or £3,800 as cheerful unflappable secretary to a young interior decorator with zooming West End business. And were he a computer programmer or a systems analyst the Saudi Arabian government would be interested in his services, to the tune of quite staggeringly large sums of money. Thoughtfully, he turned back to the Home News pages, where the oil tanker delivery men were striking for a twenty per cent increase on their basic minimum of £100 a week.

In the available evidence on Stukeley's career, there was very little reference to money: his income, his means of support, had to be deduced in more roundabout ways. If money preoccupied him at all, his diaries and notebooks gave no sign: he talked about his journeyings, about Druidical Temples and Celtic forts and 'things antienter than the Romans'. No daily scouring of *The Times* for him; no interested observation of wage-settlements and breaches of the social contract. Things were simpler in those days, for a scholar and a gentleman.

Even patronage is dead, thought Tom. Or at least not dead but buried behind the official bureaucratic anonymity of the Arts Council and the Social Science Research Council and the Department of Education and Science. I shall never address a letter, when I am older and more significant, to the Department of Education and Science pointing out that its favour has been delayed till I am indifferent and cannot enjoy it, till I am solitary and cannot impart it, till I am known and do not want it.

At fourteen or so, I don't remember ever thinking much about what I was going to do, or what I would like to do. At fifteen, I wanted to get better O-levels than Bob Taylor. At sixteen, it was becoming apparent that I was, to my own surprise and even more to that of my mum and dad, rather clever. At eighteen, it seemed to me that I stood quite a good chance of an Oxbridge place, and would have been somewhat put out to have to settle for anything else. At twenty-two, I had achieved a really very good degree, again to my own surprise, and mature and presumably rational men in advanced academic positions were suggesting post-graduate work. And I thought history was interesting and important.

Thus are decisions made, or rather, not made. At any point along the line, had one of those things not happened, I would be somewhere quite different now, doing something quite other. All very random. Perhaps a critical path method would be better: a shrewd charting of possibilities and contingent moves: if I don't get a first I will go into business/Oxfam administration/the Army; if I don't get a job by October I will join the Civil Service/a Sunday newspaper/the BBC/shoot myself. If I ring Kate tonight and if she sounds at all welcoming I'll go and see her, if on the other hand she is out, belligerent, recriminatory, not alone, I'll. . . . If the librarian in the optimistically undersized sweater passes my desk within the next three minutes I'm allowed to pack it in a quarter of an hour early and have an extra drink this evening.

'It's me.'
    'I know.'
    'How are you?'
    'I'm all right,' said Kate. There was a pause. 'I'm sorry,' she said.
    'Then I'm sorry too.'
    'What about?'
    'Nothing,' he said hastily. 'I'm just generally sorry.'
    'There are a couple of letters for you here.'
    'Ah. Perhaps I should look in and collect them.'

He lay against Kate's sleeping back and looked at Hugh Paxton's photograph on the dressing-table, illuminated by a shaft from the street lamp. Back again, he said to it, as you see. If you are in a position to see; if by any awful chance I am wrong in my spiritual and religious unbelief. I daresay you don't much care for me; your wife certainly doesn't. And yet, and yet . . . And yet she could do a lot worse, Kate. I mean well. I do love her. My shortcomings are fairly standard ones, I think. But she . . .

But she is landed through no fault of her own with some fatal compulsion always to put herself in the least favourable light. Her own worst enemy is not an empty phrase. And I don't know how fitted I am to cope with that. For ever.

Kate, an hour or two later, lay with her hands linked behind her head. You're snoring, she said to Tom, just very slightly, just enough to let me know you're there; I can't imagine why people complain about other people snoring, just at the moment it's the nicest noise I've ever heard.

I love you, she said. I know I'm difficult and cross and quite often people don't like me, but I love you. I love you more than I've ever loved anyone.

She looked at her father's photograph. Even you, and that's saying a great deal.

Laura said, 'Hello? Who's that? Oh, I suppose it's Tom.'

'Yes. Kate's not back yet, I'm afraid.'

'The thing is, that if as I gathered from Kate you were coming down this weekend, the two of you, if you could get down by lunchtime, you could come with me to Standhill. John Barclay has very sweetly arranged to take me there.'

'Standhill?'

'Standhill is a terribly famous house,' said Laura distantly. 'By, um, by Inigo Thomas. I daresay you wouldn't know.'

'Ah.' Tom considered the virtues of self-restraint, and rejected them. 'I think perhaps you mean Inigo Jones.'

There was a fractional pause. 'Of course one isn't normally allowed to see all the house but John knows the people – who are away – and the secretary is going to show us round. It is a marvellous chance to see the pictures before they go to America. You had better be here by half-past twelve, if you would like to come.'

'The family are based in the Bahamas, of course, now,' said John Barclay. 'Tax.'

'Sad for them,' said Laura.

'Henry Archer, who you will meet, runs the place, really awfully well, too.'

Barclay drove. Laura sat beside him. Shreds of their conversation reached Tom and Kate, behind; which was just as well, Tom thought, the thing in its entirety, judging from the fragments you got, would have you in a state of apoplexy by the end of the drive. John Barclay wore a wide-brimmed black felt hat and dark glasses, which appeared to impede his driving.

The journey took in a good deal of Wiltshire and one of the most agreeable sections of Dorset. Than which, Tom thought, you cannot really ask for more. He sat and appreciated. Or rather, experienced pleasure and outrage in fairly equal proportions. No sooner had you done marvelling at a sequence of shape and colour, at the interruption of a sweep of downland by the dark bunching of trees in a valley, or the alternation of brown ploughlands and the sharp green of young corn, than there arrived the discordancy of a petrol station decked out with plastic streamers like the flagship of a fleet, or the unyielding cubes and tarmac of a housing estate clamped to the edge of a village. The Lord giveth, and the Lord taketh away, he thought. Or whoever else or whatever else is responsible for setting an incomparable scene and then making sure that most of us are apparently quite incapable of responding to it. Laura and Barclay, in the front, made occasional remarks that indicated a similar line of thought, which was vaguely irritating; he did not feel any more in harmony with them than with the manifold rapes of the landscape.

Standhill was indeed a very handsome house. It stood amid parkland, the scenery re-arranged around it to flatter and display:

the long approach, leading the eye to the portico and sweep of steps; the formal gardens to right and left giving way to the park with its careful groupings of trees and pretty 'temple' with cupola on the brow of a low hill.

'I don't know . . .' said Kate. 'I've never been that mad about stately homes.' She spoke quietly; in the front, Laura was busily enthusiastic.

'Nor me. A reflex action, I suppose. Given the implications – the very unequal distribution of everything and the village removed because you don't want anything so offensive visible from your drawing room windows, and the trampling on the face of the poor and the thought that I come from the class that would have been being trampled on, had I been around at the time. But given all that, let's face it, the end product is extremely pleasing.'

'Mmn. Yes.'

'And I can appreciate Palladian architecture as well as the next man – ironically, given what I've just said about where *I'd* have been in seventeen whatever. But then, I'm a product of the historical process too, just as much as the house.'

'My . . .' said Kate. 'You never get tired of picking a subject over, do you? Some people would just have a look, and leave it at that.'

'I'm a case of educational conditioning.'

By a process that afforded Laura a great deal of pleasure, they were admitted not through the front door with the ticket-buying *hoi polloi*, but through a private side entrance. John Barclay and Henry Archer conversed knowledgeably about doors, ceilings and staircases; Archer, a man in his mid-forties, combined Barclay's faintly raffish air with the complacency of a successful stockbroker: an interesting achievement, Tom thought, done somehow by means of a style of dressing that just missed conventionality and frequent conversational reference to valuations and running costs. Laura continued to enthuse. Tom and Kate lingered behind. They toured the main rooms in the wake of a guided tour, Archer apologizing for this temporary relegation to the common ruck.

'The drawing room,' he said, 'is of course generally thought to be by way of a trial run for the double cube room at Wilton – some people think it marginally finer. Slightly smaller.'

Barclay said, 'The Constables of course stay for the moment?'

'For the moment. One can't really say how long for, though. And now let's go on to the Red Room.'

They followed him through. 'And this is the part that people don't normally see,' said Laura reverently.

'That's right. Not many of the pictures have ever been on public view. One or two of the Turners went to the Burlington House exhibition. The big Constable has always been here – it was commissioned from the painter by the Stanton of the time. The Ghirlandaio and the Giorgiones were acquired on a Grand Tour by his grandfather.' He moved ahead, with Barclay and Laura, indicating a hierarchy of value and fame within which the pictures should be viewed.

Tom and Kate lingered behind. 'The trouble is,' said Tom, 'all this was very well worth coming for. Very well worth. Let's take our time.'

They arrived presently at a small alcove in which a single picture was hung. After two or three minutes Tom said, 'I think I like this as much as any picture I've ever seen. In fact I'm completely smitten by it.'

The picture, somewhat in the style of Claude Lorrain – an anglicized Lorrain, less blue, greener, and indefinably more robust – was large, and showed an affectionately painted landscape with, at one side and very much subordinate, a small grouping of figures. These, more closely inspected, could be seen to be an upper class early eighteenth century family: father, mother and three children. Like the figures in later, more properly Romantic painting, they looked out into the landscape, in semi-profile, rather than at the viewer. There were other figures in the painting, but more distant and treated as integral to the scenery: peasant women hay-making, a man driving a horse-team, a carter. They claimed attention only after one had been looking at the picture for some while; it was a painting of a place, not of people.

Trees, in the foreground, framed the receding distances of a vale. Far away, a darkening at the horizon suggested more hills, perhaps afforested and uncultivated. The vale united the functional and the aesthetic, it was of equal interest to the agrarian historian and the art connoisseur: the formality of pre-enclosure strip fields in the middle distance – colour-blocks of fawn and gold and chestnut – were offset by the textural complexity of coppices and a laddering of hedged fields beyond. Emphasis and perspective carried the eye to a cottage tucked away here, a group of grazing cows there, the vanishing white loop of a road, a curl of smoke from a charcoal-burner's hut. It was a landscape both empty and intensely populated; it gave the impression at once of the triumph and the taming of nature. A spray of foliage in the immediate foreground was meticulously and naturalistically rendered, but one's attention was drawn from that to the more impressionistic but equally demanding port-wine glow of the coat worn by the man in the family group.

The others had joined them. Archer said, 'Spencer. Not a big name, of course, but it's an attractive picture.'

'It's the view from the house, isn't it?' said Tom.

'That's right. And Sir John and Lady Stanton and their offspring. It's going to the Mellon Collection. We hope. Between you and me – fingers crossed and all that, it's not yet cleared with the export licensing people.'

'So pretty,' said Laura, 'I love the little girls in their blue frocks.'

Tom looked at Archer. 'And they're quite happy about that?'

'I beg your pardon?'

'They don't mind – the, er, Stantons – selling a picture that seems rather to belong here.' If you turned and looked out of the window, he now noticed, a section of the landscape shown in the picture could be seen: the same distant hill with curious notch, the 'temple' with its attendant grouping of trees.

'Naturally,' said Archer stiffly, 'they would have preferred to keep the collection intact, but circumstances . . .'

'Such dreadful taxes,' murmured Laura.

'If I couldn't have kept any other single thing,' said Tom, 'I'd have kept that.'

Kate said, 'Are they very hard up?'

'Really, darling!'

Archer laughed. 'Thanks to extremely efficient financial advice – Biggard, Handley and Hope, you know' – to Barclay – 'a very satisfactory arrangement was reached with the Treasury after old Lord Stanton's death. It's a question more of – well, of diversification, you might say. The present owner of Standhill has rather wide business interests in the Caribbean and – all this in confidence, of course – it's a question of realizing assets with expansion in mind. So – unfortunately – the bulk of the pictures have to go. A nucleus will stay, of course, in the public rooms. There's an interesting negotiation going on with an American library over the archives, too.'

'Archives?' said Tom.

'Standhill,' Archer explained, 'is the only Inigo Jones house – building of any kind, indeed – to be in the happy position of still retaining all his original plans, elevations and so forth. So far as we know there's nothing missing at all, it's a most valuable collection, plus also the diary the architect kept over the building period, and his correspondence with leading figures of the time. We're talking in terms of a million dollars or so.'

'Pity the Soane Museum couldn't raise the funds,' said Barclay. 'Or the Bodleian. There have been murmurings, of course, that the Stantons might have put a lower price on them to keep them in the country. But one does see the problem, of course,' he added.

'Sometimes,' said Kate, 'people *give* things to libraries and museums. Such as my father. Of course he wasn't rich or aristocratic.'

Archer was now looking ruffled. 'Naturally the family are the first to regret . . . The Soane Museum was given eight weeks to try to match the Texas offer. Unfortunately . . . So there it is. Very sad, but inevitable.'

'Oh, quite inevitable,' said Tom, 'given human nature, from which obviously even the aristocracy aren't immune. It's interesting,' he went on, 'I can understand lions and vintage cars and antique emporia, up to a point. Vulgarization and exploitation I can sympathize with. Just about. In fact at the moment they look in thoroughly good taste. This, though, leaves you fairly staggered. It's amazing!'

'Oh nonsense, Tom,' said Laura. 'You don't know anything about how frightfully difficult it is for people to keep up old houses like this nowadays.' She gave him an icy look and went after Archer, who had walked angrily away. John Barclay looked put out. He said, 'Henry Archer is a distant cousin as it happens, his mother was a Stanton, but I suppose you couldn't know that.' He too moved off down the gallery.

Tom turned back to the picture. 'My mother always used to say, you're entitled to think what you like, but nobody's going to thank you for saying it.'

'So did mine,' said Kate. 'A bit differently put.'

'Sorry.'

'I'm not. I enjoyed it.'

'I'm quite glad we came, all the same. There's always something a bit awe-inspiring about greed on a really majestic scale.'

The next day, they walked on the downs behind the village. Kate said, 'Ma was wondering about you, over the washing-up. She was wondering if you realized how off-put people can be by outspoken-ness and if there'd be any point in you trying for a job in the civil service and she could have a word with James Hamilton only to tell the truth she wasn't absolutely sure you made an awfully good impression, that evening. And she was feeling it was a pity you were so opinionated because you're really rather nice-looking.'

Tom laughed. He took her hand. 'Well, it's a relief that I'm acceptable on one count, I suppose.'

It was early evening. The sky had cleared after a day of intermittent heavy rain; in a clear, sharp light the surrounding hills had the brilliance and detail of scenery seen through binoculars: grazing sheep half a mile away wore discernible painted numbers, the trees crowning the hillock of the East Kennet barrow showed individual outlines. There were long muddy puddles on the farm track that they were following, wide streaks of light that reflected the sky so that, picking a way past them, they walked in a circular world, the same underfoot as overhead. Birds fled past like arrows. The wind brought smells of hay and a farmyard.

Everything is all right, Kate thought. Now, just this minute, everything is all right. I could sing. The world is beautiful and I am in it and that is enough. Just for now, it is as easy and as simple to be me as it is for those birds. All I have to do is be, not feel or think.

Once, I walked along here with my father.

I am thirteen. I have breasts that slide and bounce under my jerseys; I hate them, they make me feel funny, I think all the time that people must be staring at me. I walk beside Daddy and he talks about somewhere he has been digging, about what they dug and about the people he was with, he is funny about what someone did and he makes me laugh. Suddenly, I feel as though I were someone else, not me: I feel pretty and thin and friendly. I tell him about things: about what I like and what I think and what I have been doing at school. In the middle, I remember who I really am and I say, sometimes I hate being me, I hate who I am, I wish I was someone else, anyone else. And he takes my hand and swings my arm up and down and says, we all do that, Katie, now and again, it can't be helped, that's something we all have to put up with. Some more than others, he says, but that is to himself it seems, not me. And then he sees a hawk on the telephone lines and shows me, and we stand for a moment, looking. The hawk is bright brown against the sky; I see its yellow stare and the wind ruffling its feathers and beyond it the green downs and the sun like a penny behind a cloud. I stand outside myself and see all that and everything is all right again.

'What are you doing?'

'I'm making a paper boat, aren't I? This is paper-boat-sailing weather.'

The wind, driving along the puddle, ridged it with tiny waves. Tom said, 'Go the other end, I'm sending you down an armada of unpaid bills.'

'Idiot. . . . I could never fold them properly. It's one of the lots of things I've never been able to do.' She walked to the far end of the water and watched him, folding away there twenty yards up the path. 'Go on,' she shouted, 'I'm waiting.'

'Hang on, I'm a perfectionist, Batts Road primary school champion, time was.'

And the first boat came spinning down in the force nine gale, making good time, six seconds flat by Kate's watch, to be fished out water-logged and on the edge of capsizing.

'That's not done your bank statement much good!'

'Never mind. Stand by – something with a bit more power coming up.'

And the next, veering wildly, made four and a half seconds before going aground.

'Tom! That was a page of notes or something!'

'No time to be choosy. We're racing some small craft now. Stop-watch out!'

Daft, she thought fondly, mad . . . And the cocked white hats came flying down, three of them, neck and neck. But one took off and became airborne, flew away over the fence into the field, one keeled over into the mud and was beached, leaving the winner only to be picked up by Kate. 'Slow! Eight seconds!'

Letters, scrawled in black marker pen, crept in and out of the paper folds: a C and an H and an E. She shook it open and saw – streaked now with mud and wet – a sketch of a canal lock with a narrow boat drawn up in front. A gay, pretty little sketch. And across the bottom, scribbled, Tom – love from Cherry.

And the sun went in, appropriately, shoved behind a wedge of hitherto unremarked black cloud.

She handed him the unravelled boat, walked quickly away down the track.

He caught her up. 'Look . . . She took me along the canal that day in Birmingham. She did it then.'

'Yes.'

'I'd forgotten it was in my pocket. I didn't look . . .'

'Never mind. It doesn't matter.'

But it does matter. Where there was sun and bright sky-reflecting water and grass pouring in the wind there is uncertainty and misgivings and the knowledge that nothing stays still, that one moves all the time from one moment to another, that everything changes.

# Chapter Ten

'The intellectual career of William Stukeley,' Tom wrote, 'may well provide us with a salutary instance of the manipulation of historical evidence.' May well? Either it does or it doesn't; 'may well' is journalese. Substitute 'provides' for 'may well provide'. . . . 'As Stukeley's attempts to interpret the information he had gathered move from the objective and scientific to the subjective and fantastic, as he starts to believe not what the facts suggest but what he would like to believe, we see . . .' Well, what we see is a man behaving like most people, and not like a historian, which is what he is setting out to be. Historians are not allowed to use the past for their own ends. Nor, by the same token, are blokes who happen through accident of fate to own the only complete set of Inigo Jones plans and sketches pertaining to a particular house. Nor are politicians, house agents, antique dealers, autobiographers or any other category of person that does so most of the time. '. . . Nevertheless, however tarnished Stukeley's credibility as an anti-quarian after his ordination in 1728, his early work remains as testimony to a vigorous and enquiring mind, while the pattern of his career serves as a . . .' . . . useful rung for the scholarly progress of one Tom Rider, in this present year of grace, himself involved in the same line of business. Thus do we feed one upon another.

'Well,' he said to Tony Greenway, 'I've got five chapters under my belt.'

'Great! I'd love to read it, when you've got a bit further.'

'You wouldn't. Not really. You don't have to be that polite. How's the Paxton programme coming on?'

'Quite nicely. The overall structure's worked out now, and I've got various people on tape to go with film of different crucial sites.

Helicopter shots, too. It's going to be a very *visual* programme, much more so than Teilhard was, we had a lot of sweat there thinking up shots. At least with archaeology there's absolutely no problem in that direction, it's a question of picking and choosing. We're filming down in Wiltshire at the end of the month. Will you and Kate be around?'

'Oh, I don't think we can miss out on that.'

'All well now?' said Tony delicately.

'Pretty well.'

Tony's own personal life – his inclinations even – remained mysterious and unspecified. He was attentive – slightly gallant, indeed – towards women while at the same time giving the impression that possibly these attentions were performed only in the course of duty, whether professional or social. If his taste ran rather to his own sex, there was no evidence for this either, except in the absence of any convincing demonstrations in the direction of girls. Tom was forced to the opinion that he might be in the presence of one of those rare spirits able to survive without emotional or sexual commitment of any kind. He wondered what it felt like. Where work was concerned, on the other hand, Tony gave every indication of absolute and indeed excessive commitment: he seemed frequently on the verge of nervous collapse. He worked, often, nine or ten hours a day, fuelled by enthusiasm and what appeared to be a kind of panic. He was also a prey to bouts of depression and self-doubt. During Tom's sojourn in the flat, he had occasionally unburdened himself, slumped in gloom in the mornings, drinking cup after cup of coffee, dispirited about the impermanence of what he made, about something he called 'truthfulness', about whether it mattered at all. Of course it matters, Tom would say briskly; at the other end of the room the blank screen of the very large television set reflected the London skyline through the flat's picture-window, a panorama of clouds, multi-storey buildings and the occasional aeroplane.

But at the moment, in the Gower Street pub, Tony was enjoying a spell of optimism. He had dropped in, as he often did, on the off-chance of finding Tom. He never, Tom realized, ate or drank alone; his own company (except, presumably, at night) appeared to alarm him and he took steps to avoid it as much as possible. He said, 'We shall do a day's filming at Danehurst itself and one or possibly two up at Charlie's Tump, where Paul Summers is going to talk about the finds there and its significance. Laura has been frightfully co-operative. I get the impression the sister is less enthusiastic.'

'Look,' said Tom, 'I am not seeing her. I am not writing to her. I am not furtively telephoning her. Truth to tell, I haven't much thought about her. I did go to bed with her. I don't expect I ever will again. But I can't absolutely, unequivocally promise. There. Honester than that you cannot get. I love you. I find you more attractive than anyone else. But I have, I suspect, over-developed natural urges, and from time to time they get the better of me. I'm sorry about them.'

'I see.'

'You've bitten all your finger-nails off again.'

'That's a natural urge too.'

'His parents?' said Laura to Barbara Hamilton. 'No, I haven't met them, of course they're rather a different type . . . Yes, Tom went to Oxford. Yes, it is a marvellous thing, the way everybody does nowadays.' She stared in irritation at the lawn — distressingly unmown, what had become of Mr Lucas this week? — while two villages away Barbara talked of her daughter, Olivia, satisfactorily married to a young MP said to be tipped for an interesting career. Olivia had two pretty little girls and a house in London for which Barbara had devised and procured the decor and furnishings. 'Yes,' Laura said, 'I imagine Olivia's wedding must have been lovely, you are so lucky that she's such a nice homey girl, Kate frankly is just not interested in that kind of thing. It comes of being clever, I suppose, it can't be helped.' Nellie, now, was propelling herself across the lawn, a gardening implement in her hand, stabbing infant thistles as she went. 'I shall have to go, my dear, Nellie is in the garden needing her tea and as you know I am single-handed.'

She went into the kitchen and put the kettle on. My wedding dress was heavenly, she thought, I can feel it now, that tissue-y ever so slightly rough feel, ivory raw silk, with a tiny, tiny waist and heart-shaped neck. I was so slim then. And Granny's veil and diamonds. And my hair done at that place in Brook Street.

She loaded the tray and took it out onto the terrace. She said to Nellie, 'I was thinking about our wedding, goodness knows why . . . Do you remember the awful photographer? And Mother ordering the wrong size cake from the caterers?'

I put the dress on; it is lovely; I am lovely. Everything is fuss and excitement; it is all for me. Mother says, 'Stand still, dear, don't fidget, I can't get the veil fixed right. You're not nervous, are you? There, that's better . . .' But I am not nervous: I am not anything. I don't feel anything; this is the happiest day of my life and I don't feel anything. I see the shiny black car in the drive outside, waiting, and father in his wedding clothes. Nellie comes into the room, looking funny in the sort of frock she doesn't like wearing, and a hat. Hugh is in the church now. I think of Hugh, and nothing happens. There is not that delicious, confusing rush of something there was at first, there is nothing much at all. I see Nellie looking at me; she has a funny look – she is . . . she is *sorry* for me.

Laura stands at the mirror in the dress. The dress over which we have all been so much exercised, which has been debated and constructed and reconstructed and despaired of and delighted over. She looks beautiful. She looks like a Botticelli angel; her hair shines like water in the sun. Mother is doing something with the veil and Laura stares out of the window and as I come in she turns to see who it is. Her mouth is a little sad cross button like when she was a child: like when she was a child and had got the present she wanted for Christmas or birthday and then it had turned out to be not what she wanted after all. Her eyes are miserable, and a bit scared. She says, 'You look nice, Nellie.' I laugh: because I cannot remember Laura ever saying anything like that before and because I don't think I look nice at all, in my tight, slippery blue silk dress and embarrassing hat. I want to make Laura laugh; I want to cheer her up; it is all wrong for her to be like this today.

Nothing is as it seems. Always, anyone would think, it is Laura who has had everything; as I get older, I see that it is not like that at all. Laura has very little, and sometimes she knows.

'Opinionated,' said Laura, 'and cast a blight on an otherwise perfect afternoon. When it had been so sweet of John Barclay to take us there.'

'It's a point of view.'

'Oh, Tom has points of view about everything. He's that kind of person. It's a pity. Slightly unpredictable, one can't help feeling.'

'Possibly.'

'But he is attractive, that one has to admit.' Laura studied the inside of her tea-cup and added in amendment, 'Good-looking, I mean, of course. More tea?'

'I think I'll go in and get on with Hugh's pottery sequence notes.'

Laura said, not looking at Nellie, 'How is that going?'

'Quite nicely, I think. But slow, mainly because I write at a snail's pace. It is like trying to make do with someone else's hand.'

'I could help. I could – well, you could dictate or something.'

'That would be nice.'

There was a silence. 'Yes,' said Laura. 'Well, we must do that, then.' She stood up, bent to lift the tray. 'They rang again about the television filming, some business to do with electrical things. I hope it is not all going to be a great bother.'

She went into the house. Nellie watched her go. She saw, for the first time, an absence of agility in her sister's step, the slightest suggestion of a stoop. Somewhere out of sight, but not out of recollection, there hovered a little girl with straw-pale hair, tramping with anguished expression through the splintered fragments of a toy shop.


Born Oct 17th 1952, Tom typed. He pondered, hesitated, filled in the details of his education, culminating in the First Class Honours Degree in Modern History (1974). So far so satisfactory. The typewriter (Tony's, borrowed) was a marvel of modern technology. Japanese, compact but with wide talents; it could make columns, change its own ribbon, erase its (or your) mistakes. Internationally-minded, too; dollar sign, French accents. What it could not do was extend or improve on a curriculum vitae, which is a poor bare thing at the best of times.

Currently engaged in post-graduate work on the career of William Stukeley. Engaged also to be married to one Kate Paxton about whom one's feelings veer from the proper ones of love and lust to worrying spasms of irritation and from time to time, indifference. All of which, of course, is irrelevant from the point of view of the University of the West Midlands which is looking for a Lecturer in History. The University of the West Midlands is also looking for an Assistant Lecturer in Film Studies and a Director of the Media Research Unit. The prospectus of the University of the West Midlands is quite a tome through which to browse; it makes interesting browsing, too, the diversification of higher education nowadays is remarkable, there is nothing they haven't thought of, or not much. It comes as a welcome reassurance to stumble across such familiar old landmarks of learning as the metaphysical poets, the causes of the French Revolution and

Romance Languages. Still around, for the time being at any rate. Meanwhile, the problem is how to convince the Chairman of the History Department in the University of the West Midlands that he would do well to spend his disposable cash on Tom Rider rather than anyone else.

Laura, told of this venture by Kate, is alleged to have asked where the West Midlands was. Enlightened, she went on to say that it was all rather horrid up there, she imagined, but she expected Tom would settle down all right. There is something rather splendid about Laura, considered with complete detachment. One is the richer for having known her.

Kate, washing her hands in the museum Ladies, saw in the mirror the door open and the Assistant Director, Mary Halliday, come in. Since she believed that Mary Halliday did not like her the prospect of an enforced conversation filled her with panic and she dived into the lavatory (to which she had already been), pretending not to have seen Mary Halliday. There, she sat uneasily until she heard the door open and close once more. Mary Halliday noticed the retreating back of that odd grumpy girl who was Hugh Paxton's daughter, thought it would be nice to get to know her better, but for some reason she seemed vaguely hostile . . . washed, tidied and went out again.

In the Underground, staring blankly at the row of blankly staring faces opposite, Kate thought suddenly that she had hardly any friends. If something awful happened to me there is no one, really, that I could ring up and say, look, can I come round at once, I must talk, something awful . . . But then, I am not the kind of person who would ever make that kind of phone call in any case. I don't tell people things. I've never been able to be cosy with people; other girls haven't usually much cared for me. Men have, more, which surprised me very much at the beginning, when I was nineteen or so and it first happened. I hadn't thought I was attractive, either. Being attractive for going-to-bed purposes must be quite different from being attractive for friendly purposes, which I find depressing.

Tom has been, amazingly, both.

Has been?

Back at the flat she made herself a meal and settled down with a book. When the phone rang she leapt to it. 'Kate? It's Tony – Tony Greenway.'

'Oh. Tom's away for the night – he's having this interview tomorrow morning.'

'I know. I thought, you're on your own, maybe you'd like to come out for a drink?'

'Oh. Well, actually – yes, all right, I suppose I could. Thank you,' she added after a moment.

'Right. I'll pick you up in twenty minutes or so, O.K.?'

They sat opposite one another in a crowded pub of carefully preserved Edwardian ambiance. Tony said, 'Well, here's to Tom's prospects.'

'He thought there were probably a lot of other people after the job.'

'Ah. Tell me, Kate, what took you into the museum business? You never thought of following in your father's footsteps?'

She hates talking about herself, he thought. A rare quality. Most people, it's like turning on a tap. The problem is to shut them up, interviewing, not get them going. 'Yes?' he said encouragingly, with his detached, friendly, professional look of enquiry. 'Yes, I see – it was all a bit accidental. The usual process of one thing leading to another. But I'm sure you were right not to go into the civil service. I can't see you as a civil servant, Kate.' There, he thought, that's better, she *can* unbend, it just needs the right approach. 'But you must have picked up a bit as a child, hanging around your father's digs, and just all the stuff there is at Danehurst . . . Of course I know you're not involved particularly now with prehistoric things, but even so . . . Tell me about Charlie's Tump, for instance, how much do you remember of all that? Was there some kind of moment of truth, or did they always suspect what they were on to?'

Moment of truth?

There is this moment, that I seem to have by me still, a moment when I am inside the Tump with Daddy and Aunt Nellie. It is dark inside, and a bit wet, but cosy, it is like being in a dark earthy cupboard, I pretend I am a mole, a mole in a hole, my hole, my safe cosy hole where no one can get me . . . I make myself a nest and I curl up in it and watch them dig. They are digging up a person. A skeleton person. Slowly slowly, because they mustn't spoil it. I see the bones, and Daddy brushing the earth away from the bones, and I look at my hand and think that I am like that inside, too. There is the hard part of people that is their bones and the soft part on the outside, and when you are dead the soft part goes away. Where does it go to? I ask Daddy and Aunt Nellie where it goes but they are busy, they are not listening. What is dead? The person they are digging is dead. Everybody is dead one day, when they get old. Daddy and Aunt Nellie and Mummy will get old and be dead. I am six and a half, after Christmas I will be seven. Before you are born you are inside your mummy's tummy. I think that is horrid, it is disgusting, sometimes I think of that when I am having lunch and it makes me feel sick, I can't finish my lunch.

I can hear sheep noises from outside, and birds, and Brenda talking to somebody. In here it is quiet. The dead person has been here for a long time, a long long time, I don't know how long, Daddy says they lived thousands and thousands of years ago, the people he digs. Suddenly I feel sad; it is like being not well, there is nothing I can do about it; I lie on my side and tears drip down my face and melt into the ground.

'Oh,' she said, 'I can't remember all that much. I was only about six. I suppose I must have been up there sometimes. Honestly, it's all very hazy now. I do vaguely remember a bit of fuss and excitement, and the people I remember – a woman called Brenda Carstairs who was Dad's assistant and a Spanish man who came to help, and Paul Summers who you've met. And . . .'

'Yes?' Funny, Tony thought, she's going all buttoned-up again, just as for once one thought one had got her relaxed. She's a nice girl, that's the trouble. Nice but bloody difficult. Too difficult for Tom. They won't marry, of course, in the end. 'Yes?'

'. . . oh and silly little things that aren't relevant, like Aunt Nellie giving me a trowel of my own. I adored it – I can see it now, Woolworth's, with a bright blue handle. I dug a burial mound for a dead bird with it. But otherwise it's all a bit blank, I'm afraid.'

'A Spaniard? Do you remember his name?'

'No,' said Kate.

'Paul Summers put me in touch with Miss Carstairs, which was rather nice. We had a talk.'

'Goodness. I don't expect any of us have seen her since then.'

'She teaches in Durham. Rather a gym mistress type.'

But voluble enough over a couple of drinks and a meal in Durham's plushiest hotel.

'Oh, it was a smashing dig, we all enjoyed it, Hugh Paxton was great fun to work with though he had a temper, mind, I remember him flaring up once or twice when he thought someone had done something daft. Mrs P frankly I never much cared for. One always felt he ought to have married the sister – what was she called? Nellie something – but of course Mrs P was a real sex-pot and Hugh was rather a one for the girls. Dear me, I shouldn't be saying all this – don't you go plying me with drink before we do this film thing. How long do you want me to talk for? Only a minute or so – well, whatever you like but of course there's lots to *say* about it, after all it was an important dig. Mind, once Hugh cottoned on to just *how* important there was a lot of pressure on, the appointment to the Directorship of the Council was coming up and he realized he was in with a chance so long as people knew about Charlie's

Tump. He did rush things a bit, maybe, towards the end of the summer.'

'Paul Summers I remember quite well,' said Kate, 'because he could do that thing where you put a piece of grass between your hands and blow and it makes a squeaking noise. I was deeply impressed.'

'Paxton. How does one describe Paxton? Well, to lay all one's cards on the table, I must admit that we didn't always see eye to eye. His methods wouldn't always be my methods. His trenching, for instance . . . And he wasn't a man who took advice kindly. Very opinionated. Oh, he had flair all right – one of those archaeologists who just seems to know by instinct where to put the spade in. I never know whether it's luck or inspiration. I mean, Charlie's Tump wasn't, on the ground, all that promising a site – a dozen other barrows spring to mind that might have seemed more worth doing, at the time, but Hugh Paxton has to pick the right one, straight off. And of course the burial was a secondary insertion anyway – a piece of unexpected luck. It had been tampered with in the past, inevitably – Stukeley mentions one of his contemporaries having a go at it – fascinating dig, one was glad to be there, I remember it all well – Laura drifting about in fashionable outfits, and Nellie working like a Trojan as ever. There was a bosomy girl called Brenda something, and a Spanish chap whose name escapes me. I suppose the daughter must have been around – she'd have been a small child. And it was a break-through in many ways, there was a lot of very valuable evidence and it all fits in nicely with post radio-carbon theories. But of course the person who got most out of it was Paxton himself. It got him the Directorship, no doubt about that. And Paxton was only too well aware. I'm not saying he manipulated things. Let's just put it that once he knew what he was onto he went like the clappers. He was determined to publish before the appointing committee met. It could legitimately be said that the excavation of the final chamber was done in an unholy scramble. Not that I'm going to put it quite like that for this recording of yours. I'll temper it. *De mortuis* etc.'

'I'm going to Danehurst tomorrow, to start setting things up for the filming. They're doing some helicopter shots. And I thought I'd try to have a chat with your aunt.'

I don't care for this at all, Nellie thought. Why? Hugh wouldn't mind – indeed he'd be tickled pink, I suspect. And there is nothing wrong with this young man, really, a rather earnest person in fact, he means well. The glasses, of course, help to create an impression of responsibility. So why do I have this resistance to contributing so much as a shred to what is after all a perfectly respectable undertaking? Suppose someone were writing Hugh's biography – would I feel the same? Is it a snobbishness about television? Do I think the camera will lie any more or less readily than the pen? Because both, of course, do that. Which perhaps is what accounts for this queasiness – the certainty that whatever is said will not be the truth, the whole truth or even part of the truth. And that one would not want it to be in any case, because recollection is a private matter and we all have the right to do our own distorting of the past. Collective distortion can be left to professionals.

'Well, yes, if I can be of any help. Not technical things? That's all I know anything about, really, the rest is just personal . . . A personal slant on the dig? Oh, I see. Dear, it's so difficult to think of anything that might be of interest, let's see. . .'

What one sees, personally slanted on one elbow with backside on a particularly muddy bit of ground – very awkward but the only possible position – is a section of Wiltshire subsoil larded with stones. It is dark and perpetually damp there – we have all got slight rheumatism. Hugh squats at my back. From time to time his thigh brushes against mine and it means nothing at all, for which thanks be to God. I don't feel anything, except someone's thigh. I have come through, it is all quite all right now, for always. And nobody any the wiser, except for oneself who has acquired a bit of insight into one of the more taxing areas of human emotion. I scrape and brush and Hugh scrapes and brushes and we chat away: Hugh thinks he has a chance of the London Directorship, *if* this dig is all it looks like being, *if* he can publish in time.

Going outside one blinks – the light seems of Mediterranean intensity. I stand looking down into the Kennet Valley and thinking how odd it is that what happened here once to someone else determines what happens now, to us. Kate is playing on the grass. She has the little trowel I got her, the little trowel with the blue handle. She runs up with something she has dug up and gives it to me. For you, she says, I dug it for you, Aunt Nellie. It is a bit of bottle glass, smoothed and blunted by its years in the ground. I put it in my pocket. I still use it as a paper weight.

'No,' said Laura. 'If she says no she means no. Talking to cameras wouldn't be Nellie at all. Anyway she doesn't much like television. Will this dress be all right – the colour? I have got a blue silk I rather wondered about. But don't you want to sort of rehearse it? I mean, what I'm going to say? Well, I suppose so, if that's what you feel – actually I think I'd probably get *more* relaxed, not less . . . Whatever you like. And where? In the garden. Well yes if you feel that would be nice, I'll try and get Ted Lucas to do the grass, the only snag is if it's windy one's hair is going to get a bit blown about. I suppose you want me to just remember out loud?'

Remember what?

Remember going up to the dig on a hot afternoon because one had been on one's own all day and was bored stiff. In that pink flowered sun-dress and a big straw hat and the French sandals. Wondering how they could bear it, stuck away inside those damp earthy trenches all day in the lovely weather.

Thinking, I am thirty-six. Nearer forty than thirty. Nearer being old than being young. Not believing it; thinking, it can't happen to *me*; knowing that it would. A sinking in one's stomach. Walking up to Charlie's Tump with a sinking in one's stomach.

The blue sky and the grass and little coppery butterflies and larks singing – none of it giving a damn about how I feel. Kate grubbing about with a trowel I'd let her have. Getting cross with her because she put her dirty hands on my skirt; trying to rub the stain out with a hanky.

Tom, in a room furnished like an airport departure lounge, studied a notice-board on which the forthcoming visit of a distinguished scholar was advertised alongside the activities of a Consciousness-Raising Group and a lecture on Women and the Media. From time to time he glanced furtively at the other candidates, a worryingly astute-looking trio, exuding historical acumen and charm of personality. Stukeley, at this moment, was not being particularly supportive, either. In fact, he felt like a thoroughly nit-picking subject, a piece of academic washing-up, unproductive and self-contemplative. The others, undoubtedly, were engaged on airy generous public-spirited topics, capable of infinite expansion in discussion, matters of wide concern, seminal historic issues.

He exchanged newspapers with a fellow candidate, and read an alternative view on what should be done about the car industry.

# Chapter Eleven

'No.'

Kate said, 'Oh.' She read the letter and went on, 'You don't really mind, do you?'

'Funnily enough I don't. Rejection should be more dampening than this.'

So far, after all, there had not been much of it in the career of Tom Rider. Progress had been fairly smooth. At Batts Road primary school reception class there had been a system for the encouragement of five-year olds whereby a satisfactory piece of work – sums or writing or whatever – had been rewarded by a small sticky-backed gold paper star which was pasted onto the relevant page of the exercise book. Tom, on his third day at school, had discovered the source of these stars in a drawer of the teacher's table and appropriated a handful which he plastered over every page of his book. He could not remember, now, if this ploy had been rumbled, but if it had no one had been particularly cross. Now, evidently, the free flow of gold stars was coming to an end.

On the way back to London in the train this had come suddenly to mind. And with it other blurred and fragmented scenes from school and childhood: some perhaps significant, others emphatically not. Once, slumped over a biro-scarred school copy of *Pride and Prejudice*, he had perceived suddenly the nature of wit; another time, he had sat with gathering resentment in a Religious Instruction class and recognized in himself the birth of intellectual scepticism. And he had had a fight in a seedy concrete playground with an odious boy whose face he could still see but whose name was long since lost, and come off best. And lured a girl called Sue into the long grass at the edge of the recreation ground and there made various investigations into the construction and inclinations of girls in general. And grown up and gone away and returned, in the fullness of time, to see with surprise that his native town was both smaller, dirtier and more familiar than he had thought, and that he himself was no longer so detectably of it. That he was a citizen of a larger country.

He had thought about this in the train in conjunction with other and more confused thoughts about the general nature of countries, which had led on to idle reflections about nationality and the importance or unimportance thereof and thence to the observation that he was almost the only native in the train compartment. He was surrounded by tourists: American, Japanese, German, French, indeterminate. This, of course, was explained by the fact that the train included both Oxford and the stop for Stratford in its route; it also endorsed the claims made by the British Tourist Board in today's paper concerning doubled, or was it trebled, proceeds from tourism. Interesting also was the observation that all these visitors appeared, at least to his own not very practised eye, to be extremely rich: they wore what looked like pricey clothes and were slung about with expensive cameras and baggage. He felt a sudden community with the unobtrusive but inquisitive peasant bystanders in some pre-war snap of visitors to the Pyramids or the Taj Mahal.

In the two seats opposite him, sharing his table, were an oriental couple who talked in what Tom guessed to be Japanese. Indeed, on inspection, the dozen or so neighbouring seats were all filled with Japanese, presumably of the same party. They had boarded the train at the Stratford stop, having evidently spent the night there. After a while, Tom became aware of conspiratorial talk between his neighbours, and glances in his direction. A decision was reached and the man – in his early thirties, immaculately dressed – reached in a briefcase and produced a camera, which he handed to Tom, with the request that he take their photograph. The two – the girl also was thirtyish – put their heads closer together against the midnight blue background of Intercity's upholstery, smiled with disarming confidence and Tom, after some initial alarm at the complexity of the camera, snapped them twice. There was much smiling and chatter amongst the rest of the party, more cameras – yet smaller and more intricate – were produced and Tom found himself in the position of staff photographer. Some of the girls were very pretty. He achieved great popularity; though it was unclear how much, if at all, anyone could speak English, except the man who had made the first request, who turned out to be the organizer of the party and a competent linguist. They were members of a golf club, it appeared, on a European tour and presently enjoying the penultimate three days of their English week; today was set aside for Oxford, where they would see the city, after which a coach would take them to Blenheim Palace, the grave of Winston Churchill and something vaguer listed as The Beauty of the English Countryside. Tom inspected the proffered itinerary and made various suggestions. His own Oxford background emerged, and aroused much interest. He told them what would be most worth looking at, and how to find it. The conversation shifted to a delicate probing of Tom's present situation; he told his new acquaintances about the problems of job-hunting (the girl, though unwilling to speak, evidently understood English perfectly well) and received beaming assurances of how certain he was to find himself successful. There was a pause while coffee was served – Tom, much embarrassed, had to allow his companions to pay for his – and the two Japanese began to talk energetically to each other in their own language. Tom reverted to his newspaper, but after a few minutes they were seeking his attention again.

'We would be very pleased,' the man was saying, 'if you would accompany us during our trip today. As our guide.'

'Well,' Tom began, 'it would be nice, but really I . . .'

The man, as he spoke, had been rapidly writing on a page torn from a notebook. He now pushed this across the table. Tom found himself confronted by three words in neat black handwriting: sixty pounds sterling.

He stared. Unless he was being completely crass, unless there was some enormous cultural misunderstanding, he was being offered sixty pounds to spend the day going round Oxford and a few other places with a bunch of rather nice Japanese. 'No, really,' he said. 'I couldn't, I mean I'd rather just . . .'

They were both nodding and smiling now. 'It is our pleasure,' said the man.

'Oh, all right, then,' said Tom.

'Flamingos,' he explained, 'instead of croquet mallets.' The group stared, in polite but unresponsive silence. As well they might. To stumble across the dress rehearsal of an undergraduate production of *Alice* in a college garden was the sort of thing that would happen. He tried to steer his flock quickly past, thinking in irritation that of all bloody stupid ways for a collection of expensive twenty-year olds to spend an afternoon . . .

'A dragon,' said Mr Tsuzuki helpfully, pointing. 'And a tortoise.'

'Gryphon, actually. And mock turtle. Look, I thought if we went to Christ Church Cathedral now . . .'

'It is symbolical?'

'No,' said Tom. 'At least, well I suppose you could say . . . It's a children's book, in fact, a nineteenth century children's book about a girl who goes down a rabbit-hole and meets a lot of fantastic creatures . . .' – the group gathered round attentively; one of the girls said, 'What is rabbit-hole, please?' –

'. . . and has various adventures. A good deal of the point of it is linguistic, there's a lot of play on words, it's awfully difficult to explain . . . These people are supposed to be the Red King and the Red Queen, and then there's the White Queen and – oh, and a walrus and a carpenter and so forth.'

'It is making social comment?' said Mr Tsuzuki. The rest of the group had their cameras out now and were clicking away assiduously.

'No, no. Really it's to do with chess – the game – and playing-cards.'

'Games? English drama is not making social comment, then? In Germany we saw two plays of political significance.'

'It's not typical,' said Tom, with some desperation. 'They're just students, and even as a student activity it wouldn't be entirely . . . You know, I think if we're going to stick to the itinerary we really ought to be getting on to Christ Church.'

This was turning out to be not at all what he had bargained for. It sounded on the face of it like a piece of cake: you led a group of people, admittedly of alien culture but that should be neither here nor there, round a familiar landscape and tried to give them a simple but intelligible account of what they were seeing. You assumed that they knew little if anything about either the history or the culture and tried to explain briefly but illuminatingly. It was a job that any intelligent and moderately articulate person should be able to do.

The trouble had begun at the Martyrs' Memorial.

'. . . for heresy,' said Tom, 'during the Reformation.' He stopped. Too technical. 'That is the point in the sixteenth century when the official religion of this country becomes Protestant instead of Catholic.' There was a worrying totality of incomprehension in the faces around him; the difficulty was, of course, that one's own ignorance of Japanese history was equally extensive. What was the religion, anyway? Shinto, was that right? And would there have been any parallel to the Reformation? Religious martyrdom, surely; everybody has religious martyrdom.

He ploughed on. The group, rain-coated to a man and woman (sensibly, as it later turned out) skipped nimbly out of the way of the traffic and clustered round him on the pavement. Two or three of the girls took the opportunity to plunge into the near-by Ladies.

In the Broad, it occurred to him that a short digression on architectural style would be appropriate. He stood them opposite Balliol and indicated the façade.

'Very beautiful,' said Mr Tsuzuki. The cameras came out.

'Well, actually in fact nowadays most people don't really feel that nineteenth century building is beautiful, exactly. Of course it has its supporters but taste has swung away really from that kind of thing, it's thought rather heavy and graceless – what is more highly regarded now is seventeenth and eighteenth century style. Now if you look down the other end of the street you'll see the Sheldonian, which is by Sir Christopher Wren, who is generally considered I suppose to be one of our very greatest architects, perhaps *the* greatest . . . That round building.'

Mr Tsuzuki nodded. 'Church,' he said to his girlfriend.

'No, not a church.' Tom led them on, explaining. 'And the heads are the heads of Roman Emperors.'

One of the women had good English and was more talkative than the rest. She also had a disconcerting habit of making occasional notes on a small pad, which came out now as she asked, 'This is concerned also with the religious troubles you were speaking of – the Roman Catholics?'

'No. No, I'm afraid not. It's the ancient Romans, from Italy. It's a reference to our education being classically based at that point, Latin you see was the basic language for educated people, but then the Romans also invaded this country. In about 55 B.C. . . . .'

Perhaps it doesn't really matter, he thought. After all, they're here for a day out, that's all. The trouble is it matters to me, now.

There was more architectural trouble in Magdalen. Mr Tsuzuki was dismissive. 'Not beautiful. Heavy and not graceful.'

'In fact,' said Tom unhappily, 'this would be generally thought of as rather attractive. I know it's very like the sort of nineteenth century stuff we were talking about before, but the point is that this is genuine, it actually is medieval so that makes it all right. I know on the face of it it sounds a bit perverse.'

They had lunch at the Steak Bar off the Cornmarket and the ladies were allowed a foray into Marks and Spencer. The coach, previously ordered by Mr Tsuzuki, was waiting at Gloucester

Green. 'Blenheim, Churchill grave and a mystery tour, right?' said the driver. Tom, who had been giving the matter further reflection, added his own amendment. 'Burford and the Windrush valley? O.K. then, squire, whatever you suggest. Better get off, if they're wanting the six-eighteen back to London.'

His architectural comments had confused rather than enlightened, Tom realized. On the bridge at Blenheim the group studied the front of the house and then looked to him enquiringly. He said, 'It's well thought of.' The cameras clicked and the talkative lady brought out her note-book again. Several of the girls wanted to be photographed holding his arm; he felt himself, uneasily, to be taking on the symbolic sexual role of an Austrian ski instructor. It was hard to know whether to consider oneself flattered or degraded. He conducted them slowly up the approach to the palace and gave them a brief run-down of how it had come to be built. 'Reward for winning an important battle,' said the note-book wielding lady, scribbling. 'The English people are very militaristic, yes?'

'No,' said Tom. 'At least not more than most.'

They returned to the coach. The driver, sitting on the step with a copy of *The Sun*, said 'Bampton morris dancers are in the square, I should think your party would like another ten minutes or so here for that.'

'Well. . . .' Tom began, doubtfully, but his flock was already straggling off in the direction of the thumping and bell-rattling. Mr Tsuzuki was especially enthusiastic and produced a movie camera and tripod which he set up; Tom's assistance was required in various small ways, to hold pieces of equipment and hand them over at the right moment. The camera was of such versatility and technical achievement that clearly you could have shot a full length feature film with it. Several other members of the group stood round, taking a proprietorial interest, indicating to Tom one or two finer points. He stood there, holding Mr Tsuzuki's rain-coat and something to do with a filter or a light-meter, and the whole scene seemed both ludicrous and faintly depressing. Mr Tsuzuki, in his spruce well-cut drip-dry suit, pointed the camera at the morris dancers who capered about obligingly with their bells and sticks and hobby-horses, dressed like a cross between a pierrot and the Mad Hatter. The note-book lady said, 'It is being done here all the time, this dancing, in many places?' Tom, in mounting exasperation, glared at the dancers. 'Frankly, I've never set eyes on them before, it's all fairly ridiculous, you musn't imagine this is anything at all typical.' A bystander, some tweedy Woodstock native, chipped in with a little lecture about the ancestry of morris dancing, to which the note-book lady and Mr Tsuzuki listened with attention. Tom, sulkily, helped Mr Tsuzuki shift the tripod for one final, wide-angled shot. An acolyte of the dancers was now handing round copies of a leaflet listing and describing the dances done, their provenance and implications. It included also a short potted biography of each dancer. Three of them were employed by British Leyland at Cowley, a point noted by Mr Tsuzuki. 'This is important centre of your car industry, right?' Tom nodded. 'Unfortunately a lot of problems with your car industry?' 'Hadn't we better be getting on?' said Tom. 'It's going on for three.'

Bladon crawled with coaches. The driver, impervious to the inconvenience caused to pedestrians and other drivers, backed their vehicle into a narrow lane where it sat with its roof parallel to the upper windows of a row of stone cottages. Tom, looking out, found himself staring into the impassive face of an old lady sitting by her fireside in a murky interior. There was a dresser with coronation mugs and a fifties-type radio. He looked away again in embarrassment. The Japanese were filing out of the coach and heading for the churchyard.

They gathered round the grave. 'Is not very big,' said one of the girls. Tom, sensitive to the past, felt suddenly awkward. But even the oldest person present had been no more than a child during the war; most of them had not been born. 'You would think a bigger memorial,' said Mr Tsuzuki. 'Very famous Englishman.

There is bad feelings now, yes?' 'Oh, no,' said Tom. 'It's nothing like that. I imagine this must have been what he wanted.' The group, looking disappointed, began to drift away.

Back in the coach, Tom addressed himself to explaining the significance of the landscape. This undertaking was prompted by an unwillingness that his charges should go away with a purely aesthetic impression of what they had seen: scenery, after all, is not interesting; landscape is. 'What you have to realize,' he said, doing his best to sound informative rather than instructive, 'is that everything you see is quite artificial. This is a man-made country. Very intensively used for thousands of years. Now these small fields with hedges, for instance . . .' Heads were turned politely in his direction as he outlined the processes of enclosure. The coy attempts by some of the girls to pronounce the names of villages through which they passed encouraged him to digress onto the subject of place-names. 'Thames is interesting, because it's not English. Most river-names aren't. And in the north lots of names are Scandinavian.' 'Not English?' said Mr Tsuzuki. With evident perplexity, he listened frowning to Tom's account of Celts, Saxons and Vikings, while Tom declined the proffered large cigar.

In Burford, Tom instructed the driver to drop them at the church and then find somewhere to park. He had already briefed the party about the Cotswold wool industry and continued on this theme as he led them into the churchyard. Mr Tsuzuki, relaying Tom's information to stragglers who might have missed it, said, 'Very prosperous place, many rich merchants, much money from trade.' The audience looked at the surrounding cottages, the toppling grave-stones and the comfortably shaggy churchyard in evident disbelief. Tom stationed them in front of the porch and set about a short appreciation of English parish church architecture.

'Christ! Tom!'

He looked up. A ladder, which he had vaguely noticed, was propped against one of the nave windows, at the top of which someone – whose back had previously been turned – was repairing the stonework. This person, staring down, was now revealed as Martin Laker, deeply sunburnt, and with a chisel in one hand.

'What the hell are you doing here?'

The Japanese were all now, also, watching with interest. Martin came down the ladder and was introduced, with as much explanation to either side as Tom felt able to offer under the circumstances. The Japanese all shook hands with Martin in turn. 'My friend,' said Tom, 'knows more about this kind of thing than I do – I think he'd better take over for a bit.' Martin conducted them round the church, proving a considerable hit, especially with the girls, his hairiness appearing to both fascinate and excite. When they came out into the porch again Mr Tsuzuki proposed that they should now go and have a cup of afternoon tea, and that Martin should join them as their guest. He clumped up Burford's main street in the midst of the party, incongruous amid the pastel raincoats (which had come out now, in response to a heavy shower) in his workman's dungarees and heavy boots. The party almost completely filled the tea-shop, with Martin ensconced in the middle at Mr Tsuzuki's table, tucking into paste sandwiches and small, pink iced cakes. In response to the beaming interest of Mr Tsuzuki's girlfriend, he took various of his mason's tools out of his pockets and described their use; other members of the group craned to hear, or rose from their seats to stand around him. Detectable in their interest, though, was an element of kindly patronage. Tom, who had planned at this point to give them a quick run-down of the sixteenth century and the dissolution of the monasteries prior to the drive back to Oxford, which would take in Minster Lovell, sat in silence.

They parted from Martin outside the tea-shop, after more handshakes all round and a short photographic session. Martin entered into the spirit of this with great good humour, putting his arm round the girls' shoulders and beaming broadly. Tom said, 'Well, 'bye then, hope we didn't interrupt your afternoon's work too much. Love to Beth.'

Martin grinned. 'Not at all. Worth every minute. Sometime you must tell me just exactly how you got involved with all this.' He clumped away down the street.

When he had gone Mr Tsuzuki said, 'A very charming person, your friend. You have known him long?'

'We were students together, at Oxford.'

There was a pause. Mr Tsuzuki looked perturbed. 'Your friend is also university graduate?'

'That's right.'

After a moment Mr Tsuzuki went on, 'He is finding it difficult, then, to get employment? Suitable employment.'

'Oh,' said Tom. 'Oh, I see . . . No, no. It's not like that. He wants to do that kind of thing – stone-carving and metalwork and stuff. It's purely a matter of choice.'

They had been joined now by Mr Tsuzuki's girlfriend and one of the other girls. Mr Tsuzuki broke into rapid Japanese, to which the girls responded with sounds of dismay and regret. Tom said again, 'Really, it's what he would choose to do. He's just not the sort of person who would want an office job.' His companions shook their heads sadly and one of the girls asked if his friend had perhaps had bad luck with his examinations.

'No,' said Tom. 'As a matter of fact he got quite a good degree.' There was no point in persisting with the struggle, he could see. He followed the group back into the coach.

It now began to rain quite heavily. The coach splashed along the Windrush valley lanes, occasionally having to pause and shunt to and fro in order to manoeuvre tight corners, at which points the driver, who would have preferred the main road back, glanced balefully at Tom. The Japanese stared out at the dripping greenery. Tom indicated points of interest.

At Minster Lovell, it had stopped raining, though clouds hung sullenly overhead; the ruins seemed suspended in a watery bowl of river, lush sodden growth and grey misty air. The group picked its way fastidiously over the wet grass. Tom gave a curtailed explanation of what they were seeing. One of the girls, who had evidently not taken in much, said, 'Is all broken down. What a pity.' 'Well, yes,' Tom said, 'but it's rather nice, all the same, isn't it? Of course, we've been fond of ruins, in this country, ever since – oh, since the eighteenth century. I suppose it's partly because we've got so many, we've had to make the best of them.' He had intended this as a light-hearted remark, but nobody smiled. The party stood about in the grassy quadrangle formed by the shattered walls, and gazed up at the stonework and its cloak of ivy. Pigeons walked about cooing in the window openings; a pair of jackdaws tumbled around the bared remains of a fireplace, high above their heads. The noise of the river, a dozen yards away, was nicely answered by the rustle of a line of poplars. Hackneyed lines of verse came into Tom's head. It occurred to him that there was no way, really, in which to explain the English response to places like this to anyone unfamiliar with it. Did you have eastern ruins? Well, yes, Indian ones, certainly. Kipling's jungle city. But of course Kipling is anthropomorphizing in an English way. The city is Indian, but the response isn't. The fact is, of course, that what you feel about what you see depends not on what it is, but who you are. A place is an illusion. Here we stand, these people and me, looking at quite different things.

Mr Tsuzuki was glancing at his watch, in fact. 'I am thinking, perhaps . . . ?' 'Yes,' said Tom. 'Quite right.' They trooped back to the coach and re-embarked.

He parted from them eventually, at Paddington. Final photographs were taken, against the background of Platform I departure board. Addresses were exchanged; hands were shaken. The party left in a fleet of taxis, and Tom, by now genuinely sorry to leave them, made his way into the Underground.

He felt disgruntled, both with himself and with the way the day had turned out. He hadn't done at all well. He had bewildered rather than enlightened. Whether through accidents or circumstance or personal inadequacy he had managed to give an impression of a place in which the theatre was childish, the amusements quaint and irrelevant, the landscape baffling and the history incomprehensible. In which university graduates were obliged to repair churches and famous men were insufficiently honoured. In which, apparently, nothing is quite what it seems to be; whose architecture is either pretending to be what it is not, or in a state of disintegration.

They would have done better, Tom thought, with a competent guidebook. And I should feel less frustrated at not having been able to do with any aptitude something which after all I never intended to do in the first place.

And then, of course, there had been the matter of squaring things with Kate. Of accounting for what in the end amounted to an entire missing day, since she had expected him to phone her from the flat that morning, instead of which he had appeared just in time for dinner. And, on the face of it, a tale of twenty-five accidentally acquired Japanese sounded fairly implausible. She stood there with that expression of incredulity, and honestly he gave his account and could hope only that it might be received in the spirit in which it was given.

# Chapter Twelve

Tony, with assistants and camera crew, had gone down to Wiltshire, where they were based at a pub in Marlborough. From here, he telephoned Tom and Kate at frequent intervals to complain about the weather, his own creative misgivings, and Laura. Laura, it seemed, had destroyed what Tony considered the period charm of the Danehurst garden by importing a firm of contractors to mow the lawn, cut the hedges and weed the beds. Also, she kept inviting the team to sherry parties to meet her friends. This, Tony said, depressed the camera crew who preferred beer and took up a lot of valuable time; she doesn't seem to realize, he complained, that what we're actually doing is *working*.

'Naturally,' said Kate, 'what does he expect? Ma has always found people's tendency to work a nuisance. It stops them doing other things that she might be wanting them to do. Let's not go down this weekend.'

'Oh, come on – it might be interesting. Anyway, you'll get all hell from Laura if you don't.'

Kate groaned.

Paul Summers, who was currently engaged on a dig somewhere in Yorkshire, had declined to make himself available for filming at Charlie's Tump at any time other than a weekend, to Tony's annoyance. The cost of this to the BBC, in overtime all round, would be considerable. However, it was impossible to sway such commitment to the job in hand, and Tony had had to settle for a major filming session on the Saturday, with possible extension to Sunday if the weather or other circumstances made this necessary. On the Friday, there was to be filming at Danehurst and round about.

Laura telephoned, twice, to say that both Kate and Tom were expected by Friday evening at the latest. Help was required for various unspecified tasks.

On Friday morning Kate announced suddenly that she had agreed to go into the museum on Saturday morning to help with the packing of some things that were being lent out for an exhibition.

Tom said, 'You can't.'

'I can. I am.'

'Laura is going to say why can't someone else do it.'

'She can say.'

What Laura in fact said was that in that case she would make do with Tom and Kate would have to follow on later. 'I'll pick you up at the station. You must learn to drive, Tom, it's so odd – someone who doesn't drive.'

Kate said, 'Just say you won't. You don't have to.'

'Oh, I might as well. I can always get Tony to come and take me for a drink in the evening.'

It had become hot. A summer of fitful weather had stabilized to produce a period of long sunny days culminating in still, balmy evenings. Wiltshire was as languid as some southern European pastoral scene, the trees sending long shadows down heat-sodden fields, cows clumped together with swishing tails.

Laura, at the station, was wearing a flowered dress and straw hat; glimpsed first at a distance, on the other side of the car park, she was a girlish figure, so that for a moment Tom found himself looking at her with natural appreciation until he realized with a jolt who it was. She drove them back to Danehurst fast, saying they mustn't waste a moment of the garden on such a heavenly evening.

'I thought there was a job you wanted me to do.'

'Oh, it can wait till later. There's just some furniture I want moved before tomorrow.'

She brought drinks out into the garden and sat down in a reclining chair on the terrace. 'You do yours, Tom – you know how you like it. Sherry for me.' She closed her eyes and leaned back. 'Perfect. Summer at last. The sort of day that should go on for ever.'

The garden, certainly, had been rather drastically tidied up. The lawn, neatly shaven, reached away to the clipped yew hedges; through the gap could be seen a section of the flower-garden beyond, a square of hazy blues and greens and golds, an impressionistic blur of colour. Nearer at hand, some plant with trailing ropes of periwinkle blue flowers smothered part of the terrace; Laura sat with her sandalled feet among them. The rose growing up that side of the house was covered with delicate, scented blooms. Yellow butterflies rose and dipped above the big border at the side of the lawn. Swallows chattered overhead. Down by the summerhouse a blackbird was thrashing a mangled worm against the grass.

Laura's cat appeared suddenly through the gap in the hedge, with something in its mouth. She slunk tigerishly towards them across the lawn to the terrace where she put down her burden, now revealed as a mouse, not by any means dead. After a minute she began to shunt its twitching body to and fro across the paving stones with one paw, purring loudly.

Laura opened her eyes. 'Oh, you bad Heloise. Another poor mouse.' She watched for a moment or two and then closed her eyes again.

Tom said, 'I'm afraid I can't really stand this.' He got up, feeling slightly sick, and finished off the lacerated mouse, disposing of it at the back of the flower border. The cat looked on with manifest resentment. Laura said, 'How brave of you, Tom. Of course, I never imagine they're feeling much by that stage. Could you be very sweet and throw me over that cushion. Thanks.' She tucked the cushion behind her head and stretched out more comfortably. 'I tried to get Nellie to join us, but she's been feeling a bit under the weather these last few days and she thought she'd stay in her room. Tell me, now, how did your interview go in that place?'

'Oh, not too badly. But they appointed someone else.'

There was a pause. Laura said, 'Do help yourself to another drink.' Then, 'What will you do if you *don't* get a job?'

'That's an interesting question.'

'Of course I didn't know Hugh when he was your age, I was so much younger than him . . . So I don't know if it was at all like that, not that there's really any kind of comparison. I read something in the paper the other day about it, obviously it's not just you. What does happen to people who don't get jobs?'

It seemed a good idea to make the second drink quite a lot stronger than the first. 'Oh, I should think they just fester away in private,' said Tom, 'trying not to be a nuisance to other people.'

'Kate was quite lucky, I suppose. Though of course it's different for a girl anyway.'

The temptation to ask why was removed by Laura going suddenly into the house to check the dinner preparations. She was gone for some time and in her absence Tom put his feet up on a second chair and set to appreciation of what was indeed a particularly pleasant evening. The light had taken on a filmy quality, both muting colours and making the far seem nearer so that the downland hung at the end of the garden rich with detail: sheep, trees, the dark ring of a barrow. And the garden itself glowed and murmured and breathed out indefinable honeyed scents. It must be around midsummer, possibly midsummer night itself. And the sense of ripeness was having a slightly disturbing effect on the senses – though admittedly a couple of drinks might have played their part. Vague yearning feelings. Kate? But no – the feelings when examined a little did not seem to have anything much to do with Kate, which was disturbing in itself. Cherry? Well, just a bit, maybe, but only in a rather general sense. No, not really her either. Perhaps in fact they weren't really to do with sex at all, or even love, though there seemed to be an eerie connection. Another drink would perhaps settle the stomach in some way.

Laura came out again to say that supper would be ready in a

few minutes, and did Tom feel up to coping with those chairs now. She led him upstairs. 'They're in the attics, I'm afraid, where you haven't yet penetrated, but the thing is we shall need them for tomorrow, there just aren't enough in the drawing room.' A ladder had to be hooked to a hatch opening. Laura said, 'Shall I go first? Then I can find the light switch.' She swarmed ahead of him up the ladder, with admirable agility; she had extremely handsome legs, seen to advantage from this angle and viewed with absolute detachment, just as pleasing objects. Tom, averting his eyes after a moment or so and following her up through the hatch, thought: of course being around in a time when all women wear jeans I probably suffer from leg-deprivation. He thought of those forties film stars, all leg and bright lipstick. Not that that was Laura's style at all.

There was a light on now, and Laura was saying should she go down and stand at the bottom and he could hand the chairs one by one. He pulled them to the hatch – nothing was either heavy or particularly unwieldy – and lowered each one carefully into Laura's outstretched arms. 'Lovely. That's the lot. Now it's just a case of getting them downstairs.' She disappeared to the kitchen again, leaving Tom to manipulate the chairs.

Nellie, it seemed, didn't after all feel up to joining them for supper. Laura took a tray through to her room and then decided that it would be nicer to eat out on the terrace. She loaded food – and a bottle of white wine – onto a trolley which was wheeled out through the drawing room.

'I love alfresco eating,' said Laura. 'Not that one often gets the chance, here.' She filled their plates from the trolley. 'Lots of salad? You do the wine, Tom dear, please. It's as good as being abroad. I've often thought of going to Portugal or somewhere. Permanently, I mean. A lot of one's friends have. I've always loved abroad, in some ways one feels more oneself in those kind of places.' She sighed. 'Danehurst is an albatross, in many ways. Of course, Nellie wouldn't like it.'

'No,' said Tom. 'I imagine she wouldn't.'

'Perhaps eventually . . . Of course I suppose that's something you could do, if you don't get a job here.'

'Yes, I suppose I could.'

'You've really done awfully well so far,' Laura looked across at him thoughtfully, sipping wine, 'going to Oxford and everything. Your parents must have been thrilled to bits. Did you love it?'

'Well,' Tom began, 'yes and no. By then I'd picked up this habit of working quite hard which . . .'

Laura cut in. 'I used to know someone who was a don at your college – a man with a beaky nose called Masterson, did you know him? He wasn't really a friend, just someone one used to come across at dinners and things, rather nice. Of course in my day it wasn't so much the thing for girls to go to university, but I daresay it's great fun now.'

'It has its points.'

'I used to go and see Kate sometimes when she was at college. Actually I always thought there was something a bit bleak about it – all those girls in little poky rooms with their dirty washing everywhere.'

'The dirty washing I never noticed.'

The meal was really extremely good. The wine too. But there was no way, now, short of barbarous incivility, of getting on the phone to Tony in Marlborough and suggesting a jar in the pub. Laura had moved on to the subject of social mobility and the wisdom engendered by experience. 'Lots of Kate's friends were girls from just quite ordinary homes, which of course is such a good thing when they settle down all right. Some of them come unstuck I daresay but really one of the good things about nowadays is the way people are so much more adaptable. One often thought in the old days that more should have been done – not of course that I really remember before the war much but one was much more aware as a child of things being, well, sort of more uneven. People were awfully hard up. But you know, Tom, one thing one does realize, getting older, is that change is inevitable.' She filled their glasses and stared reflectively out over the garden. 'Barbara and I were talking only yesterday about how much more *confident* people are nowadays – ordinary sort of people. Mind you, Barbara is a bit older than I am so she remembers before the war better. And of course having known lots of different types one has had the opportunity to notice, and think about it. What?'

'That's interesting.' Or words to that effect.

'One wonders,' said Laura thoughtfully, 'where it will all end.'

'Yes, one does indeed.'

'Of course in many ways one had fewer opportunities oneself even. Not that I would really have wanted a job or anything like that – I often think Kate is really awfully tied down. But one travelled so much more, which does make such a difference.'

'What sort of difference?'

'To one's outlook.' There was an implication, here, that other outlooks had been examined, and found wanting. 'I'll just pop in and get our puddings. You might as well finish off that bottle of wine. I shan't have any more.'

The meal finished, Laura decided it was getting chilly. They moved into the drawing room, Laura now engaged on recollections of continental holidays, both with and without Hugh. Kate seldom featured. Indeed, considering that Kate was the link accounting for their being together at all, it was odd how rarely she was mentioned. Laura, of course, was not a person who devoted much thought to cause and effect. She was on about the perversities of memory, now. 'It's funny how attractive it always seems looking back, like when you were a child it was always nice weather, and yet at the time one didn't feel it was so very marvellous. But now you wish you were back there – everything seems brighter and better and people more interesting and fun. We had such a super time in Le Lavandou with the Wentworths, Peter and Mary – you wouldn't know him, he's rather a well known philosopher who was a friend of Hugh's. The most heavenly summer. But then it was only the autumn after that Hugh had the beginning of his illness, and of course one had no idea that was in the offing.' She sighed. 'So unexpected.'

'The wheel of things.'

'What?'

'Sir Thomas Browne. Somebody in the seventeenth century. He puts it rather well – "remember the wheel of things". Just when you think everything's going along nicely, it'll go into reverse.'

'Is that the one you're writing your thing on?'

'No. A different bloke.'

'By the way, there's some whisky in the drinks cupboard. Do help yourself.'

'Thanks.'

'Well, it does all seem somehow rosier, looking back. I daresay other people get that feeling.'

'He says things about that, too. "Great examples grow thin, and to be fetched from past times. Iniquity comes at long strides upon us".'

'I don't know how you can remember all that kind of thing. I never could learn poetry.'

The whisky was going down very nicely. Tom ceased to regret that drink with Tony, whose conversational responses could, in their own way, be equally haphazard at times. Laura, though, had a particularly fine mastery of the off-the-mark return.

Tom said, 'I've written up quite a lot of my stuff now – forty thousand words or so. This is the satisfactory part – producing something out of what always looked like the most irreconcilable set of constituents. Seeing that the apparently irrelevant does in fact fit in. Rather like cooking – I always used to be amazed to see my mother conjure a cake out of eggs and butter and cornflour.'

'It would be flour, actually. Self-raising flour. Well, that's good that you're getting on with it. So then you'll have to think seriously about what comes next. You're rather set on staying in England if you can?'

'Not absolutely. But I suppose given the choice I'd prefer to.'

'I can't think why,' said Laura with a yawn.

It seemed suddenly time to take a more active part in the conversation. 'Well,' said Tom, 'if you'd really like to know I'll tell you. May I?'

'Love to hear.' The look she gave him did not indicate an unusually intense interest. 'Oh, you mean a drink . . . Well, yes, help yourself by all means.'

'Right, then. Let's see what kind of sense this makes.' He tipped some more whisky into his glass. 'First of all, there's the language, which seems to me rather well devised to do what it sets out to do. Of course, our own processes of thought – yours and mine both, which is interesting – are conditioned by its use, so I daresay I'm prejudiced there. And then there's the matter of what's been done with it, the fact that quite a few capable people, over the years, have made extremely effective use of it. Oh, I could read anywhere, I know. But I've always got a certain kick out of the relation between the place and that to which it gives rise. By which I don't of course mean the scenery.'

'Hardy,' said Laura. 'That's all set in Dorset, isn't it? We used to know a woman who knew a relation of his. Her name's quite gone out of my head – the relation, I mean.'

'Ah. What a pity.' There is a certain fascination, Tom thought, in talking to – if that is the right preposition – someone who has never, apparently, actually listened to what is being said. It accounts, presumably, for a quite remarkable edifice of self-deception; a monument, indeed. 'Do tell me if you remember. And then there is also the matter of the place itself – considered quite apart from its literary spawnings. The national stage-set, the background or whatever you like to call it. And that has also always seemed to me notable in a number of different ways – it's beautiful, often; it's remarkably various for such a small country; and to anyone with any sense of the past, impressively suggestive. A palimpsest; the original one, in fact. However, scenery is not enough for a thinking person, as I'm sure you'll agree, so we'll move on to what might be called the nitty-gritty, nowadays – in other words what it all adds up to. And that seems to me not inconsiderable. There's political stability and a fair degree of tolerance and a certain capacity to admit mistakes. And, you may well be adding by now, complacency. That's a point, I concede. But I'm not meaning to be complacent – a book-balancing job, this is supposed to be, no more nor less. For my own edification – I'm merely trying to examine my own responses, which is a good thing to do from time to time. We all ought to know how we stand, and why. Where was I? Oh yes, what's satisfactory and what isn't. And there's a great deal that isn't, of course. Satisfactory is a comparative term – nowhere's perfect. And of course if you had pronounced political views to either left or right you would be making noises of protest at this point.'

'Actually,' Laura began, 'I'm . . .'

'Quite above politics. Absolutely. So am I, for present purposes. What we're concerned with now is what one might think of as the outcome of it all, so far. The end product of all the ingredients (back to cooking again, I see) – language, history, ambiance, culture, the lot. I'm using rather pretentious words, I'm afraid.'

'You're a bit drunk.'

'Oh, very possibly. And for all its shortcomings, which I'm only too ready to admit, I find the end product not unattractive. Oh yes, there's plenty to make the gorge rise – Rhodes Boyson and Wedgwood Benn and Edward Short and Ken Russell and the Institute of Contemporary Arts and practically the whole of the Midlands and *The Guardian* women's page and a good deal else. But being . . .'

'Is the Institute of Contemporary Arts that place in Piccadilly?' said Laura.

He looked at her with admiration. Nice one. 'But – as I was

about to say – being a bloke of low political drive I'm unlikely to do a lot of trying to do anything very active about any of those or anything else, which is in itself I concede a count against me. Low political drive is probably a bad thing. In that, I suspect I'm of my time, or of the times. Even a few years ago, I gather, someone like me would have been more likely to take his indignations to the barricades than to reflect on them in private. Interesting, that. Not only are you a product of the whole long process, but of your own immediate bit of it too. On the face of it, there doesn't seem to be much room left for freedom of spirit. And yet, and yet . . . And yet you see it seems to me that someone like me inherits a great deal of freedom of spirit, quite apart from all the other freedoms that haven't even been mentioned . . .'

'John Barclay went to Russia last year,' said Laura. 'Apparently over there. . . .'

'Yes. One had heard. And given all that – given certain feelings of respect and affinity and curiosity and interest, I feel an inclination to stick around and see what happens. Just that. Assist at the historical process. And the other thing, of course, is that for better or for worse and like it or not I happen to be a manifestation of the place myself. As also are you, only the difference between us – one of several differences – is that you don't really give a damn about it and indeed for two pins you'd bugger off to Portugal, whereas I have these rather confused umbilical sentiments. And I . . .'

'Talk too much,' said Laura, smothering a yawn.

'I daresay. And now I come to think of it I really can't imagine why I'm telling you all this.'

'In vino . . .'

'How true. And perceptive. However, since you aren't going to remember longer than tomorrow it doesn't really matter.'

'As it happens I've got rather a good memory. But never mind. I won't come out with embarrassing reminders.' She looked at him, thoughtfully. After a moment she went on, 'You aren't going to marry Kate, are you?'

In the buzzing silence that followed he took some more whisky. 'I suppose I'm not. But I'd rather almost anyone than you had pointed it out to me.'

Laura got up. 'I think I'm going to bed, if you don't mind. I've had a bit of a wearing day and tomorrow's going to be busy. You come up when you feel like it.' She went round the room picking up glasses and switching off a light or two. Leaning over him to check the catch on the french windows she over-balanced slightly and laid a hand on his arm. 'Sorry, Tom.' There was a little gust of a rather agreeable perfume. At the door she turned and looked back at him. 'I feel guilty leaving you on your own like this – sure you don't mind? Just give me a knock if there's anything you want, won't you?'

There was a fair bit of whisky left. Enough to put paid to the next hour or two, anyway.

He woke to the most fearful cacophony of birds outside the window. And blinding light. And a headache to beat all headaches. And along with the headache accompanying miseries like nausea and cramp in the legs and a general feeling of being only tenuously connected with the universe. And as he lay pole-axed in this dark night of the soul, there swam into the head the most amazing and unnerving image: the image of Laura, of Laura seated at a dressing-table in her underclothes, one arm raised above her head, holding a hairbrush (thus revealing the curve of an inadequately covered breast), her face turned to his with an expression of . . . Of what? Of expectation? Of annoyance? Of surprise?

He shrank in horror beneath the blankets. What was this, for God's sake? The product of a fevered imagination? Or had – hideous thought – had there come to pass last night in those lost whisky-sodden hours some appalling scene that he no longer remembered except in these horrifying fragments?

The underclothes were vivid. Flesh-coloured, lacy, and esoteric.

Camiknickers. That kind of thing is called a camiknicker. How do I know that? he thought wildly, I've never heard of them before. Kate wore the bras and briefs familiar to anyone.

She sat there, Laura, undressed, in a murky light from the bedside lamp, hairbrush in hand, looking at him.

He groaned.

The image, of course, was also that of any television advertisement: the pretty, under-dressed woman, in a situation of suggestive privacy. Hairspray; deodorant; soap.

Racked by uncertainty, his head pounding, he got up and dressed. He did not know how he was going to look her in the face.

# Chapter Thirteen

The cameras were being set up in the garden for Tony's interview with Laura. The fine weather was lasting, though the forecasts had talked of thundery showers. Tom stood with Tony on the terrace.

'Kate was held up, I hear.'

'She'll be down after lunch.'

'You look a bit low. Anything wrong?'

Tom stared gloomily across the lawn. 'It's just possible,' he said, 'that I may have made a pass at Laura last night. In fact it's remotely conceivable that more than that might have happened.'

'Good Lord. I see. Well.'

There was a silence.

'*Possible*. What exactly does that mean?'

'I can't remember. I was pissed, totally. There's just a kind of impression. Which might or might not be imagination.'

'Ah. Very awkward for you.'

'Quite.'

'You can't ever be absolutely sure?'

'No.'

'And you couldn't – er – ask?'

'Christ, no.'

'I see your problem,' said Tony. 'I certainly do.' He put a sympathetic hand on Tom's shoulder. 'Well, I'd better get on.'

Laura – whose manner gave no clues that were in any way helpful – had come out of the house and was greeting the cameraman with the graciousness of a senior actress. She moved across the lawn with Tony, discussing problems of lighting and the disposition of chairs. Tom went into the sitting room and slumped on the sofa with the newspaper. The headache was beginning to wear off a little; he wished he was somewhere else. Anywhere else would do, really. Suppose he suddenly remembered an ailing grandmother and just upped and offed? But Kate was coming this afternoon.

Kate.

Another problem.

They drove to the point where the trackway to Charlie's Tump led away from the road, and left the car in the layby there. The BBC cars had apparently braved the inconveniences of the track. Kate set off for the Tump without looking to see if Tom was following, walking quickly in that dogged way of hers. He was reminded of the first time they had come here. They had hardly spoken since she had arrived a couple of hours earlier; she seemed sullen and he had left her alone. Now, he did not attempt to catch up with her.

From this point it was impossible to see the barrow, positioned as it was not quite on the crest of the hill but at a point slightly below, and hidden by a piece of rising ground before. The track, snaking ahead between cornfields, seemed indeed to vanish at that point. To the right, a quarter mile or so away, the clump of trees crowning the East Kennet long barrow made a dark patch against the long pale swelling of another field, rooks circling above it. He and Kate had walked up there once, and he had found the site more evocative than the Tump, combining as it did the two mythic stage-settings of under-world and sylvan glade. He had remarked on this to Kate, who had said, 'Or it's a mound with some trees planted on it . . .' Now, looking across at it once more, he wondered if Stukeley had ever walked up this particular downland way and, if so, what he had seen. The scenery of the classically-fed imagination? Or a 'Sepulchre of the Ancient Britons'? Or a suitable site for the application of certain pre-conceived theories?

Barrows, of course, have always had their own mythology. That which cannot be explained is a subject for fantasy: the homes of the Little People, the sites of buried treasure, the graves of Arthurian heroes who will rise again. Even, absurdly, a hiding-place for Charles the First.

They had reached the crest of the lower hill now and the Tump itself came into view, with its stone threshold and dark maw and the white track winding towards it. Just ahead, the BBC cars were parked in a gateway, having reached the nearest point possible; beyond, a line of distant figures humped equipment up the last stretch of the hill. At the top, Tony stood silhouetted against the sky, a stooped Napoleonic figure staring down at his marshalled forces. From time to time he shouted some instruction; the wind had lifted his hair in a coxcomb from the top of his head. Once or twice he looked upwards, shielding his eyes with a hand. The sky had partly clouded over, as though shut off by a slowly tilting lid; the light had drained from the eastern half of the landscape, while the rest remained bathed in sunshine, an odd effect like illustrations of an eclipse in a school text-book. Somewhere along the Kennet Valley, a stone building was caught in a shaft of sunshine, a point of emphasis which somehow gave an air of contrivance to the whole scene: the fields, the sky, the dark slash of the valley, the clustered farms and cottages. It ceased to be a piece of countryside and entered a tradition of painting. Tom was reminded of the picture at Standhill – the carefully arranged view with figures in the foreground, the representation of an inhabited world. This piece of Wiltshire, too, had for the moment the same docility, the same suggestion of order and obedience, in which utility and aesthetics combined to please.

She could sense him behind her, some way behind. Not bothering to catch up. She thought, I'm cold, why am I so cold? It's quite a nice day, quite sunny.

Clouds coming up, though. That, she supposed, would muck up their filming. And there indeed was Tony on the rim of the hill above the Tump, staring across the valley at the cloud bank. Presumably Paul Summers was up there too, who was going to be filmed talking about the excavation.

When I was a child, she thought, it used to seem miles coming up here. An endless walk. Hours. Now, it's just ten minutes or so. Nothing is ever quite what it seems to be, that is what being grown-up adds up to, that is the one thing you do find out. That, and that you can't count on much.

She had always thought this a primitive place, faintly threatening. Coming up with her father and others once, when she was a schoolgirl, she had wandered off and found them gone when she got back to the Tump; in panic she had fled down the path, experiencing that atavistic knowledge of pattering, following footsteps somewhere out of sight. Today, stumping upwards, not looking back – only Tom's footsteps, now, and those felt rather than heard – she saw it as indifferent, a scene hostile to life, peopled only by sheep and birds, that might always have been thus. The barrows and trackways suggested a victory of nature over man, rather than the passage of time. All dead; all gone. Everything goes.

Tony and his entourage, scattered about the Tump itself, looked not so much incongruous as irrelevant. There was some kind of fuss going on around one of the BBC cars, which had apparently got stuck in a muddy gateway; the driver wrenched the wheel, someone else heaved at a bumper. Further away people were setting a camera up at the entrance to the Tump: an entrance that was itself in fact an illusion since behind the two huge blocks and the lintel stone that formed the doorway the internal stonework had long since collapsed. Kate thought of lying curled up in there, as a small child, with her father and Aunt Nellie; that was before the place had assumed for her its aura of desolation. Then, it had been somehow different.

It's futile, all this, she thought. Pointless. I wish they weren't doing it; I wish I hadn't come up. She planned to wait for Tom at the fence before the Tump: to wait inadvertently as it were, to take his arm, start talking . . . Planned, and then, when she got there, climbed over and went plodding on towards where Tony Greenway stood with the others.

I don't like that wire fence, it spoils the uninhabited effect. We shall have that in shot if we pan away from me to the view down the valley. And if we pull back instead we shall get that corrugated iron thing in the corner of the field.

Better to put the camera the other side, pan left from me over the top of the Tump, nothing obtrusive there. The joy of filming is that anything can always be made to appear otherwise. With a bit of care and application. You can always get what you want in the end.

I don't like the look of that sky, not one little bit. That, of course, is the one thing you damn well can't do anything about – the bloody weather. Are you ready, Mike? he said, let's go, I'm worried about the light. O.K., Sue?

The mouth of the barrow behind him, he began to talk to the camera. 'Charlie's Tump, this little hill is called. Charles the First is supposed to have hidden here, in flight from Cromwellian troops – or at least that's been the local story, down the centuries. He didn't, of course – there's not a shred of evidence to suggest that he ever came near the place. But it has generated its own myth, like so many prehistoric sites. Because of course what it really is is a barrow – a Neolithic long barrow. And its real claim to fame is that it is here that Hugh Paxton excavated the grave goods that have since come to be known as the Danehurst hoard. The dig that established his name. And the dig that in many ways consolidated modern archaeological theories about Wessex. Paul Summers worked here with Paxton that summer . . .'

Cut. And re-assemble cameras and people for the next shot. That sky is getting very dicey.

★

This is all fairly boring, Tom thought. Standing here not quite being able to hear Paul Summers give a run-down on prehistoric Wessex to a camera, some people from the BBC and a few sheep. And Kate, who is not listening. And by the look of that sky it's going to come chucking down any minute now.

I must say something. Ask. I've got to know. I have known, for weeks now. Later, back at Danehurst. But there'll be so many people around. Why is Paul Summers crawling around in front of the Tump now? Oh, I see – he's supposed to be looking inside.

'. . . not unfortunately restored and preserved like West Kennet. The entrance remains but the chamber had been largely destroyed by early barrow diggers and little is now left. If we look at this scale diagram of the interior of the barrow we shall get an idea of the lay-out.'

And cut again. 'O.K.' said Tony. 'I know, I know, Mike. You can't see a damn thing. Pack it in and get the camera back to the car before it starts coming down.'

The tilt of that cloud lid had accelerated, bringing with it rumbles of thunder. There was a sour yellowish light. The group around the Tump broke up and began hurriedly to head back to the cars; even as they did so warm rain started to fall. There was a flare of lightning. The girl with the clipboard ran helter-skelter for the gate, a jacket slung over her head; the others followed at a more dignified pace. Paul Summers said, 'Well, I daresay it could change again equally suddenly.' There did seem to be a malign triumph about the rapidity with which the storm had broken.

They crowded into the cars. Tom and Kate were squashed into a big Volvo with cameraman, lighting man, Tony, and the clipboard girl: rain thumped down on the roof. The girl said, 'I'm petrified of thunder, I know it's silly.' She sat with her hands over her ears. There was reminiscence of other disastrous filmings. Someone brought out a flask of brandy which was handed round. Kate sat silent; when anyone spoke to her she made a brusque, awkward rejoinder; Tom felt a gush of irritation. The noise without was deafening; beyond the windows of the car there was nothing but a wall of water. Tom said cheerfully, 'How much is all this costing the BBC?'

It slackened, at last. They climbed out into the dripping land-scape.

The girl said, 'Phew! Thank God that's over,' and then, 'Funny smell. . . .' Looking up towards the Tump, they all became aware of some re-arrangement of the large stones at the entrance. Paul said, 'Hello! What's happened up there?' He made off up the track again, followed by the others.

The lintel stone, they saw as they got nearer, had cracked through and toppled across the entrance, bringing with it a cascade of soil and smaller stones. From the wreckage protruded the hindquarters of a dead sheep; another lay close by. That peculiar acrid smell of burnt wool was accounted for. A bolt of lightning had struck the stonework of the Tump, and with it the group of sheep that had huddled there for shelter. The party gathered round, impressed. Someone said, 'Bloody good thing *we* didn't think of sitting it out here.' The clipboard girl took one look, walked over to the fence and was discreetly sick into the long grass. Tony said fretfully, 'Well, I hope to God those shots we did manage to get are going to be O.K., because there's going to be no re-shooting of that particular angle. Are you all right, Sue – why don't you go back to the van?' Paul Summers speculated aloud about the chances of getting the entrance restored. It was suggested that someone had better make contact with the local farmer. Sue, with Kate and one of the men, set off down the track. The others followed singly, picking their way through the watercourse of creamy mud resulting from the storm.

Tom, looking back, saw Tony bring up the rear, considerably separated from the rest. The Napoleonic image, if pursued, suggested now the retreat from Moscow. He was hurrying down, his stoop exaggerated – perhaps by the slope of the hill. And behind him, above the Tump, as though to emphasize the caprice of the physical world, the sky had cleared to an intense and cloudless blue. Sheep were already grazing once more unconcernedly around the Tump, yards from their former companions.

'What rotten luck,' said Laura. 'Typical. And now it's perfectly fine again.' She was exhilarated, a little overwrought; Danehurst teemed with people. In the kitchen Mrs Lucas and a sister-in-law prepared food, paying token and slightly cynical attention to Laura's frequent entrances and instructions. Kate disappeared to talk to Nellie, who was remaining in her room for the time being. Tom retreated onto the terrace with Tony's assistant, Sue, an attractive girl, now recovered from her attack of sensibility at the Tump and amusingly tart about the rest of the company. Within, the Hamiltons were in bright conversational assault upon the cameraman.

'I only came onto this programme last week, because someone's on holiday – I don't entirely get where everyone fits in. You, for instance.'

Tom said, 'Oh, I'm just incidental.'

'And the prickly girl – she's the daughter, right?'

'Mmnn.'

'A bit grumpy – you can't get much going there.'

There was a pause. The girl said, 'Oh, Christ, you're not . . .'

'Not to worry – you couldn't know.'

'Trust me . . . Now you're going to loathe me, and quite right too.'

Brown eyes turned on him, filled with genuine remorse and compunction. Tom said, 'I'll see if I can rustle up another drink without letting us in for being generally sociable.' She was a thin girl with straight, fair hair. Not a bit like Kate. A little like Laura, oddly enough; Laura twenty years ago.

A buffet lunch was served in the dining room. Others had arrived: John Barclay and a couple from Marlborough. In a somewhat ill-assorted party, conversation periodically withered. Tony, evidentally ruffled by the morning's events, seemed unable to concentrate on what was said. Nellie came in and sat somewhat apart. Laura and Barbara Hamilton vied to outdo one another in sprightliness. Kate remained silent.

To Tom, the whole day had begun to be somehow macabre. Never having previously thought a great deal about Hugh Paxton, he was now acutely conscious of his absence. It seemed an interesting instance of the power exercised by the dead: in this case the ability to fill a room with people most of whom had never known the person in question. To determine not only how they spent their day, but how several of them had been spending a good number of other days. He looked at Tony, who was rather dazedly listening to Laura. Laura, though, in mid-anecdote, had fallen suddenly silent, as though forgetting what she had been about to say, thus allowing Barbara Hamilton neatly to occupy the vacuum.

I can't remember what Hugh looked like, she thought. I can't see him any more. Oh yes, there is the photo on the dressing-table, I know what that looks like, and all the others in the albums. But I just can't see him any more. He's gone.

And in sudden panic she clutched the glass in her hand, jerking it so that the wine tilted over onto her skirt, dark drops on the blue silk, and she not noticing, nor hearing Barbara Hamilton either, staring with wide surprised eyes at all these people.

'What?'

'A hankie, Ma, you've slopped wine onto your dress.'

★

It's nothing; it doesn't mean anything; he only met her today, he'll never see her again.

Or will he?

She has hair like Ma's; that straight, fair, fine hair. She makes people laugh; she makes Tom laugh; I never make people laugh.

I've got to talk to him. Before we go back to London. Before we start another week in which we don't make love once and most evenings he goes out somewhere on his own. Or we go out together to meet someone because he doesn't want to be with just me.

'I wonder myself,' said James Hamilton, 'why you didn't see fit to include a legal figure among your set of influential chaps. One of the great judges. You've a bias towards cultural thought, if I may say so – surely moral and social viewpoints can't be left out, I mean if as I gather you embrace religion, at least with de Chardin and Archbishop Temple. Just a notion. Not of course that one isn't going to watch the series with enormous interest in any case. But speaking as – well, as the not-quite average viewer, I suppose one must concede – I would have thought . . .'

Would you, now? thought Tony, with his concerned and attentive look, his young-man-to-older-and-more important-one worried inclination of the head. I daresay. But since I didn't devise the damn series, merely some of it, since in the last resort I'm a nuts-and-bolts man, no more nor less, that's hardly the point. And since I'm too knackered just now to explain that, and I've got too much to think about anyway, if we're going to pull anything like a respectable amount of film out of this hellish weekend, then the best thing to do is to sit tight and let you go on enjoying a flight of fancy as man of creativity and insight. Christ, what a gathering! No wonder the poor old sister looks a bit baffled over there in the wheelchair.

Better today. Quite a bit better. Less of that buzzing in the ears; limbs more in contact with oneself. Oneself – ah, whatever that may be – oneself more inclined to look around and sniff the air. And goodness knows there is enough to look around at today. Such a spread has not been seen at Danehurst for quite a while now – no wonder Laura has been so tetchy these last few days. Though today she has been in a better frame of mind, if a bit over-excited. Like the cat that's eaten the cream, when she brought breakfast this morning. One wondered what was up.

And there is something amiss with Kate. But as ever she will go to the stake rather than say.

It would have been interesting to have witnessed this curious little drama up at the Tump; like some mythic revenge of the gods, or an outbreak of Shakespearean symbolic weather. So the lintel stone is broken, the entrance destroyed . . . Well, Hugh would no doubt say the place has served its purpose now, anyway – he was never a one for sentiment. False sentiment.

What is done is done, and we live with our mistakes. He said that once. About a bad decision over a trench, actually. I can see him now, scowling down into a bit of – a bit of Norfolk, I think – with that fan of white lines around his eyes, from screwing up his face in the sun, and his chin peppered with black stubble. We live with our mistakes.

Laura is beginning to look a bit distracted, now. We shall pay for this, when all the commotion has died down. It'll all end in tears, as mother used to say. Silly expression: a denial of life.

The lunch disposed of, Tony set briskly to the redirection of his team. The visitors, relegated to a position now of onlookers, subsidiary to the real business of the day, drifted through to the drawing room. Coffee was served. The BBC party went into conclave; Mrs Lucas and her sister-in-law picked their way past them, ostentatiously unimpressed.

Tom met Kate outside the study door, coming from the kitchen.
'Oh, hello.'
'Hello.'

'I don't seem to have seen much of you.'

'No.'

'A funny kind of day.'

'Yes. You've found someone to talk to, anyway. The fair girl.'

There was a silence. Tom said, 'Shall we go in here? It seems to be the only room not crawling with people.'

The room was lined with glass-fronted book-cases, which reflected the garden – the lawn and the flower-beds and the yew hedge brightly overlaying the sombre ranks of *Antiquity*, Proceedings of the Prehistorical Society, the Victoria County History. From time to time figures walked across: Tony, Sue. Kate picked up a piece of pottery from the desk and stood running her finger round its rim. She said, 'Perhaps it's better if I go back to the flat alone.'

'Is that what you think?'

She said, 'I suppose so.'

'Is it what you want?'

She turned away and stared out of the window. 'No. But I think it's what you want.'

There was an insidiously ticking grandfather clock in one corner of the room; on one wall, a collection of eighteenth and nineteenth century prints of Avebury; perched on a filing-cabinet, a Roman amphora. Kate said, 'Isn't it what you want?'

He wanted to put out a hand, touch her arm. But it would be the wrong kind of touch; she would know that well enough. 'It may be the best thing.' Lame; appallingly inadequate.

There was a silence. Kate said, 'I imagine it's not so much anything I've done as what I am?'

'Kate, look I . . .'

'Don't, just *don't* say you're sorry.'

'I wasn't going to.' That's right, he wanted to say, get angry, it'll be therapeutic, a purgative. And I deserve it.

But she didn't. She stared across the desk at him; there was hurt in her eyes, and something else as well. Something disconcerting; a detachment, a look of assessment.

'I'm too much to take on,' she said. 'Aren't I? You did love me – that was true, I know that – but I'm difficult and cross and awkward and when it comes to the crunch it's more than you reckoned with. And there's Ma.'

'Kate, it's you who's obsessed with your mother, not me.'

'Quite, but that's something else you don't want to get involved in.'

'Let's not argue,' he said. 'Not now.'

'You don't want a nasty painful scene that might lodge in the mind?'

'I don't expect you do either.'

'No,' she said, 'I don't. But I'd rather have that than not look things in the face.'

'Ah. Well, yes, I suppose there's a case for that.'

'A case! Oh, Tom.'

I wish this was over, he thought. I wish it was next week, or next year, even.

'You're an evasive person, you know, just a bit,' she said.

'Evasive?'

'You duck things, where you can. Issues. Responsibilities, even.'

'Such as?'

'I'm sorry – having said that I can't think of anything specific. It's a state of mind I'm talking about, more. You're a very un-committed person.'

'Go on,' said Tom sourly. 'This is interesting. A good bout of character assassination is salutary, I don't doubt.'

'I haven't got anything to lose, have I? I've lost it already.'

There was nothing he could say to that. Or do. Except avoid her eyes.

'I don't mean to assassinate. Just understand. And you are, you know. You're against things rather than for things, and even when you're against them you just turn your back and walk away. You're a looker-on. You keep out of things. You step out of the way and make a wry comment.'

'It comes of growing up in a temperate climate, I daresay.'

'That's exactly the kind of thing I mean,' said Kate. '*Quod erat demonstrandum.*'

'All right,' he said after a moment, 'you've got a point. Maybe I'd have been different in more strenuous circumstances. A child of the times?'

She shrugged.

'Or perhaps it's an innate tendency? I still think the climate may have something to do with it.' His head was throbbing now; a timely reminder of last night, and serve him right, too. 'You should have been here yesterday evening – I drank too much of your mother's whisky and harangued her about the same kind of thing.'

'About the *climate*?'

'Sort of. Mercifully I can't remember too much now.'

There were voices outside the door. Kate said, 'You'll go back with Tony tonight, then?'

'I suppose so. But let's meet up in a week or two, Kate – let's have a drink and see what . . .'

'Mmn. Maybe. I may have my holiday then.'

'Oh,' he said. 'Where will you go?'

'I haven't the faintest idea.'

The door opened. Tony said, 'Can I come in? I'm rather thinking this room might be better than the drawing room to do the sequence with Paul Summers – the rest of the stuff we'd hoped to have done up at the barrow. Yes, sitting at the desk might be nice – Mike, what do you think?' People gathered in consultation; Laura appeared, concerned about dust and untidiness; Kate vanished.

Tom went into the drawing room, there being clearly no alternative but to subject himself to the Hamiltons. 'Isn't this fun?' said Barbara Hamilton. 'Do let me give you some coffee.' He sat in gloom on the sofa, guilt and depression now added to the many ills of the day. From through the open door came the sound of Tony's voice, telling people what to do. Presently it was replaced by Paul Summers saying loud, carefully phrased things about Wessex and Hugh Paxton and the state of mind of British archaeologists in the nineteen fifties.

I'll go and see the Lakers for a bit, he thought. Or something. Bugger off for a week or two.

Kate came in, said, 'Oh, I thought Aunt Nellie was here,' and went out again at once.

Through in the study Tony said, 'Cut.' Then Paul Summers, 'Sorry, I got myself tied up there.' 'Not to worry, we'll go again.'

Tom conversed with Barbara Hamilton and her husband and marvelled at his own ability – hitherto unsuspected – to do this without being in any way aware of what they were talking about. From the garden came a curious wooden knocking noise; someone laughed. He looked out of the window.

Sue and a presently unoccupied BBC man were on the lawn, stooped over a long wooden box from which they were taking the component parts of, apparently, a croquet set. That knocking noise was accounted for. Sue, setting up a hoop, made some experimental shots; there was laughter and banter. Barbara Hamilton said, 'Croquet – what fun! I had no idea Laura had a croquet set, do let's have a game.' Tom followed them onto the terrace.

There was argument about the placing of the central stick. Sue said, 'This was Tony's idea – he noticed the box in that old summer house at the bottom and thought it would be nice to set it up. He thinks it adds to the house's Edwardian atmosphere.' She giggled. 'I must say I'm glad I wasn't an Edwardian, I'm hopeless at it.' She swung wildly at a ball, missed, and sent it skidding down the lawn through the gap in the yew hedge. 'Oh God, now where's that gone?'

Barbara Hamilton said, 'Of course the thing is to cheat wildly, that's half the point. Darling, I'll take you on. You and – er – Sue against me and Tom. Or Kate – wouldn't you like to play?'

Kate, standing now on the terrace, shook her head. Tom said, 'Actually, I'd prefer really . . .'

'Oh, come on, be a devil.'

He took the proffered mallet; presumably one could do this kind of thing in a semi-trance as well.

Nellie had fled from the house and its activities. Insofar as it is possible for anyone in a wheel-chair to flee. She had taken herself to the small orchard at one side of the drive, to the front of the house, and sat there under an apple-tree, reading. After a brief well-being in the middle of the day she felt, now, disordered again, unwell. She wished all these people would go away. Trying to concentrate on the book, she was disturbed by an odd noise: an odd, familiar yet unreckoned-with noise. She closed the book, listened. Began, after a minute or so, to trundle herself round the outside of the house towards the garden.

In the study, Paul Summers completed, finally and satisfactorily, his piece. Tony said, 'Lovely, let's have a break now.' Laura, who had been watching from the door, made remarks of congratulation and approval. She had not, in fact, listened, being taken up with thoughts prompted by the sight of Hugh's books, murky behind the glass of the case, Paul Summers's tanned face and the greyish clouds racing in reflection across the surface of the books: a not entirely random sequence concerned with the possible sale of some books which after all nobody read nowadays, sunshine, the price of air tickets to Corsica, and this villa of the Hamiltons in which apparently there was room for one more. But now, breaking into this, there came a perplexing, evocative noise: she turned towards the door, frowning. From the garden were heard a thwack, a feminine squeak, a burst of laughter. Tony said, 'Oh Laura, is it all right, I suggested they put up that old croquet set before we do those shots of the house – it adds a certain something.' She walked through the drawing room and out onto the terrace without replying.

How dare they! They had no business, it really is the limit.

Nobody's touched the croquet things for years, not since . . . well, not for ages and ages. I never did care for it, a silly game that brings out all the worst in people.

She stood on the terrace. The Hamiltons, Tom, the fair-haired BBC girl – knocking the ball now, inexpertly, turning with a cry of anguish and bumping into Tom so that he has to put a hand up to steady her. And – coming round the side of the house, one hand trundling the chair wheel, the other held up to shade her eyes against the sun which has suddenly blazed out, low in the sky above the garden wall – Nellie.

They are playing croquet: Hugh, Laura, the Sadlers. Laura's idea. She has been all day in one of those states of heightened animation – vivacity which could topple over any minute into something else. A mood long familiar, to those who know her best, and dreaded. The croquet is unwise; a game for people of steady temperament only.

I stand at the side of the house, watching. It is good to get outside, all week we have been shut up in the study; so much to do, so much sorting, so much writing. Hugh says, 'God, Nellie, what would I do without you.' He looks up now, from the lawn, and waves. And Laura, as he does so, misses her shot.

And turns on him. He thinks – we all think – she is going to hit him. His arm comes up across his face. My stomach turns. He says, 'Laura, what the hell are you. . . .' Perhaps she did hit him, it is hard to see. And now she is shouting, awful things, frightening things, about me, some of them. Everybody stands there; it is as though time had stopped. I say, 'Laura . . .'

And she goes into the house. She looks as pretty as a picture, her pale hair and that blue dress. Her face I cannot see.

'Sorry,' said the girl. 'Was that your foot? And now I suppose I'm going to get clobbered.' And she yelped as Tom whacked her ball away into the flower-bed. 'Dreadful game,' said James

Hamilton. 'Red in tooth and claw. Is it me now?' Tony, standing on the step to the terrace, restless, called out, 'We'll have to put a time-limit on this, I'm afraid – I want these garden shots before we have any more weather disasters.' And Laura, an edge to her voice, was saying something about could people not send balls into the border, it's not doing the flowers any good.

Kate said, 'Aunt Nellie?'

And now they all look across at the wheel-chair, where she is oddly leaning to one side, her head at an angle, as though, everyone thinks for a moment, she has dropped off to sleep.

And then Laura is pelting across the lawn towards her, saying something that no one catches. And the mallets are dropped. And Barbara Hamilton says, 'Oh *no* . . .' And Tony, looking across the lawn at Laura, whose face is turned now away from Nellie with an expression no one, not even Kate, has ever seen before, says 'Where's the phone? Not to worry, Laura, it'll be all right . . .'

But it is not all right, at all.

# Chapter Fourteen

Tony said, 'Oh, we retrieved a fair amount. Enough, anyway. It won't be what I'd have liked, but there it is. God, of all five-star disaster weekends . . . I went to the funeral – it was the least I could do, I felt. Laura was shattered, you know. Completely shattered. Funny – one would never have realized she was so devoted to the sister, it didn't somehow come across. But she must have been. Like a zombie – we had a bit of a chat but I don't think she even knew who I was, really. A wretched business. By the way, I gather you and Kate . . .'

'Yes.'

'Permanently?'

'I'm afraid so.'

'Well, I'm sorry to hear it. Nice girl. But I daresay in the end . . . These things happen, anyway. I understand she's staying down at Danehurst for a bit – prop up Laura and so forth. Look, Tom, there's something I'd like to have a talk with you about, if you could spare an hour or two one evening.'

The summer, which had so recently, it seemed, begun, was fading into autumn. It was hard to remember, now, those bright green spears of spring that first weekend at Danehurst; the sharpness of the young corn in the downland fields, the vibrancy of the garden. Now even London, more or less impervious to seasons, suggested the onset of other things – withered grass in the parks, heavy, drooping trees. And Stukeley was all tied up, pretty well, bar some final re-writing and chores like index and bibliography. Work, as things had turned out, had been the best antidote to – well, to a great many uncomfortable emotions that lurked, like dormant bacteria, to spring into action when the conditions were right. Guilt and regret and misgivings. And, from time to time, relief and a faint sense of exhilaration. Things move on; not always for the worse.

He received in the post one day a large envelope from Japan. Inside was a stilted note – from which of Mr Tsuzuki's group he could not make out – and three coloured photographs. In one, he stood outside the Cornmarket branch of Marks and Spencer, flanked by two beaming Japanese girls, against a window display of red, white and blue beachwear ingeniously arranged to form the cross and diagonals of the Union Jack. In the second, he was posed alone outside a petrol station near Burford. Framing his head was a sign, lettered in glowing orange, drawing attention to cut-price petrol: the words 'Four Star Reduced' hung around his right ear. The petrol station itself, gaily flagged, was moored like a giant pleasure-steamer between thatched and mullioned stone cottages. The third photograph showed himself and Mr Tsuzuki, both grave-faced, watching the morris dancers. Tom was holding Mr Tsuzuki's raincoat and some photographical equipment and looked like a priestly acolyte in attendance at some bizarre religious ritual.

His days in the British Museum were numbered now; wasting away like the meagre remains of his grant in the Midland Bank. The expiry of both, one felt, merited some kind of celebration – an initiation ceremony perhaps, the emergence of economic man after his long and expensive apprenticeship. Other cultures do these things better.

As it was, the events were marked by nothing more notable than a large bill from the lady who had typed the thesis, and a letter from the Bank in which a faint tone of threat was veiled by the deference due to a client of no account (in every sense) but incalculable potential. Tom wrote to his mother to expect him home for a prolonged autumn holiday, to the employment exchange in his home town, and to the Lakers.

*

'You never did tell me about your Jap friends.'

'It would take too long.'

'Cherry was asking after you.'

'Ah. Give her my love. I thought I'd look her up at some point.'

Martin was engaged in the restoration of a derelict manor house in one of the more picturesque villages. The house, formerly the property of a landowning family who had gone to seed in the thirties, converting estates and valuables into cash and yachts, was a mere shell with hints of its vanished charms. The village had decayed with it, due to some legal tangle preventing the family from selling cottages, which in consequence were rented and unrepaired. The legal problems were now cleared up, but galloping disintegration had put off buyers for several years. Now, apparently, the whole lot had been acquired by a Dutch businessman, and was to be painstakingly restored. Tom, for a week or so, joined Martin on the site, helping out with the more unskilled tasks. Once, the new owner arrived to see how things were going. The stereotyped vulgar tycoon that Tom had expected turned out to be a slight, diffident man, deeply concerned with craftmanship and deferential towards Martin. They toured the building, locked in discussion of stone and timbers: no expense was to be spared, no trouble was too great. The Dutchman's fortune, apparently, came from the manufacture of a new kind of aluminium alloy used in aircraft construction.

'Stay on a bit,' said Martin at the end of a week, 'since you're at a loose end. You're just beginning to pick things up – that paving wasn't half bad.'

'It's tempting. But I think I'll push off home.'

'Anything in the offing?'

'Not a lot. There is one thing. I'll have to think about it.'

A period of reflection, he had thought. A time for taking stock. He walked about the town – saw it with eyes that were both of now and of then. Accompanied by other, younger Toms, he observed and remembered: the cinema, scheduled for demolition, had acquired a certain period interest (if there wasn't already, there presumably would be, a Thirties Society); it was also the place where he had brazened his way into his first X certificate film. The enormous Batts Road primary school playground was not so at all: a small puddled area of grey tarmac, merely. The heroes of yore, the wits and blades of the second year sixth, were men with mortgages and life insurance and evenings spent in front of the telly. Observation of how things are was contradicted by knowledge of how things once appeared to be: where, in that case, did the truth lie? Is the world as we see it, or as we have known it? A confusing point, he thought, and one that presumably perplexes others too.

But in the meantime, it seemed more appropriate to think about the future. He wrote letters, made telephone calls. Stukeley, two swollen typescripts, bound in inferior grey cardboard, arrived and was despatched to meet his fate at the hands of learned men: there was nothing more to be done about him.

Once, he wrote to Kate, who did not reply.

He said to his parents, 'There's this programme this evening I'd rather like to watch. All right with you?'

The title was suspended against a glittering backcloth of gold cups and jewellery: Treasures of Time; Hugh Paxton, archaeologist. Tom's mother, alerted by the tide sequence, said 'Paxton? Wasn't that . . .'

'He was her father, that's right.'

'I thought that was a pity, Tom. Dad and I really took to her.'

'So did I.'

'Well, it's a shame you didn't see it through.' She stared at the screen. The camera, airborne, swept across verdant landscapes, dwelt on selected features. 'Lovely country. The Yorkshire Dales, look – remember that trip we did over there?'

Tony's voice introduces other voices, who in turn expound and explain. The viewer is painlessly conducted to inconvenient or obscure places, given a bird's eye view of Maiden Castle and Cadbury, a peek inside Maeshowe. It is the converse of Tony's motorway map; this is a mirror England where roads and buildings do not exist, a place of turfed bones and melancholy stones, of scrawled markings in a field of corn, of a million broken pots. 'The splendour of Wessex', someone says, and the screen shows weaponry and brooches and a great gold drinking-cup. Accounts of what Hugh Paxton said and did are neatly inter-cut with the basic descriptive task: information must be given, but not offence, people don't like to be made to feel ignorant. It is all very skilfully done.

And there, suddenly, is Danehurst, with the croquet set laid out on the lawn – that shot must have been taken just before . . . 'Nice house,' says Tom's mother. 'Did you go there, dear? What are those iron things for, on the grass?' 'It's a game': what you can't see, of course, won't know, is that a few minutes later someone died. And here is Laura, sitting on the wicker chair, by the yew hedge, talking. 'Good-looking woman,' said Tom's father. 'The mother, is that?' 'Mmnn': the mother, yes. And now – juggling with time once more – we are up at the Tump. Tony's voice tells us where we are, and why, and the camera is generous with a view from which much is excluded: inharmonious items like the BBC cars and the barbed wire fence and people and dead sheep. Except that they of course have not yet happened. 'Lovely country,' says Tom's mother again. 'Look at those wild flowers.' 'Yes. Just after that some sheep were struck by lightning.' His parents jerk their eyes from the screen, incredulous – 'Never!' 'Honest. We were there.' 'Well,' says his father, 'there's a thing – and it looks as peaceful as you like.' They turn back to the picture, well and truly hooked; Paul Summers peers into the entrance of the Tump and Tom's mother wants to know now if that is real. 'Or, I mean, is it something they arranged for the film, like?' 'Oh no, that's real.'

Or was, because of course now that is no more either, or at least no more in that particular form. And now we jump back to Hugh Paxton's study at Danehurst, with Paul Summers discussing, in pleasant, measured tones the man's contribution to a discipline. 'Of course,' he says, 'radio-carbon dating is the great watershed in twentieth century archaeology. It came at the right moment for Hugh Paxton. He . . .' He holds a little bronze pin or something, taps it absent-mindedly on the desk once or twice as he talks: behind his head the glass of the book-case reflects the garden. What you cannot see is Laura, standing in the doorway; Tony, in the arm-chair; Tom and Kate, who will not thereafter say a great deal more to one another, outside in the garden. 'Who's that?' says Tom's mother. 'Just a man.'

And now we are out of doors again. It is the end, the summing-up. Voices pronounce; the camera roams the landscape, rooting out lumps and bumps and circles and trackways like white blood-vessels on green hill-tops. A carefully selective view of things; again, much lurks off-stage. There is music; the credits roll: that's that. 'Very interesting,' says Tom's mother. 'I enjoyed it – some lovely photography.' She plumps up cushions, makes ready for bed; it is nearly twelve, culture is a late-night offering.

Tony said, 'Well, I suppose it could have been worse. Not quite what one would have liked, but the background traumas didn't show, which is the great thing. By the way, have you . . .?'

'Yes, I have. I think I would.'

'Right, then. Of course you realize to begin with it would be a bit routine. Research, mainly. But that's your line, isn't it?'

'I suppose it is.'

'Come down here, then, and have a chat with some people. Very good to know we may have you around.'

On the other side of the windows of the London train, the country was autumnal: bleached and harvested. It had a cropped and tidy look, as though it had had its fling and would now go meekly enough into hibernation. To Tom, conditioned by the calendar of the educational year, September seemed always a time of renewal rather than of completion. A beginning, not an end. He sat, now, in contemplation of the landscape, whose ambiguities he was beginning to appreciate, drinking the measure of British Rail coffee which had cost what felt like a sizeable proportion of his remaining assets, and experienced a certain zest. Which could come only from perversity of spirit, since it was not justified by anything in the immediate circumstances. Prospects, insecure; liquidity, proving unreliable; status, not clear. Notwithstanding which – and the atrocity of the coffee, the torment induced by a heating system apparently designed to roast the thighs of passengers, the ghoulish satisfaction of the station announcement that the train was running approximately twenty-one minutes late – notwithstanding all this, it was possible to look out of the window with pleasure, and to feel a distinct twinge of well-being. I'm not altogether without resources, he thought: we shall get by. We might even enjoy ourselves in the process.

# *He just wanted a decent book to read ...*

Not too much to ask, is it? It was in 1935 when Allen Lane, Managing Director of Bodley Head Publishers, stood on a platform at Exeter railway station looking for something good to read on his journey back to London. His choice was limited to popular magazines and poor-quality paperbacks – the same choice faced every day by the vast majority of readers, few of whom could afford hardbacks. Lane's disappointment and subsequent anger at the range of books generally available led him to found a company – and change the world.

*'We believed in the existence in this country of a vast reading public for intelligent books at a low price, and staked everything on it'*
**Sir Allen Lane, 1902–1970, founder of Penguin Books**

The quality paperback had arrived – and not just in bookshops. Lane was adamant that his Penguins should appear in chain stores and tobacconists, and should cost no more than a packet of cigarettes.

Reading habits (and cigarette prices) have changed since 1935, but Penguin still believes in publishing the best books for everybody to enjoy. We still believe that good design costs no more than bad design, and we still believe that quality books published passionately and responsibly make the world a better place.

So wherever you see the little bird – whether it's on a piece of prize-winning literary fiction or a celebrity autobiography, political tour de force or historical masterpiece, a serial-killer thriller, reference book, world classic or a piece of pure escapism – you can bet that it represents the very best that the genre has to offer.

## Whatever you like to read – trust Penguin.